even weirder than before

even
weirder
than
before

A NOVEL

SUSIE TAYLOR

BREAKWATER
P.O. BOX 2188, ST. JOHN'S, NL, CANADA, A1C 6E6
WWW.BREAKWATERBOOKS.COM

ISBN 978-1-55081-771-3

A CIP catalogue record for this book is available from Library and Archives Canada

We acknowledge the support of the Canada Council for the Arts. We acknowledge the financial support of the Government of Canada and the Government of Newfoundland and Labrador through the Department of Tourism, Culture, Industry and Innovation for our publishing activities. PRINTED AND BOUND IN CANADA.

 Canada Council   Conseil des arts
for the Arts   du Canada
 Canada
Newfoundland
Labrador

Breakwater Books is committed to choosing papers and materials for our books that help to protect our environment. To this end, this book is printed on a recycled paper and other controlled sources that are certified by the Forest Stewardship Council®.

MIX
Paper from
responsible sources
FSC® C016245

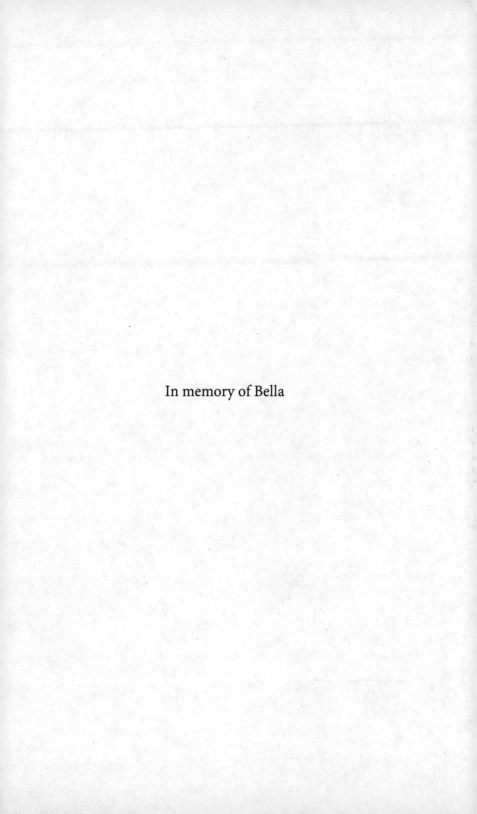

In memory of Bella

one

Miss Blake is standing in front of the class with her eyes closed and her head bent in supplication. She is mouthing the words to the Lord's Prayer as the principal reads it over the intercom. I'm watching Wanda Wayne, her desk is in front of mine, make tiny braids in her hair and trying to ignore the fact that, in the seat to my right, my friend Cathy has her hands held together palm to palm with her fingers pointing heavenward. We are all waiting to get a good look at the new kid who is waiting at the back of the class.

After Miss Blake and Cathy mumble "Amen," Miss Blake beckons the new kid to the front of the room, and he slouches up, reluctant and full of attitude. His hair is dark and spiked on top. He has a rat tail running down his back, his ear is pierced. There has never been a boy like this in my class before.

His name is Damon Jones.

At recess Cathy and I huddle next to the building, watching boys play foot hockey with a tennis ball. Most of the girls stand around in groups and watch as Damon joins the boys' game. The only girl playing is Wanda. She was new three

7

weeks ago on the first day of classes. She's taller than half the boys, and she swears more. The tiny braids she made through the morning swing around her head as she runs for the ball.

Damon scores, shooting the tennis ball past Kevin and between the makeshift goalposts of two empty pop cans. I can see Darlene and Jenny whispering behind their hands, and I know by the end of the day Damon's name will be etched in red pen on both of their pencil cases.

During lunch, which I eat at home, Mum stands at the kitchen counter, staring out the window, and doesn't come sit with me.

"I'll get something later," she says. She is in one of her moods when she doesn't speak and only half hears anything I tell her.

"There's a new kid at school," I say.

"That's nice," is her only response to this astonishing news.

I see Damon emerging from a car parked outside of the school. The Cure is pumping out of its speakers. Damon notices me staring and half smiles in my direction. As the car pulls past, my knees feel weak; the driver is around sixteen and has long black hair, shaved underneath. She's wearing a black T-shirt, leather studded jacket, lots of eyeliner, and multiple earrings. It's me. It is me as I imagine myself in the future. She drives past; the car billows smoke and she/me is gone.

When the bell goes, I join the lineup outside the door of our classroom and wait for Miss Blake to come lead us in. Two boys at the back are mercy fighting, and one of them falls against the queue sending the rest of us stumbling forward like dominos. A hand grabs my upper arm in the crush when someone tries to steady themselves. I turn around, and I see that the hand belongs to Damon. He looks at me, but Miss Blake is yelling at us all to settle down, so we don't speak.

"Are you sick? Your face is all red," Cathy says loudly as we take our seats. Physical contact with Damon has left me blushing violently.

Wanda overhears Cathy, and she turns around to check out my burning cheeks. Miss Blake says, "Eyes to the front, Wanda!" Wanda rolls her eyes up so only the whites are visible, and I feel laughter rising up. Miss Blake glares at me, her mouth in an over-exaggerated frown like a clown. I bite my lip and cast my eyes towards my math book.

I am contemplating Damon's arrival and walk right by my father's car without considering the strangeness of its presence at 3:45 p.m. on a Monday afternoon. It is his shoes that stop me in my tracks. They are placed by the door neatly, side by side. Inside the house there is an absence of the usual sounds of the radio playing and Mum calling out to see how my day was. There is a wrongness about everything, and my ears start ringing like they do if I'm about to faint or jump from the high diving board. Dad comes through from the living room and sees me standing on the threshold. "I thought I'd be gone before you got home," he says. I take in the scene before me in the kitchen: an abandoned onion half-chopped on a wooden board; the dishcloth crumpled on the counter mid-wipe; and at this early hour, an empty wine bottle on the table, a red ring staining the tablecloth where it was previously placed.

My father leaves slowly. I wish he would just get in the car and drive away, but instead he trails from bedroom to car with white shirts on hangers. I retreat to my bedroom and watch him through a crack in my door as he folds underwear and places it precisely in an old suitcase. My mother sits on their bed with silent tears streaming down her face and her hand clasped over her mouth. Each second Dad is still here my gut twists. "Get out!" I want to scream at him. When he has finally finished packing, I creep to the top of the stairs and watch as he kisses my mother goodbye. Now he walks out the door, and we are left behind.

The next few days unravel slowly. Mostly there is deep silence, sometimes punctuated by telephone calls. Reverend Winter, from the church we go to at Christmas, comes and talks to my mother in low tones. He smiles at me when he leaves and tells me he's praying for us all. Elizabeth, my older sister, is alerted of our father's departure and makes plans to come home from university for the weekend.

I answer the phone, and Dad makes no attempt to explain his absence. "Can you tell Mum I've paid the mortgage? How is she?"

"Where are you?" I ask him.

He is at Pat's apartment. My father is a biology prof at the university, and Pat is one of his grad students.

Pat used to come to our house for dinner. She'd arrive with her blue-rimmed eyes and glossy wet mouth, looking like a white lab rat with her pink tongue darting in and out as she popped in a grape or cube of cheese. Mum tried to get Elizabeth to be friends with her. "She's so sweet and she seems lonely." Elizabeth and I hid upstairs whenever Pat came mooching around. Pat was always sucking up to Dad and wanting to talk about mouse gestation periods or fungal infections of the nose. When she stopped showing up, my parents never talked about it.

I stop answering the phone and stay in my room, listening to my Walkman and taking occasional breaks to make cups of tea and remove cold ones from Mum's bedside.

Inside the house, the air is stale and the curtains remain drawn. My mother stays in her bedroom, occasionally getting up to pee, or calling out to make sure I have gotten up in time for school.

Outside the house, life continues as if nothing has changed. I still have a math test on Thursday. Candice gets her period at school and brags about it. Wanda gets a detention for saying "Shit" in class. Elizabeth comes home for the weekend, does dishes, cleans the house, and goes back to university. Damon Jones does well in school and beats Cathy on the math test. She immediately takes against him and says he must have cheated. I draw hearts with *Daisy + Damon* on small scraps of paper, then flush them down the toilet, watching our names swirl away together. In the evenings, Damon skateboards. I see him glide by my house on crisp fall nights, and I listen for the sounds of wheels on pavement. I listen and wait.

two

"Why didn't you call me straight away? What a bastard!" I know this is Olivia, partly because I recognize her voice and partly because she is the only one of Mum's friends who uses "language," which is what I hear Mum saying to her now.

"Language, Olivia."

"For fuck's sake, Sheila!" And, for the first time in two weeks, I hear my mother laugh. Olivia did not bring a Bible to share with my mother, like Reverend Winter, but gin. This seems to be working much better.

They are in the living room when I get home from school. Mum is looking white and blotchy pink, but she is wearing real clothes, not just her dressing gown. Mum has her feet resting on the coffee table, even though she is wearing shoes. They go quiet when I come in, and Olivia asks how school was. I can tell they are both waiting for me to leave the room so they can keep talking.

"You're better off without him. I never knew how you put up with him," I overhear Olivia say as I come down the stairs a few hours later to poke around the fridge.

The gin bottle is empty on the counter. I tip the last drop onto my tongue and feel it burn. Mum and Olivia are drinking white wine now.

"An expert in the naked mole rat. I thought you were making a joke when you told me that's what he did. What normal man wants to spend all day thinking about something that looks like a flaccid penis?" Olivia's voice has gone back up; she's forgotten I am downstairs.

"He does work hard, Olivia. People tell me he's a brilliant man all the time."

"This won't be the first time. It never is."

Mum ignores this. I have noticed she does this a lot when she talks to Olivia, only hears what she wants to hear.

Dad calls Olivia the "Feminazi." Olivia is different from my parents' other friends. They are all people from the university who come around to dinner parties when a visiting lecturer is in town to talk about high beaver mortality rates or a rise in Australian rabbit populations. Mum met Olivia when my parents first moved from England to Canada, and they lived next door to each other in a small apartment building in Don Mills. Olivia taught Mum how to make coffee in a percolator and lent Dad her shovel the first time his car got blocked in by the snow plow.

Mum used to ask Olivia to the dinner parties to even out the numbers if one of the biologists didn't have a wife. During one of these parties, Olivia and Dad had an argument about affirmative action, which Dad says is just sexism against men. After that Olivia stopped being invited over with the university crowd and started coming to visit Mum when Dad was away for work. Dad says Olivia's voice gives him a headache.

"I just need to be patient. Everyone knows the man always goes back to his wife."

Olivia clicks her tongue at this. "Sheila," she says, "you shouldn't take him back even if he comes begging."

I am at Cathy's after school a few days later, and with wide eyes, her mom asks me, "How are you?" Adults keep asking me this, except for my parents. "How's your mom holding up? I feel so bad for her." I can feel her wanting to pull out confidences from me.

"I'm fine. Mum's great." Cathy's mom looks at me with pity, like I'm too young to see what's really happening in my home.

Cathy and I slink away from her mom, up to Cathy's bedroom.

"Are you okay? You know, your dad will probably move back in. I've been praying for that."

Cathy gets all tight lipped when I mention Olivia bringing over gin, and I regret telling her this as I'm doing it. They don't have any booze in the house, something to do with Cathy's uncle. Cathy doesn't probe any further and changes the topic to more familiar ground.

"George is so handsome, don't you think?"

"He's okay. I like Kevin Taylor." I don't tell her about my crush on Damon because I don't trust her.

Cathy draws a bunch of M.A.S.H. boards on a piece of paper. It's a fortune-telling game everyone at school is playing. The letters stand for Mansion, Apartment, Shack, or House. We play until Cathy ends up living in a house married to George, with a Ferrari and fifteen children, and rich. I end up in a shack married to Murray, the fattest boy in our class, with two children and a station wagon. We are on welfare.

After M.A.S.H. Cathy shows me a magazine with instructions on how to create kissable lips and flirty eyes; she wants to use it to get ready for the upcoming autumn school dance. I flick through it. Mum always says fashion magazines are a total waste of money when she sees me eyeing the glossy covers at the grocery store checkout. Cathy's mom is always buying her magazines and special shampoo and jars of Noxzema. When she got her period, her mom came home with new jelly shoes and a seventy-colour eye-shadow kit to celebrate her womanhood. When I got my period, all I got was a pack of thick maxi pads.

Hailstones pelt the playground on Friday afternoon. At recess we are kept inside. I watch the tiny cubes of ice melting on the asphalt and long to scoop them up with my hands. Wanda sets up her own M.A.S.H. board and puts *Axl Rose* down four times for her husband.

"That's cheating," Cathy says.

"It's not like a game you can win," Wanda replies.

"It's not how you're supposed to do it. It's against the rules."

I make up my own board writing down *Robert Smith*, *Morrissey*, *Sting*, and a *D*. If anyone asks, I'll say the D is for any of the guys from Depeche Mode, but it's really for Damon.

I stare at the back of Wanda's head during last period. Her hair is shiny and thick like in shampoo commercials. Sometimes she grabs it and piles it on top of her head; when she lets go, it tumbles down like a waterfall. Mine is always full of static and sticks flatly to my face. I try casually playing with my own hair like Wanda does, and a bunch of dandruff drifts down onto my desk.

The Friday before the Thanksgiving long weekend, we have regular classes in the morning, then after lunch the autumn dance takes place in the school gym. I spend my lunch break locked in the bathroom applying and reapplying eye makeup. Mum has always been disapproving of makeup for girls my age, but she's lying in bed and has no idea what I'm doing to my face. Elizabeth gave me some makeup when she was home—half a used lipstick and black mascara and eyeliner she never uses anymore since she switched to brown. The eye makeup gets smudgy and has a racoon-like effect; the lipstick is easier to use, but I keep finding I've touched my lips and there are smears of it on my fingers. I wear my jeans, Elizabeth's old jean jacket, and a U2 T-shirt she got me last year. I'm nervous and excited. I've never cared about the dances before, but just the slim chance that Damon might ask me to dance makes me feel light-headed.

Cathy is wearing her lime-green jelly shoes and her new favourite blouse. It is covered in a crazy peach-and-baby-blue geometric design that vaguely resembles swastikas. She wears it with a thin plastic belt that cinches it at the waist. I tell her she looks nice.

"Lesbo!" she says, but I can tell she's pleased.

You can go to the dance or play board games in the library.

Wanda is opting for the library. She has arranged to play cards with two asthmatic boys from grade seven and seems perfectly content with this.

"I don't want to hang out with those bitches," she says, looking over at the other girls as she saunters off to the library.

Peony Wong has volunteered as door person. She will

collect tickets, then spend the dance adding up money in the peace and protection of the secretary's office.

The gym is decorated with the construction paper cut-outs of leaves the grade ones made for a parents' meeting held earlier in the week. Pumpkins sit on a table where you can buy fifty-cent pops. The regular overhead lights are turned off. Mr. Dean, the grade seven teacher, has set up an ancient disco ball that casts flashes of light across the floor. It is still daylight outside, but artificial evening in here.

Everything is going okay. The girls are on one side of the room and the boys are on the other side. Mr. Dean is the DJ. He plays "Jump" by Van Halen and a bunch of the boys start leaping around. "Girls Just Want to Have Fun" comes on, and Candice, Tiffany, Jenny, and Darlene squeal and run to the middle of the dance floor. They stand in a circle, not actually dancing, just shuffling from foot to foot with their arms held out and their hands wiggling around. They look like a bunch of dogs begging for treats.

I stick out my tongue and pant in dog fashion and waggle my paws/hands in front of me. I'm imitating the other girls' dance moves when I see Damon looking over and smiling. I smile back, and then when I turn around, Candice is walking towards me and my hands are still waggling.

"Who do you think you are, you stupid ugly cow?" Candice hisses at me.

I can't think of a reply. I see how she looks at me, with disgust. My limbs seem heavy, and the more I want to disappear, the more my body seems to swell and take up space. I wish I could suck back the last thirty seconds and un-imitate her. Miss Blake glares at me. Mr. Dean is beside us.

"Everything okay here, ladies?" He puts one hand on Candice's shoulder and one hand on mine.

Candice beams at him with her good-girl smile.

"Fine," she says, smirking. "I'll see you later, Daisy." She walks away, sending me one long look over her shoulder.

"You're in for it," Cathy says. She's already inching away from me, and I don't blame her.

I don't cry. I won't cry. Miss Blake joins Candice and the other girls in a circle and bops around to "Dancing Queen."

I slink in the shadows at the edge of the gym. No one asks me to dance. Cathy goes to help Peony with the final tally of the door money. I watch Candice and Darlene head out the door of the gym together, giggling behind their hands. They laugh and shoot disgusted glances at me when they return. I can hear them from where I'm seated on a side bench pretending to be retying my shoelaces.

"Her mom never lets her come to sleepovers. I think it's because she wets the bed," Candice says.

"She tried to make out with Cathy once. Cathy's mom saw and told all the other parents. My mom told me," says Darlene.

"I heard she does it with hot dogs!" Candice says this loudly, and it makes Darlene laugh so hard she starts coughing and has to produce her asthma inhaler.

The lights come on in the gym, and we all go to pick up our bags from homeroom. Mine is on the floor. It was new this year, and a satisfying army green that I had fought Mum to purchase instead of a crafty one made out of brown corduroy. It's covered in what I first think is mud, and then I realize is dog shit.

"What's that smell?" Candice says loudly. "Did someone have an accident?"

Miss Blake can see what's going on. She gives me a dirty look like I've rubbed my own backpack in dog poo. "Have a good weekend!" she says and goes across the hall to chat with Mr. Dean.

Candice and her friends leave in a swirling, cackling horde, and I hear Candice out in the hall say "Poopsy Daisy," and Darlene copy her, croaking out "Poopsy Daisy" in a sinister voice like Freddy from *A Nightmare on Elm Street*.

Cathy hands me the plastic grocery bag her lunch came in, and I shove my books in it. It smells vaguely like ham. I am very careful not to touch the shit, but I feel filthy. Cathy leaves me. She says she can't stay and pats me on the back. I'm left alone to deal with my shit-encrusted backpack. I take it and sneak round the back of the school. I wait until everyone is gone, then I pry the lid of the dumpster up and hurl my bag into it. The lid of the dumpster clunks shut, and I hear something above me. Damon is climbing down from the school roof.

"Tennis ball," he says. He throws the ball at me, and it hits me in the stomach. I realize I was meant to catch it.

"Sorry, sorry," he says, and then we both laugh.

"What are you doing here?" Damon asks me.

"Nothing," I say too fast. "Have a great weekend," I say even more quickly before heading away from him.

I walk very slowly towards the house. As much as I want to wash my hands, I'm dreading my mum's questions about where my bag is. If I tell her the truth, she'll say, "You shouldn't have let them do that," and unhelpfully point out that I shouldn't have made fun of anyone's dancing.

Dad's car is in the driveway. I don't know what I'm going to walk into. He might be here to collect more clothes, or maybe they want to sit me down and have the divorce conversation like it happens on TV. When I come in the door, the radio is on and there's the smell of spaghetti bolognaise coming from the kitchen. My dad is working at the dining-room table with a glass of wine beside him. "Hello, Daisy," he says.

No one says anything about his return. We just pretend like nothing is unusual about us all being here for dinner together. We sit down at the table and start to eat.

Dad asks me if I have done something to my eye.

I don't say anything.

Mum says, "You're a bit young for makeup, aren't you, Daise?"

My father stays for two weeks. One night the phone rings at 2 a.m. and I listen as his car rumbles to life in the driveway.

I find Mum standing in the dark living room, staring at the departing tail lights. "He'll be back. I just need to be patient. Pat is being difficult."

Olivia comes over, and when Mum makes excuses for my father, I hear Olivia say, "He's an asshole, Sheila. You're way better off without him."

three

Mum discourages me from wearing my watch to school in case I lose or break it.

"What's the point of having it if I can never wear it?" I ask her.

"I suppose it's up to you," she says. She's been getting up all week and hovering in the kitchen as I get ready in the morning. It's a relief to see her standing up. Mostly she silently drinks tea as I cram in toast. Today she actually takes the time to cast her eye over what I'm wearing and notices the watch. I thought she'd be pleased I'd started wearing it.

Everyone else has a Swatch. Candice has five, Cathy has two, even Wanda has one, she has written *G N'R* on the rubbery strap with a black magic marker. The morning of my last birthday, when Mum handed me the wrapped box, it was the wrong shape. Instead of a Swatch I got a plain watch with a silver face and a black strap. I don't know why I expected anything different. In grade six everyone had a Cabbage Patch. Mum went to the bazaar at church and came home with a "Crochet Kid." A hideous doll with a head made of old nylons that smelt like old lady. It wore a green crocheted jumper that you couldn't take off. Its nylon legs flopped back and forth where they had been sewn to its permanent clothing.

I wear the watch despite Mum's concern. The black watch strap looks punk rock against my wrist. Miss Blake makes us put our heads on our desks and gives us a lecture about the importance of personal hygiene before we head out to change for gym. "At the age you are at, your bodies are changing. Pheromones start developing." I like the way the leather smells salty, and I give it an experimental lick as Miss Blake talks.

The change room is actually just the girls' washroom closest to the gym. It always smells like wet paint, even though the concrete walls haven't been painted in years. When the bathroom door opens, it swings directly into the main hallway and gives a clear view into the room. The only space sheltered from view is the big communal shower room in the far corner. Candice, Darlene, Tiffany, and Jenny change there. The rest of us find a space against one of the short walls and hope we are out of sight from the doorway.

I can hear Candice and her friends proudly showing off stubbled armpits and comparing sticks of deodorant. They are laughing and snapping each other's bra straps. Wanda strips off fast and doesn't seem that bothered standing around in her bra. But then her bra is black, with a T-strap back. Cathy has a white cotton bra with lace trim. It's clean and athletic looking. Her mom just went out and bought it for her, so she didn't have to suffer the indignity of trying it on under the fluorescent lights of the Sears change room. Peony goes into a cubicle with a toilet to change. I'd like to do the same, but it makes it seem like you're hiding some physical defect, hair growing down your back or a third nipple.

I have bigger boobs than most of the other girls and an embarrassing patch of black pubic hair. My bra is a hand-me-down from Elizabeth; it is elastic and beige and smells of old deodorant. It looks like it came from the lost and found at an orphanage. I'm wearing a long shirt, so I can slip off my jeans and pull on my shorts without anyone seeing any of the black hairs that sometimes curl through the cotton of my underwear. I take off my T-shirt really quick and pull on the one I've brought for gym in practically one motion. I only have to expose my yellowing bra for a few seconds. I try and time this move when everyone else is busy tying up shoes or taking off their own shirts. I think about putting my watch in my jeans pocket, but we all leave our clothes hanging on hooks in the bathroom and anyone could come in and go through my stuff. All the other girls leave their Swatches on for gym class, and I decide to keep my watch on too.

Miss Blake lines us up for skills drills. Cathy serves the ball at me, and I duck when it comes hurtling down. I manage to return the ball to her a few times. I can't stand the way the volleyball feels when it slams against the insides of my wrists. My wrists are red, and my veins are sticking out disgustingly. A ball from Darlene and Jenny comes bounding over and hits me in the side of the head. "Heads up, Daisy!" Miss Blake shouts afterwards.

Rachel and Everett do the best at spiking, so they get to be team captains. They call out names, and soon there are only four of us left. Everett picks Cathy, Rachel picks Peony, Everett picks Murray, and I shuffle over, unchosen, to Rachel's team.

"Something smells like poo," says Derek Fletcher, as I join the group of kids on my team, and everyone laughs, even nice Kevin Taylor. The ball is coming towards me, and I start to run in its direction. I see Tiffany in my peripheral vision. I stumble over Tiffany's foot, and she pushes me away from her, so she can get to the ball. I fall sideways; the back of my arm and hand slam against the ground. Candice laughs. I can't tell if Tiffany tripped me on purpose. She says sorry, but doesn't offer her hand to help me up. When I stand up I can see cracks running through the face of my watch. During the rest of the game, I just try and stay away from the net and move out of the way if the ball comes towards me.

At home I put the watch back in its box and shove it far into the back of my underwear drawer. All through dinner my wrist feels naked, and I dread Mum asking about it. I can't fall asleep, worrying I should have confessed to Mum about it. The phone rings late, and I can hear Mum speaking into it. I put my ear against the heating vent in my room; this way I can hear her down in the kitchen. She keeps saying, "I understand, Donald." When she hangs up and comes upstairs to bed, I put on my headphones so I don't have to listen to her crying.

"It's not based just on looks, it's personality too," Tiffany tells Cathy, Wanda, and me. I think this is meant to reassure me. She has joined us for group work. Candice is rating all the kids in our class on looks and personality. She writes the results in a Care Bears notebook that she reserves especially for this purpose. "I know your scores," Tiffany confides. I am four out of ten, and Cathy is a five. Last year I got invited to three more birthday parties than Cathy, so I'm a little surprised she beat me. Wanda doesn't even blink when Tiffany tells her she's a six.

Later that day Miss Blake gets called to the office, and we're told to stay in our seats. As soon as Miss Blake shuts the door behind her, Candice gets up and grabs a thick marker from the *World's Greatest Teacher* mug on Miss Blake's desk. Everyone is watching. She heads to the back of the class and grabs my new bag. She holds it up triumphantly and starts writing.

"That's mine," I say.

"What are you going to do about it, Daisy?" Candice looks at me and starts unzipping my bag.

Packed inside are a bunch of maxi pads, as well as a pair of clean, but bloodstained, underpants Mum made me take to school "just in case." The shame of having these things spilled out on the classroom floor is unimaginable. I stand up and walk to the back of the class.

"Sit down. You'll get in trouble," whispers Cathy.

I glance back towards my desk, and Wanda gives me a smile.

When I reach Candice, she holds my bag towards me. I go to take it, and she snatches it away. Everyone laughs. It's juvenile, but effective. I can see she has written *Daisy is a* and hasn't had a chance to finish.

"Give it to me," I say quietly.

Candice just laughs, and I see she is about to dump the contents of my bag all over the floor.

I reach out and slap her hard across the face. She has not been expecting this from me and just stands there with her mouth open. I'm shaking with rage. "Come on, hit me back, Candice," I say to her. I want her to hit me, so I can hit her again and again. Candice just puts her hand to her cheek and stares at me. The class goes absolutely silent.

"Holy shit!" I hear Damon say after what seems like forever.

Then there is the sound of the door opening, and Miss Blake has my arm and is pulling me down the hall to the principal's office. "Who do you think you are?" she keeps asking me.

My hand tingles like it's filled with fireworks, and I seem to float behind Miss Blake like an oversized helium balloon. I watch as a single maxi pad slips from my bag onto the floor. I disown it without a second thought. Miss Blake is focussed on heading to the office, so there is no stopping.

I wait for a very long time outside Mr. Holder's office, listening to the occasional rise in inflection of Miss Blake's voice. When she leaves the office, she gives me the evil eye, and for the first time ever, I'm told the principal is waiting for me.

He talks for forty-five minutes. It takes me a while to realize that he's enjoying this. He likes the sound of his own voice and sees me as an impressionable audience. I can't hear the words at first. It occurs to me somewhere near the middle of his diatribe that we are talking about the difficulties of divorce and how he won't bother my mum with this. And, obviously, this is so unlike me that it must be the atmosphere at home. Mr. Holder doesn't give me a detention, but assigns me to write a book report for him on *Jonathan Livingston Seagull*.

The book is only 144 pages. It doesn't take me long to write the report. I hand it in a week later. Mr. Holder lectures me on being a team player, and then says, "We'll speak no more of the incident," when he sends me back to class.

When I return from Mr. Holder's office my desk has been moved. Miss Blake is sorting out a new seating system where we all have desk buddies. Instead of our desks being in six rows, there are now three big rows of double desks. Miss Blake acts like this is her idea, but classes have been moving desks all week, and we know it is just a new school policy. Cathy has moved to the front of the class to sit next to Peony. "Mom wants me to sit up front, because of my eyes. It's nothing personal, Daisy." My desk is pushed up next to Wanda's. Wanda finishes Candice's graffiti on my backpack with the word *crazy* and draws a bunch of stars and flowers all around the words. I like *Daisy Is a Crazy*. I tell Wanda this will be the name of my first band.

Wanda is addicted to reading and bubble gum. During class she is either illegally chewing gum or has a book or magazine opened up inside of her desk that she reads while Miss Blake explains fractions or talks about the structure of the Canadian government.

We're doing math, and Miss Blake's back is to us when Wanda eases a piece from the forbidden pack of Hubba Bubba in her desk. It is grape flavoured, and when she pops in a piece I am engulfed in the purple scent of it. When Miss Blake turns from the board to look at us, Wanda's head is down, reading the open copy of *Murder on the Orient Express* she has balanced on her legs.

"Wanda, come up here and solve this please."

Wanda eases her book into her desk before she stands. The gum in her mouth is hardly chewed yet. I imagine it still plump and square. Wanda walks slowly up to the board and takes the piece of chalk Miss Blake hands her. She stares at the problem and does not speak.

Miss Blake gives her "Everyone Needs Math" speech; everyone from an astronaut to a cleaning lady. Wanda's mom works as a cleaner at the local hospital. When Miss Blake turns to face the rest of us and can't see Wanda behind her, Wanda chews her piece of gum with exaggerated pleasure. Miss Blake turns around to see why the class is smiling, and Wanda's lips become motionless, her face an insubordinate mask.

"Now you've wasted all of our time, you can go sit down, Wanda. Kevin, come up here. I'm sure you can show us the answer." Wanda sits down, and I give Miss Blake the finger under my desk.

Mum is up in the morning going through the careers section of the paper. "I don't qualify for any of these. No one wants shorthand anymore," she says as I pass by her on my way down to the basement laundry room. I'm hoping to find some safety pins. The more silver safety pins you have holding your jeans tight from the ankle up the better, but I can't find any. I notice a faded black T-shirt of Dad's poking out of the top of a bag of old clothes. Mum uses these as rags for polishing shoes and cleaning behind the back of the toilet. I take off the shirt I'm wearing, an uncomfortable green striped one with a scratchy collar, and put on Dad's old shirt. I shove the stripped shirt into the bag of rags.

I think I can sneak by Mum and grab my jacket without her noticing what I'm wearing, but she looks up irritably from the paper when I come back upstairs.

"What are you wearing, Daisy? Don't you have anything

clean? You can't wear that shirt to school. What about that pink sweatshirt? I haven't seen you wear it in ages."

"Mum, I like this."

"Daisy!"

"I've got to go, Mum. I'll be late for school."

"No one cares what I think anymore," she moans, and I shut the door with more vigour than I intended, making it slam. Hot tears come up, but I blink them back and grind my teeth together.

Wanda sits in a cloud of strawberry, and the smell is sweet and tempting. I'm starving too, having abandoned my toast because of the morning discussion. Hunger and the guilt about disappointing Mum are both making my stomach rumble. However much I rustle papers, when I feel a loud gurgle coming on, I know other people must be able to hear it.

My stomach lets out a particularly embarrassing and loud sound, like thunder followed by a bubble bursting. Wanda does her trademark eye roll and sticks her hand holding the half-eaten pack of gum out under my desk. I shake my head and say just audibly, "No thanks." My mouth waters at the thought of that first burst of flavour.

Miss Blake raises her head; we're supposed to be silent reading. I finished my book a week ago, and I'm staring at a page and picking a word and seeing what other words I can make from the letters in it. In "peninsula," there is "in," "pen," "sale," "nine," "penis"; probably more. Wanda offers the pack again.

"Take a piece. Don't be such a chicken."

I take the gum this time. The flavour explodes inside my mouth, the sweetness rushing over my tongue. The first few chews release sugar and the taste of red, and fool my stomach into silence. I am careful only to chew down occasionally and mostly just to move the lump of gum around with my tongue. I'm thinking about chickens and rooster penises, and wondering exactly where the egg comes out of the chicken. I am distracted and have started carelessly working the piece of gum between my teeth. Then I hear it:

"Daisy Radcliffe, come here."

Miss Blake points at the wastepaper basket. I let the gum fall from my mouth, still red, juicy and soft, into the garbage can.

"I'm disappointed in you, Daisy," Miss Blake says, as she writes my name in squeaking letters up on the black board under the ever-present word *DETENTION*. She wrote the word on the board the first day of class and underlined it twice in blue.

I have never stayed behind for a detention before. Some kids have their name written up on the blackboard all the time for running in the classroom, talking, or passing notes. Today it is me for chewing gum, Curtis for running in the hall, Everett for talking in class, and Damon for writing on his desk.

Curtis, Everett, and I have to write out lines. I am supposed to write out, "I will not chew gum in class," fifty times. Miss Blake has presented Damon with a rag and a spray bottle, and told him to go around the class scrubbing graffiti off the desks. I only have six of my fifty lines done, and my hand is crampy and I feel panicky.

"I'm going across the hall for two minutes. No talking! None. What-so-ever."

As soon as Miss Blake is gone, Damon comes up to

Wanda's desk and looks at the big love heart with *W. W. + A.R.* that Wanda has etched into it with the point of her protractor. Damon makes no attempt to scrub off the red ink she has repeatedly applied to the groove. He watches me for a few seconds.

"You're doing it wrong."

"What do you mean?" I whisper my reply, although Damon is just using his normal speaking voice. I also move my sheet to cover a discretely pencilled *D.R. loves D.J.* written in faint and tiny letters on the corner of my desk.

"Miss Blake can't hear you," he whispers back to me. Then he shows me how to write the sentence on one line and just copy each word fifty times underneath. I finish my columns of *I, will, not, chew,* and *gum* just before four o'clock. Everyone else has had more practice, and they finish early and are all staring at the clock, watching each minute slip by and waiting for Miss Blake to free us.

She calls us up one by one, and I am last. I carry the page up to her desk. She makes me stand there for a few minutes while she counts the lines and looks closely for mistakes.

"Put it in the garbage, Daisy." I throw my piece of paper in the metal bin; the smell of rotten oranges drifts up as my paper floats down, landing on top of the abandoned and wasted wad of gum I spat out earlier.

"You may go now, Daisy."

"Thank you," I mumble, and gather my things and get out as fast as I can.

The schoolyard is almost empty. Cathy and I were going to go to her house tonight, but she didn't wait for me. Wanda is sitting alone on a swing in the playground, spinning and unspinning around. We are banned from this as it is supposed to weaken the chains.

"You want to come over?" she asks me.

I don't tell Mum Wanda's parents are both still at work when I call to tell her where I am.

"Miss Blake is such a loser. I can't believe she gave you a detention."

"She hates me. I think she likes Mr. Dean. She was in his class for half of Detention."

"He always wears track pants, and you can see his thing."

"That's so gross."

"I swear I've seen him with a hard-on."

"Wanda!"

"Oh, come on. Like you haven't noticed. Murray had one the other day in class. I could tell because he put his ball cap on his lap to cover it up."

"What happens if a boy gets one in front of the class? Or at a funeral or something?"

"I guess they just hope no one notices?" says Wanda. She takes a pencil and sticks it at her crotch and starts moving it up and down. She makes sound effects, a long *bloop* that rises in tone when the pencil goes up and descends when it goes down. Laughter takes over. When I catch my breath, I let out a tiny *bloop*, and we start laughing again.

Wanda's mom comes home and feeds us chips and cans of Pepsi. She says I have beautiful eyes and offers to "do something" with my hair.

"So who's the best-looking boy in your class, Daisy? Wanda won't tell me anything!"

"Mom, please. There are no good-looking boys in my

class. I've told you this a hundred times." Wanda sighs.

"Come on, give your mom a hug."

Wanda sighs again, but drapes her arms around her seated mother's shoulders and pecks her on the cheek. Wanda makes a random downwards *bloop* sound, and we both start giggling.

"You girls are cracked," her mom says.

Dad is at the house when I get home from Wanda's. He is picking up socks and his good suit. Mum is ironing a shirt for him to take with him. He gives me a pen from the North American Rat Conference and a pack of complimentary airplane peanuts. I hide in my room and put my ear against the heating vent, but all I can hear from them is a sad murmuring.

four

Miss Blake gets us to write our names down on little pieces of paper and puts them in an empty fishbowl. Sonny and Cher, the goldfish she brought in to be our class pets, died the first week of school, and she didn't replace them.

Technically you can opt out of the gift exchange for religious or other (your family is too poor) reasons, but no one does. She calls each student up, and we each pull a name out of the glass bowl, a waterline stain still around its edge. Miss Blake writes the names down, so no one can cheat and pretend they didn't pick out the name of a kid they hate. I don't care who I get, as long as it isn't Candice. I pull Murray's name from the hat. We're supposed to keep the whole thing secret, but by the next day, most of us know who our Secret Santa is.

Mum tries to get me to buy a packet of marzipan fruit from the German deli for Murray.

"No way."

"Why not, Daisy? It's cute. Look at the little banana. And you love marzipan."

"It's for a boy. It can't be cute. And marzipan is weird."

"I don't see what's weird about marzipan. And we're here, and it will save us time."

"No. I can't."

Mum and I are shopping for things to send belatedly to her parents in England. The deli is busy with the Saturday crowd and women ordering huge amounts of cheese and cold cuts for upcoming parties. I look around the store. There are chocolate apples, different kinds of black licorice candies, and more marzipan—this time pigs. I consider the pig, then I remember that I am buying this for fat Murray. I convince Mum to buy us a small Christmas tree in a pot of dry brown dirt with Styrofoam glitter balls twist-tied to its limbs, hoping this will cheer us both up.

In the Italian Market, Mum sees the pyramid of festively decorated panettone boxes, puts down her half-full shopping basket, and leaves the store. She walks past Mrs. Davis from church, who is calling out her name, and crosses the parking lot only pausing for the slightest moment to look for oncoming cars. I hurry after her, giving a brief nod and smile at Mrs. Davis.

When I reach Mum, she is sitting in the car with her head resting on the steering wheel. "Your father always bought panettone at Christmas. He'd eat exactly one piece and wouldn't let me throw it out until it started turning green."

"Panettone tastes like sawdust," I say.

"What's wrong with me, Daisy? Why did he leave me?" I rub her back and pass her the tissues I find in the glove compartment.

Mum sends me to the pharmacy with a list of things we

need. I pick out a box of chocolates for Murray. It's the cheap kind in a big fancy box, the ones that look good but taste like sweetened candle wax. It's better than nothing. And it's not like I can give Murray the unopened pack of fruit-flavoured bubble bath I got from Secret Santa last year.

The gift exchange takes place the last day of classes, four days before Christmas. Everyone is talking about their holiday plans. "Okay, class," Miss Blake says, and everyone ignores her. Miss Blake slams a metre stick down on her desk to get our attention.

"You all need to sit down and be quiet, or we're not going to do this."

Peony hands out the gifts. We have to wait until everyone has theirs, then we get to open them. There is an awkward moment when Kevin Taylor's gift appears to be missing, but Everett remembers it's still in his backpack. My gift is tiny, wrapped carefully in gold paper and tied with red ribbon that has been curled into a mass that is larger than the actual gift. Wanda fidgets beside me as it gets placed on my desk. I recognize her handwriting on the tiny folded piece of wrapping paper that acts as a card.

It's half a heart pendant. Wanda kept the other half for herself; it says *Be Fri* and my half says *st ends*. It is one of the best gifts at the exchange. These pendants are popular; you can only get them from the Consumers Distributing catalogue. Candice has one that she shares with her big sister that says rite ter.

When I get home from school, the Christmas tree and its pot are missing. There is a trail of pine needles heading out of the house towards the garbage bin.

Mum is wrapping the gifts she bought to send to England. "I don't know why I'm bothering. They won't make it until practically Easter."

She is using masking tape, and it must be old because it keeps unsticking.

"Look what Wanda got me." Mum eyes the pendant.

"Wanda isn't really your best friend, is she? You just met her. You don't want to hurt Cathy's feelings."

It turns my skin kind of green after the first couple of days, and Mum notices. "You'll get a rash if you keep wearing that, Daisy."

I keep wearing it. I take the pendant off the thin chain it came on and wear it on a leather cord around my wrist.

On Christmas Eve, I light cranberry-scented candles and even put on the album of the King's College choir singing in saintly voices to try and festive things up. Mum makes me take the album off, claiming it makes her too emotional. Elizabeth puts on an old Beatles record, but this makes Mum weepy too. We eat our Christmas Eve dinner of smoked salmon in moody silence.

On Christmas Day, Donald comes first thing at 9 a.m. before he and the Rat drive to a resort in the Muskokas to spend the holidays. He comes in for a quick cup of tea and a Marks & Spencer minced pie, as none of us have done any baking. It is very awful having him here. He gives each of us a card with a cheque inside: me, Elizabeth, and Mum. It's like receiving a Christmas bonus. Mum gives him a Gordon Lightfoot CD and looks meaningfully at him when she hands it over. Elizabeth and I jointly give him an Old Spice soap-on-a-rope. When he leaves, Elizabeth and I each enact a fast and obligatory hug, and slink away from the door and back into the kitchen. He and Mum stay in the hall saying goodbye for an uncomfortably long period of time.

Then we go to church.

It's what we do every year, even though none of us enjoy it. We sit at the back, and halfway through Mum starts crying. The tears just roll down, and of course people notice. She doesn't go up for communion, so we all just stay kneeling and waiting for this to be over. At the end of the service, as everyone else bustles out to get the turkey on, we wait. Elizabeth and I give stony stares to any unwelcome well-wishers, and then we leave by a side door, avoiding happy holiday families and the deacon dressed up as Santa.

five

Greensborough High School is the academic school. There are two other high schools in town; one is the technical school where they teach hairdressing and auto shop, and the other is the school with the swimming pool that the athletic kids go to. It's close enough to our school that the group of us planning to attend Greensborough are sent to walk there without adult supervision. The other kids get bussed off for tours of their future high schools.

I'm cold and nervous as we trudge down the snowy streets. I'm wearing a pair of steel-toed combat boots that I liberated from Elizabeth's closet, and my feet feel numb when we arrive. We've been told to report to the main office. In a self-conscious and terrified clump, we enter through one of the student entrances and make our way down the hall to the main office. The older kids stare at us. They look alarmingly adult. "Look how young and cute they are!" I hear a girl say as we walk by. There's a couple making out in the semi-privacy of an open locker door, and it's hard not to stare at them. Damon whispers, "Get a room," as we walk past, not quite loudly enough for them to hear, but loudly enough that I hold my breath in case there are ramifications for his comment. When we get to the office, the secretary points at some chairs and says, "Wait." We wait.

A tall boy in a school jacket comes into the office, and the boys go off with him. The girls wait longer, and the secretary shoots us dirty looks like it's our fault no one has come to collect us. Eventually, when the wait is becoming unbearable, my vision sweeps in. It's Damon's sister, my future self, with her glorious hair, black leather jacket, and blood-red lips.

"Children, children, gather round," she says, ignoring the secretary's glare.

I follow blindly as she streaks ahead of us down the hall. She shows us the cafeteria, takes us to a Drama class, interrupts a Band class. We walk right past the science rooms and the gym. She knocks on the door of an English class and introduces us to a teacher by his first name, Gerry. He sits on top of his desk, wearing jeans, and no one raises their hand, they just speak when they have something to say. We leave Gerry's class and troop out to the smoking section, where the girl lights up and gets us to introduce ourselves. When I croak out my name, "Daisy," lisping the S, a nervous habit, she smiles.

"I know who you are," she says, looking me up and down. "You beat up the bitch in your class. Damon's my brother, he told me all about it."

I don't know what to say, so I just smile.

"She didn't beat her up," Cathy says.

Cora, as we have learned her name is, flicks her butt away. She looks at Cathy and says, "Did you say something?"

Then, as we stand there, a guy comes over and bums a

smoke off Cora. He is good-looking. He has long hair and tight jeans, and I try hard to avoid looking at his crotch. Wanda is alert. She's standing beside me, and it's like a wave of electricity passes over us. This is the kind of boyfriend she has been looking for, not the preppy boys we saw in the classrooms earlier. She flicks her hair behind her ear and then pretends to be listening to something Cathy is saying about the school's excellent music program, but we are both taking in every word Cora and the guy say.

"You hear about Weiner?"

"Oh my god. Yes. He's lucky he didn't get arrested."

"Just cautioned. He's grounded for months."

"He's always doing such stupid stuff."

"That's Weiner for you."

The guy is done his cigarette, and he grinds his butt into the ground.

"See you in Band, Cora."

"He's in Band?" It escapes Cathy's mouth, and I can imagine an incredulous thought bubble surrounding her words.

"Second trumpet," Cora tells her, and I briefly consider taking music.

When I get home, Elizabeth has arrived for the weekend. I can hear them up in Mum's room.

"I got an interview," Mum says as soon as I come in the room. All her clothes are strewn across the bed, and Elizabeth is fingering an orange-and-brown silk blouse.

"It's all just a bit dated, that's all, Mum. It's not that they aren't nice clothes, but you want to look modern."

"Not like I haven't worked in two decades, you mean?"

"Well," says Elizabeth, "yes."

The three of us stare at price tags and look through racks of clothes. Nothing is quite right. Mum is getting discouraged. Entering the sixth store of the day, Elizabeth banishes Mum from the racks and sends her to the change rooms. My job is to make sure Mum doesn't leave without trying on whatever Elizabeth gathers.

I'm overheated in my jacket and feel like I could slump from the chair I'm sitting on to the carpet, which is alarmingly littered with loose pins and bits of thread. A sales woman tries to help and produces a purple pant suit with padded shoulders.

"Thanks," says Mum curtly. She takes the suit into her stall, but does not try it on. It is like a miracle when Elizabeth appears holding the items she's found, a grey boucle skirt and jacket, marked down, and a sky-blue blouse to go underneath it. Mum eyes everything, then taking in the reduced price sticker, agrees to try them on.

We leave the store triumphant. This is my moment, Elizabeth and I have discussed tactics.

"Mum."

"Yes, Daisy."

"Can I get my ears pierced?"

For a moment I think she will say no. But she looks from me to Elizabeth.

"Yes. And I'm going to get mine done too."

We enter Noah's. Noah's is the fancy hairdresser's. They play loud music, and when we walk in, the smell of expensive floral shampoo hits us. Noah's has dim lighting, and ladies sit chatting as red dye gets brushed into their hair. At Hair for You, where we usually go to get my bangs cut, all you can smell are the chemicals they use to do the perms.

Amanda takes our money and shows us the studs we can choose from. I choose a plain steel pair, and Mum goes for ones that have a green cubic zirconium in them. It's all women in here, except for one male hairdresser who's wearing really tight pants and calls Mum "darling" when he has to nudge past her.

"Just squeezing past, darling," he says.

The woman who pierces the ears is called Vanessa. We have to wait for her to finish with one of her hair clients. Her eyebrows are plucked into thin arched lines, and her own ears are pierced three times on each side.

She is delighted Mum is getting hers done.

"It's about time, honey. You will love it. Change your earrings and you can change your whole outfit. I can do some-thing about the grey in your hair too, if you want."

Mum goes first. Vanessa spends a lot of time making sure the dots she has placed on each one of Mum's earlobes are even. She gets Elizabeth and I to approve the placement of the marks, and then she dabs Mum's ears with rubbing alcohol and gets out the gun. Mum closes her eyes. I don't watch, but I know it's done by the noise that sounds a lot like a stapler.

Vanessa turns to me.

"Okay, sweetie, your turn now."

"It hardly hurts, Daisy, just like getting a shot," Mum says, but she looks very pale, and the male hairdresser has ushered her to a chair.

The metal is cold against my ear, and I am focussing on holding still. Vanessa shoots in the first stud. As she is setting up the second one, I realize I can't hear properly and my vision is getting fuzzy. The gun goes off, and the other ear is done. I get off the stool and everything goes black. I wake up lying on the hairdresser's shiny black floor with Vanessa's long curly tresses hanging around my face as she gently slaps my cheeks.

"Okay, chicka, you're fine. We caught you on the way down. Just a little shock. It's all done now."

"Daisy, Daisy, are you alright? Say something to me, Daisy."

I try to say I'm fine, but I feel so ridiculous lying here on the floor that I start laughing, and it tips over into laugh-crying. When I start, Elizabeth does too, and neither of us can stop. Every time we look at each other, it gets worse. We are both laughing and weeping on the floor, and Mum is still fussing,

"Daisy, you're hysterical. Stop laughing, Elizabeth, it's not helping. Pull yourself together."

I see Candice walking past the store with her mom, clutching several large, full shopping bags. Candice looks at me and Elizabeth surrounded by concerned hairdressers handing us tissues and patting our shoulders. I look her straight in the eye, and she turns her head away not wanting to meet my gaze.

On Valentine's Day we have a small class party. We sit at our desks eating chips and cinnamon hearts off of paper towels. Miss Blake plays CHUM FM from a portable radio. Wanda asks me if I like Damon.

"No," I say. "No, not all." I feel my cheeks getting hot as I lie to her.

"I knew it. You'd be good together," Wanda tells me, and I feel a surge of pride.

I see Cora pick Damon up from school. I start to walk over in her direction. I'm deciding if I'm brave enough to say hi. I see Mr. Dean marching towards her car and divert my route. I think he is going to yell at Cora for smoking out front of the school; you can only smoke in the staff room and in the back teacher's parking lot. I am surprised when Mr. Dean leans down, smiling, to talk into her window. Cora laughs up at Mr. Dean and blows smoke out of the side of her mouth so it doesn't head in his direction. Damon gets in the car and doesn't even look at Mr. Dean. Cora sees me and waves as she pulls out, but Damon stares straight ahead through the windscreen.

Mum is on the phone when I get home from school. She didn't get the job she interviewed for. "Not as much recent experience as the other candidate," she says to me, getting off the phone. "How am I supposed to get experience if no one hires me?"

There are a bunch of flowers Dad sent sitting in a vase on the dining-room table. Mum is not sure if he sent them on purpose or if his secretary doesn't know he's left her and just placed the order like she does every year. Halfway through supper she gets up and puts her still full plate next to the sink.

six

"Daisy, come here and talk some sense into your mother."
It's Olivia. I have walked into a white-wine-fumed discussion.

"What's Daisy going to do if I'm working for March
Break? Hang around here all day by herself?"

"What's she going to do if you don't take the job? It's not
like you two were heading off to Florida."

"Oliva wants me to fill in at her office as receptionist for
a week, but it's over March Break."

"Do it," I say. I have been dreading a week of Mum and I
stuck in the house together.

It is the Sunday night before Mum's first day of temping.
The batteries in my Walkman are dead. I scroll through the
stations on my clock radio. I come across the talk show *Sex
with Sue* and turn the volume right down. I can just barely hear
it. I'm listening, rapt, when Mum starts tromping across the
hall towards my bedroom in what must be high heels. I quickly
twiddle the dial until the speakers admit static fuzz with only
the occasional line of a French pop song making it through.
Mum knocks lightly, but doesn't wait before opening the door.

46

"You're sure I'll look alright tomorrow?" she asks me. She's wearing her interview outfit and newly polished black pumps.

"You look great. That looks perfect."

"You think so?" The radio emits a particularly loud buzz, and Mum looks at it, then me. "Are you alright? You look a bit flushed. Don't answer the door to strangers tomorrow. And if you use the stove—"

"Mum. I'll be fine."

"Well, alright." She surveys my room. "You could spend some time cleaning up in here." She eyes the piles of clothes on my floor, my desk covered in dusty bits of paper.

In the morning, Mum wakes me before she leaves; I wish her luck, then close my eyes and sleep until noon. I get up and walk from room to empty room. I look out the front window. It's warmer today, and the accumulated snow has formed into brown slush that lies in ridges across the road. The sidewalk is a slick of water-covered ice. There is nothing to do.

I head back into my bedroom and lie on top of my unmade bed. My eyelids feel heavy and my limbs warm. The feeling comes, a tingling in my thighs, my armpits gets sweaty. I know girls can masturbate, but I don't really know how. I experimentally put a finger down into my underwear, but I feel embarrassed. I go to the bathroom and wash my hands.

I put the plug in the bathtub and turn on the taps. Using my hand to test the temperature of the water, I feel the pressure and I remember something I heard. I make sure the water isn't too hot, then get into the bath. Lying on my back, I scoot my bum down until I'm right down at the faucet end of the bathtub. The water is halfway up my ears when I lie back. I put my left leg straight up in the air, and my right I sling over the side of the bathtub. The water pours down over my crotch. At first it just feels nice, like the comforting pleasure of putting your hand over the end of the hose, and then something starts to happen. I've never felt this before—it's a sensation that sweeps through me; at first it comes down through my fingertips and down through my body. The thoughts in my brain shut off, and all I can do is feel the pleasure of the water coursing over me. My body bucks up, and I pull away from the tap—the feel of it suddenly too much. I'm throbbing like I have a second heartbeat. A wave has splashed all over the bathroom floor, and water is going straight down into the overflow drain from the still running tap, and I'm laughing, my body filling with relief and a physical joy.

The other kids show off Piglets from Disneyland and accumulated chair-lift tags on the zips of their ski jackets. "How was your break? What did you do?" Wanda asks me.

"I read and took long baths," I tell her.

Now March Break is over, all anyone talks about is the grade eight overnight trip at the end of the year.

"I need these back by the last day of April. Make sure your parents sign the permission slip. Just handing in a cheque isn't enough." Miss Blake lays the form across my desk.

I take the permission slip for the week-long trip to Quebec and fold it in two. I have to decide if I'm going to participate in this rite of passage. Mum is on the phone when I come in. I point at the slip, and she nods as I place it beneath the salt shaker. Later it is stuck to the fridge with a Union Jack magnet, but Mum doesn't mention it and nor do I.

Elizabeth sees it when she arrives home on Friday.

"You'll have fun," she says.

"I'm not sure I want to go," I say.

"There are just so many things that could go wrong. What if she gets her period?" Mum says.

"Nothing will go wrong, and she'll take some Tylenol and use a tampon." They both look at me.

"She doesn't use tampons yet," Mum says.

"You should start," Elizabeth says. Today she takes no prisoners.

Mum and I look at Elizabeth. I imagine getting stuck for a week sharing a room with Candice, or worse, Miss Blake.

"It's so much money right at the moment," Mum says.

"What about Dad?" Elizabeth says.

"You could ask him on Wednesday when he comes to take you for dinner," Mum says hesitantly to me.

"I'll ask him," I say, deciding Elizabeth is right and I should go.

I get ready too early, nervous at having a date with my father. I wait with my jacket and shoes on at the front door. He shows up late. "There's a flea infestation at the lab. I've got to get back. I can't take you for dinner tonight. Some other time, okay?"

Mum stands behind me with a pile of short-sleeved shirts Dad requested that she pull out for him. I can smell detergent coming from them; they are freshly washed and newly folded. He gathers the shirts, and leaves.

In the bathroom I fill the sink with water and then light the corner of the pink permission slip. Pieces of light ash rise slightly in the air and then fall into the sink. I have to drop it before the entire thing is reduced to ash. The last part is too damp to burn, so I crumple it into a tight ball, wrap it in toilet paper, and stick it in the bottom of the garbage.

Wanda, Peony, Murray, epileptic Brittany, the two poor kids Ken Smith and Lisa Kelly, and I stand in the back of Mr. Dean's class while he takes attendance. There are not enough desks for us to stay in Mr. Dean's classroom. He sends us to the library to work on our assignments. Miss Blake wants us to make up tourism guides for Quebec with pictures and little captions. This way we'll get to learn about all the places our classmates are going this week.

"Do we get marks on this?" Wanda asks, but Mr. Dean ignores her question.

On Wednesday, Wanda finds a big coffee-table book about the architecture of Quebec, sticks a copy of *Anna Karenina* in the middle, and settles down to read. The librarian ignores us. Brittany didn't show up to school today. Peony is knitting a Bonhomme scarf using a complicated method involving straws and wool. Ken, Lisa, and Murray are looking up rude words in the dictionary.

"*Anals*," says Murray. "It just goes on about something year by year?"

"That's annals, dumbass," Lisa says, grabbing the book from him. "You're looking up the wrong word."

Culture in Quebec, I write, *has got to be better than this.*

Wanda announces her book is boring. The sun shines outside of the library windows. It's the first warm day of spring.

"Let's get out of here," Wanda says to me.

"We'll get in trouble."

"No one will notice. We'll come back before home time."

The librarian is in the staff room. She spends more time there drinking coffee than in the library.

"Leave your jacket and grab a Duo-Tang." I follow Wanda's instructions. In the hall we pass the staff room, the smell of smoke leaking out from under the bottom of its door. We keep heading down the hall. I figured we were headed to the girls' washroom, but Wanda keeps going.

"Act casual," she says.

A teacher and a janitor walk by us and don't even give us a second glance. The hallway is clear. Wanda slowly opens one of the school's side doors, grabs my arm, and pushes me through. She slips outside after me. We duck down and walk by the windows of the grade seven classroom. Once we're clear of the windows, Wanda heads to the alley that acts as a shortcut between the school and one of the residential streets. It cuts between the yards of two suburban houses. I follow a few steps behind her. I stand in the short stretch of path waiting for someone to come yelling after us, but nothing happens. All I can hear is blood beating in my ears and the sound of Wanda breathing.

Despite the warm weather, we are starting to get cold in the shade; we didn't bring our jackets. There's an old gate in the fence on one side of us; it's overgrown with shrubs, but Wanda and I force it open. We push through twiggy branches and find ourselves in a sun-filled back garden. The curtains are drawn, and it doesn't look like anyone is home. I look over the fence. I can't see a car out front. At the back of the yard, there is a patio bordered with large planters made out of old railway ties that block the wind. We hunker down and sit behind one of the planters in case someone comes out of the house.

I grin at Wanda. I feel the sun burning through my jeans, and I'm thinking about the summer.

Wanda leans forward and hauls a crushed pack of cigarettes from her back pocket. She flips up the squashed cardboard lid, and I see the top of one cigarette poking out through silver foil. Wanda takes out the lone cigarette. It is bent into a curve, and in places, the paper is wrinkled. Wanda fishes out a book of matches from inside the remains of the pack and gets me to hold the cigarette while she lights a match. She takes the smoke from me and puts it in her mouth. It won't light properly, just flares for a moment, and then goes out. She drops the lit match and examines the cigarette. There is a crack in it. She breaks off the end of it and lights a second match. This time the loose bits of yellow tobacco at the end start to glow; Wanda inhales steadily, and then exhales smoke. She proffers the forbidden cigarette, and I stick the damp filter in my mouth and breathe in. I can taste Wanda's lip gloss.

Not much comes out when I exhale. Wanda takes the cigarette from me and takes another deep drag, then extinguishes the remains in one of the planters. She buries the butt under a small mound of soil and sticks a dead leaf above it stalk down, like a tiny flag. No one even questions our absence when we return to the library.

The Game starts two weeks after the other kids return from Quebec. The rules are unclear to me, but it twists my stomach just watching it take place. Not everyone plays; those of us who usually stick to the sidelines don't participate, and Wanda, who is good at Red Rover and Murder Ball, avoids this. Darlene and Jenny are observers too, shaking their heads no when Candice calls out to them.

The Game always takes place on the basketball pad by the back door of the school. No windows face this area. The door where the senior classes line up is here, but the area can't be seen by Miss Blake casually looking out of her window. For a lot of the Game, the players stand around kicking the cracked surface of the concrete. Eventually, a group of boys decide to chase the girls. They'll go for the pack, but once they've managed to separate out one girl, they'll ignore the others and focus on their lone victim.

Wanda and I sit on the players' bench by the side of the baseball diamond. We have a view of the proceedings here, but are far enough away we won't be mistaken for participants. I look up at the sound of feminine screaming. Three boys, Brett, George, and Tony, rush towards a group of six girls who have momentarily let their guard down. Candice is facing the wrong direction and doesn't see them coming. She steps back, and the boys fill the space between her and her friends. She takes off across the school ground; a pack of boys pursue. Candice is fast. She runs to the left and soon clears the hidden part of the school grounds. The teacher acting as recess monitor blows her whistle when Candice gets close to the edge of the school yard boundary. This ends the pursuit, and the boys lope back towards the basketball court. Candice bends over catching her breath, then slowly follows behind the boys.

The other players wait for Brett, Tony, and George to return. None of the other boys hanging around are serious players. They take part in the initial chase that separates someone out, but not the shirt lifting. That is always done by Brett,

Tony, and George. There's about five minutes left of recess when the boys lunge again. This time it's Tiffany they pursue. She's not fast, and instead of running the same direction as Candice, where eventually she'll become visible to the teacher in charge of us, she runs straight back past where Wanda and I are sitting, towards the track field that can't be seen from anywhere except the back end of the school. I hear Wanda swallow when Brett gets close enough and grabs Tiffany's arm. She's stopped running and is surrounded by the three boys. They pull up her shirt exposing her bra. Usually, this is the end of it. I look away, but I can hear the taunts. "Show us your titties, show us your titties, show us your titties."

"Brett," I hear Candice yelling. "Stop, that's enough." The boys ignore her, and I look back. Tiffany's face is covered by her T-shirt, her hands held up in the air by Tony. Brett reaches out and pulls the side of her bra over her left breast so her nipple is exposed. It points out, vulnerable like the nose of a mouse. I look away back towards the school. Mr. Dean has come out the door at the back of the school, and he is watching.

He notices my eyes on him.

"Enough, boys," he yells.

The bell rings, and Wanda and I walk slowly over and join the lineup. Tiffany joins the back of the line. I'm afraid to look at her.

Throughout the morning announcements the next day, Miss Blake is unusually solemn.

"Class," says Miss Blake, "before our spelling test, we're going to do something different this morning. We need to talk about what you are all doing during recess." There's a knock at the door, and Mr. Dean stands there along with all the girls in his grade seven class.

"Mr. Dean is going to take all the boys back to his classroom, and the grade seven girls are going to join us. Off you go, boys. Get up so the girls can take your seats."

The boys get up and shuffle out behind Mr. Dean. I hear him say, "Don't look so terrified. I know how it is. Boys will be boys, eh?"

The grade seven girls take the vacant seats among us. They look pale. None of us want to be in this room right now.

Miss Blake sits on her desk. "I'm sorry we have to have this talk, and to be honest I'm disappointed in all of you grade eights. I thought you all had more respect for yourselves. I need you to understand that the game the grade eights have been playing is wrong. What you were doing could have had serious consequences. Your bodies, your breasts, are not things to be flashed around without thought. They are a special part of you."

I purposefully block out the rest of what she says. I make a thundering sound in my ears. I can do this if I concentrate hard enough and vibrate the muscles across my forehead. I have my hand up over one ear. Wanda notices before Miss Blake and jabs me in the leg. I drop my hand.

"Boys, men, will take any opportunity. That's why I'm particularly disappointed in you girls. Boys sometimes can't control their urges. Does anyone have anything they want to say? Candice?"

"I'm sorry, Miss Blake. We won't play anymore."

"Tiffany?"

"Sorry, Miss Blake," Tiffany whispers while still looking down.

"The rest of you."

"Sorry," we collectively mumble.

"Good. We'll say no more about it then."

seven

Miss Blake is getting us to vote on a theme for our grad. She is writing suggestions on the board. *Silver and Gold*, *Putting on the Ritz*, *Shoot for the Stars*, *Top of the Class* are all her ideas. Candice suggests "Oriental Nights."

"We can decorate the gym with paper cranes and paper umbrellas. The banquet is always at Mr. Lee's, so it makes sense." Miss Blake writes down *Oriental Nights*.

"Do you have any ideas for 'Oriental Nights'?" Miss Blake asks Peony, and Peony just shakes her head no. *Shoot for the Stars* wins.

"We can make stars with all of your names on them, and maybe some rockets and a few planets. How about a big moon hanging over the stage?" Miss Blake spits a little as she plans it all out.

Mum is watching the news with the paper on her lap. They are showing footage from a pro-life rally today at the Morgentaler clinic. Protesters wearing woollen hats like tea cozies are holding up signs depicting bloody dead fetuses. Mum's circling job ads.

"Mum, I need something to wear to grade eight graduation."

"Can't you wear that dress from Sheena's wedding? You've only worn it once."

It is a cotton dress that reminds me of the costumes on *Little House on the Prairies*. The dress is tight in the neck and flattens my breasts. I try it on and show it to Mum.

"That's a beautiful dress and you look so pretty in it," she says, barely glancing up.

"It's not like what the other girls are going to wear."

"I can't help if it these North Americans make such a fuss about switching schools."

"It's too tight."

"Try holding your stomach in."

I lift my arms above my head and hear the satisfying rip of fabric as the seam in one of the armpits tears apart. I stretch my arms higher, making the tear longer.

Mum looks up at me properly.

"You did that on purpose."

"I didn't!" I lie.

At school Cathy shows me a picture of her dress in the Sears catalogue; it's pink with a ruched top with sparkles and a sticky-out tutu skirt. At Wanda's her mom is cutting down an old shiny peach dress she once wore as a bridesmaid.

"It's going to have one shoulder strap and a tulip bottom," she explains to me, pinning the hem as Wanda stands on a kitchen chair.

"What are you wearing, Daisy?" Wanda's mom asks me innocently.

Mum has sewn up the rip and the rough hand-stitched

seam rubs in my armpit like punishment. Mum and Elizabeth sit on the couch, and I come down wearing the repaired garment.

"It's really not great," Elizabeth says.

"Don't you have something she can borrow? What did you wear?"

"That terrible white dress. I spilt fruit punch down it," Elizabeth says, and then mouths, "on purpose" to me.

"I don't need to go to grad," I say.

"It is a lot of fuss for grade eight," Mum says hopefully.

"You're going," says Elizabeth. "Both of you," she says, shooting Mum a warning glance.

"I'm not wearing this dress," I pronounce.

"What about your black dress?" Elizabeth says to Mum.

"That dress is ancient. And black, it's a bit funereal."

"Daisy won't mind that. Funereal is in."

They observe my face. I am perfecting a smearing technique with eyeliner.

It is a relic of Mum's from the sixties. Sleeveless black velvet with a simple cut that comes just to my knees. The fabric is stiff enough that it holds in my gut, and I don't feel self-conscious with the way it reveals my new, more curved shape.

"I knew I kept that for a reason," Mum says.

"Do you like it, Daisy?" Elizabeth asks.

"Yes," I say, and I'm not lying. Mum drives Elizabeth to the bus station, and I go to see her off. Back at home, the light is blinking on the answering machine. There is a message for Mum asking her to call and arrange a time to come in for an interview at the town hall. They are hiring a new front desk clerk. We whoop. Mum calls Olivia to come celebrate, and I try my dress on for her.

"You look fabulous!" Olivia tells me, and Mum pours me a half-glass of wine. The first few sips taste like cat pee and perfume, but then I stop noticing the smell and it's finished before I want it to be. Before I take off the dress, I stand balancing on the edge of the bath so I can see myself in the mirror. I take in my reflection for a long time.

The ceremony is hot and long. Mum and Elizabeth sit in the audience, and I sit next to Wanda at the front. Peony gives the valedictory speech. She talks about what great friends she has made during grade school and how we will always keep in touch as we grow older. She's moving to Calgary and no one has her address.

The other girls are crying and standing on the lawn of the school, saying how much they'll miss each other. I'm not crying. Elizabeth, Wanda, and I stand in a corner and watch Candice's mom organize group shots. She tries to get me in one, but Elizabeth saves me by saying we have to go find Mum, and we simply walk away. Wanda's parents take a picture of me and Wanda. Her mom makes us put our arms around each other's shoulders, and I pick up the scent of Dove's Baby Soft perfume. I take a picture of Wanda, holding a rose and mini foil graduation balloon standing in between her smiling mom and dad.

Cora catches my hand as I am walking by her. "That is a cool dress."

There's a party at Candice's. Her dad has a basement bar with a fancy stereo. Pop and chips will be liberally supplied. Everyone's invited, although some of us are expected not to attend. I walk home with Elizabeth and Mum.

I keep Mum's black dress on and lie in the dark, listening to Kate Bush and wondering what is happening at Candice's. When I wake in the morning, the clock says 10:00 a.m. and I'm wiping sleep from my eyes. I don't know what time I fell asleep. I'm still wearing my grad dress, but I'm under the covers.

"Daisy! Daisy!"

"Mum, you're supposed to knock." I pull the covers up to my chin hiding my dress.

"I got the job. I have a job!" She flounces in and opens my curtains. "Come on, get up. You're wasting the day."

I pull the covers over my head, and she leaves the room humming.

eight

"I can get you in to art camp, if you want? One of the campers broke their arm and pulled out. Carmen says one of the perks of the job is getting your kids in municipal programmes without having to line up for hours."

"I'm too old for day camp, Mum."

"You can't just lie in bed all day when I'm at work. It's not good for you. You'll get all fausty. I've got to go, but we'll talk about it when I get home."

"I'm going to Cathy's youth-group barbeque tonight."

"I thought you didn't want to go."

"I changed my mind."

At Cathy's house we pray before eating the hotdogs and potato salad her mom has piled on the picnic table. I stand in a circle with the kids from Cathy's church and we hold hands. I feel my palms sweat in the loose grasp of the boy to my left and the girl on my right. They all say grace, and I watch an ant crawl across the top of my shoe.

A blind speaker comes after dinner. In Cathy's living room, we eat bowls of ice cream, and he tells us how lucky he is to be blind in Canada as his wife projects pictures of semi-naked, blind children lying on dirt floors and covered in flies. He gestures to the opposite side of the room from where the screen is; no one corrects him.

I stay after the other kids leave, and Cathy picks up the acoustic guitar she is learning to play. She plays "Kumbaya" and I make up dirty verses. "Someone's pooping, my lord, kumbaya…someone's peeing my lord, kumbaya." She laughs. "Someone's fucking, my lord," I sing, and she stops playing and tells me I should go home.

Wanda spent the first two weeks of the summer holiday in Barrie with her cousins. One of them did her hair for her. I feel a little shy with her at first, when she shows up at my house. Her hair is bleached blonde, and she's wearing new, very tight jeans and feather earrings. We walk to the park. We're walking past a grown man inside his car stopped at the intersection. He whistles at Wanda through his open window. He looks her up and down, and she tosses her hair. "Don't look, Daisy!" she says, realizing I am staring back at him. He has a bald spot and is wearing a golf shirt.

At the park we find a bench facing the water and wait for something to happen. I am hoping that some boys will show up, or maybe the Dickie Dee cart will come by, and we can buy popsicles. I tell Wanda about "Kumbaya."

"Someone's murdering, my lord, kumbaya."

"Not so loud, someone will hear."

"Someone's stripping, my lord, kumbaya," Wanda sings more loudly, and a passing woman with a stroller shakes her head at her. Wanda is quiet.

"You know, it's true. Someone is stripping, and I don't see why God shouldn't love them," Wanda says.

"Daisy! Don't forget I'm going out tonight. You'll have to get your own dinner, and I want you home by five. No calling from Wanda's. I want to know you're safe at home before I go out."

"Daisy?"

"Okay, okay," I call from beneath my blankets.

The mail arrives at the house at around 10 a.m. and I pick it up from the floor where it has landed. There are the usual bills, but today there is also a blue envelope that has African stamps on it and Dad's handwriting. The seams are just holding together where they have been licked and stuck together. I'm holding the letter up to the sunlight when Wanda arrives. She takes it from my hand and holds it up to see if she can make out any words.

"I can see writing, but it's too messy and I can't read it," she says.

"Mum's been in a good mood recently, and she's supposed to go out with people from work tonight. This could ruin that."

"Maybe you should just hide it from her?"

"What if he wants to move back in?"

I fill the kettle and my hand shakes.

"Are you sure?" Wanda says as she hands me the envelope. It only takes seconds to unseal it when I hold it over the steam coming out of the kettle's spout.

"I'll just stick it back together once I know what's inside," I tell Wanda.

My research is going well. I have found a colony that is surprisingly resistant to ear mites....

The entire letter is about his work, except for one paragraph about a stomach bug that he caught when he first got there.

Say hello to the children for me. Love, Donald. The letter ends.

"He doesn't even mention Elizabeth and me by our names." I read the last line to Wanda.

"Maybe he forgot them?" Wanda says.

"Why did he bother to send this?"

"Get rid of it."

"I can't. That's illegal."

"It's illegal to open someone else's mail, and that didn't stop you. I bet letters get lost all the time on the way from Australia."

"Kenya, he's in Kenya."

"Whatever. If it's not going to help her to read it?"

"It will just make her mad and then sad."

Wanda and I shove the letter between two slats of wood on the porch floor. I want to make it look like our mail man dropped it and it slipped down there accidentally, just in case Mum finds it.

When she gets home, Mum rifles through the pile of mail absentmindedly. "The day that I've had, Daisy. Someone's been stealing stop signs, and people are up in arms. It's not like the town is out taking them down at night. And dog licences, I had to get Carmen to show me again how to issue them. This lady came in to register three poodles. Who needs three poodles? Surely one is more than enough. Carmen says it slows down in the fall and that starting in the summer is like trial by fire. People come out of their houses and start finding things to complain about. I need this drink tonight."

"Who's going?"

"Carmen, I've told you about her. Nancy, Marjory, the mayor's secretary, Glenda, if she gets off on time. She was still waiting for the mayor to get back from lunch when I left, and she can't leave until he's signed a bunch of stuff. And Grahame, he just started too. I don't think Carmen warned him it would be him and all women. He's a historian, well, an archaeologist. Doing a survey on land that's up for development. He's got an NDP sticker on his car. Carmen keeps joking around that he's single, but he's not my type."

Mum changes three times before she heads out. "I won't be late."

When she comes in at midnight, I am still up and I hear her humming to herself.

It was raining too hard to go to the park, so we took the bus to the mall. Wanda and I are sharing an Orange Julius and watching a little kid sit on top of a blue snail that rocks back and forth when you put quarters in it. His mom is digging through her purse to find one. I used to ride this snail, but my favourite was the mini movie theatre, a small box that Mum would plug a quarter in so I could sit inside and watch ancient black-and-white cartoons. The little cinema is still there, but has a big out-of-order sign hanging off it. We talk about these, but both of us are watching three teenage boys, older than us, on the other side of the snail. One is the guy from the smoking section at the high school.

"Second trumpet," Wanda finally says to me.

They're standing outside of the record store. Wanda slurps down the end of the Orange Julius.

"Come on."

The boys talk loudly when we walk past them, and Second Trumpet nods his head at Wanda. Even though it's Wanda he nods to, I feel a flip flop in my stomach. Wanda's jeans are really tight, and when I walk behind her it's hard not to stare. I stand next to Wanda, flipping through the hanging rack of posters. There are cute kittens, ladies in bikinis, the Beatles, and David Lee Roth showing his bum. We're flipping through half-heartedly when Second Trumpet arrives behind us, wearing a nametag. His name is Nick. "You need any help?"

"We're just looking," I stammer out.

"You need anything, come find me," he says, looking at Wanda.

We're going through the records, and Nick returns and comments on the Journey album Wanda has pulled out.

"That's a classic."

"That's my parents' music. I prefer something harder."

"You like G N' R?" He is eyeing her Swatch band.

"Yeah, and Steven Tyler."

"What's your name?"

"Wanda."

"I'm Nick."

"I know," says Wanda, pointing at his nametag.

"You look familiar?"

"I've seen you around."

"Do you go to Greensborough High?"

"No, Clearview, but I'm thinking of transferring." Clearview is the jock high school. I admire Wanda's seamless lie.

"Cool, I got to get back on cash, but can I get your

number? We could talk about music sometime?"

"Okay." I feel pretty invisible at this point in the proceedings. Nick pulls a pen from his back pocket, and Wanda writes her number on his hand.

"See ya," she says.

"I hope so," Nick replies, and we walk sedately until we are out of sight and then start running and skipping through the mall to the bus stop.

The bus home takes forever as it winds down all the little streets. "I bet he tastes good. I bet he tastes good/bad like black licorice," Wanda says.

It has never occurred to me that boys might taste like something, although I've always figured Wanda tasted like artificial strawberry or maybe raspberry jelly powder.

"What flavour do you think I am?" I ask Wanda.

She looks at me. "Salt and vinegar, for sure."

Wanda is sitting on the edge of our blanket at the park painting her toe nails Vixen Vibe red. Nick is watching her and occasionally taking a long blade of grass and sticking it in her ear. He's wearing a jean jacket with the sleeves cut off. They listen to Aerosmith, a yellow set of earbuds split between them. Nick plays air guitar. Nick humours my presence like I am some kind of little sister. I read and try to ignore them, especially when Wanda has to keep moving Nick's hands when he tries to wiggle them up the short leg of her cut-off jeans.

They make out, and I close my eyes and listen to the occasional slurp or slap of ill-timed lips, but mostly I hear the sound of Wanda slapping Nick's hand away at regular intervals and her cautioning him when his hands travel under her clothes. "Nick. Nick!"

"Weiner's allowed to use his dad's car again," Nick tells Wanda.

"How come he got grounded?"

"He set off a bunch of fireworks behind the Yonge Street Motel. He had this idea the strippers would all come rushing out to see what the noise was. They thought it was gunshots and called the police. No one pressed charges, but his dad had to come pick him up at the station. He's driving us to Wonderland on the weekend. You want to come? You can come too, if you want, Daisy."

"Cool," says Wanda.

"I'll see," I say.

"That means no," says Wanda, and I shrug. She knows Mum won't let me go without calling Wanda's parents to see who's driving.

Nick leaves to go to work, and I gather up his cigarette butts and put them in the garbage.

The day they go to Wonderland, I decide I'm going to dye my hair black. I'm sick of my natural hair colour, mousey brown. I've wanted to do this for ages, but I always chicken out at the last minute when I remember that scene in *Anne of Green Gables*.

I bring the radio into the bathroom and turn it up. I have two of the old towels Mum makes me sleep on when I have my period. I open the package up and peel the gloves off of the paper sheet of instructions. I prop the instructions up behind the taps of the sink. I smear Vaseline along my hairline; Wanda told me to do this. I skip the allergy test and mix the contents of the two vials that came in the packet together and work the thick lotion through my hair. It drips down my face a bit, and I dampen one of the period towels and wipe away the drips. There's a light grey mark on my face, but it isn't too noticeable. The dye smells toxic and chemical; I open the window to let some air in. I have to wait for twenty minutes. I take off the plastic gloves and sit on the side of the bath.

I decide to clean up a little while I'm waiting. I pick up the gloves and put them on the beige counter. I wash a clump of hair dye from the sink; the gob of dye goes down the drain, but leaves behind a purple stain on the basin. I scrub at it, but nothing happens. I glance over, and I see the dye on the gloves. The dye is seeping into the counter beneath them. I pick them up and throw them in the bathtub, but they have left a telltale mark. I take the towel I've been using to wipe my face and use it to wipe the counter. It turns out there is quite a lot of dye on the towel, and it smears across everything. My scalp feels hot, and when I breathe in, the air is heavy with chemicals. I start to get sweaty; I can feel drips of dye start to run over the Vaseline barrier and onto my face. Not my *eyes*, I think, and grab the clean white hand towel. I use it to save myself from going blind.

The timer goes, and I decide I need to rinse out my hair first and then try and clean up the mess. The gloves meant to protect my hands from the dye are wet, and there is dye on the inside of them. "Fuck it," I say out loud, and throw the gloves in the garbage bin. I use my bare hands to try to wash out my hair in the sink.

My hands are turning grey, and drips are spraying up onto

the mirror and splattering the white paint above the sink. I feel desperate, and the wind coming in the open window is now making me cold. I take off my clothes and get in the shower, trying to keep the black run-off from my hair away from my body. I regret skipping the allergy test. I dry off using the scratchy old towels. My skin is grey, but doesn't seem to be inflamed. I try to remove the worst of the dye from my face using some old exfoliant of Elizabeth's. I rub too hard, and my forehead looks red and raw. Mum gets home while I'm still cleaning the bathroom. I have a drip stain running down one side of my face and what looks like carpet burn on my forehead.

Mum looks at me first, then she surveys the drip stains on the wall and the grey smears in the sink and across the counter.

"What were you thinking?" she says to me. Then she starts digging in the cupboard, getting out rubber gloves and noisily slamming the container of Ajax on to the counter. I retreat to my room.

I hear her laughing on the phone to Olivia. "The worst of it is, she looks ridiculous."

I'm still in bed when Mum gets home from work the next day.

"Are you okay, Daisy? Is it that time of the month?" she asks me.

"Maybe," I reply.

"I'll get you a towel to lie on," she says.

She brings me a cup of tea. I lie on the hard towel, which gets bunched up beneath me, and tears form in my eyes.

The next day in the shower, I wash my hair and more grey water swirls down the drain. I return to bed.

Mum comes and sits on my bed after work.

"I'm not that mad about the bathroom," she says. "What's wrong?"

"I can't tell you."

"Why don't we go out for dinner?"

"No thank you," I say, and lie back down.

She brings me a sandwich and a Mars bar. I eat the Mars bar.

Wanda calls and tells me about Wonderland. She says it was boring and that Nick won her an enormous pink hippopotamus that she doesn't know what to do with. Also, she almost puked on one of the roller coasters. I've never been on a roller coaster; I've always been too scared. She asks me to come over, but I say I am not feeling well. She asks me about the hair dyeing.

"Don't ask," I say.

Two days later Wanda walks into my room and opens the curtains. "Your mom let me in," she says.

She sits on the edge of the bed. "Are you mad at me?" she asks.

"No."

"Let me see your hair."

I sit up.

"It looks cool," she says.

"My mum says it looks ridiculous. I'm so ugly." I ooze self-pity.

"Nick dumped me," says Wanda. "He found out I was only fourteen."

"I'm sorry."

"It's okay. I didn't like him that much."

Mum knocks on the door, and we dissolve into giggles.

I wash my hair. Wanda tells me not to brush it, just to run my hands through it. Instead of clinging all staticky to my face it actually has some life. Wanda uses Mum's hair spray and back combs it into a black crazy mess. She makes up my face with pale concealer covering the grey streaks from the dye. Holding my face delicately with the fingers from one hand, she uses her other hand to carefully make up my eyes.

"At least you're up," Mum says, surveying Wanda's handiwork.

At the donut shop in the plaza I drink coffee with one sugar. Wanda drinks a Coke. When the cashier goes to the back room, Wanda pushes coins into the cigarette vending machine. Up on the pedestrian bridge that crosses over the highway, Wanda teaches me how to inhale. On the third cigarette, I am inhaling without coughing, but I feel a little nauseous. "That goes away after some practice," Wanda assures me.

The nicotine and the caffeine have pumped me up, and I need to move. Instinctively, we head to the park, laughing our heads off at nothing, and then we play on the swings. Some younger kids avoid us and the families act like we don't exist, and this makes us laugh even more.

We lie together on top of a picnic table, staring up at the trees.

"We're going to have fun in high school," says Wanda.

"Are we?" I ask.

"We're going to blow everyone's minds," she says. I almost believe her.

nine

I can't open the lock on my locker. I turn it left, then right, then all the way around again. I forget the combination and pull out the piece of paper I have it written on.

"Move over." Wanda does it for me. She takes a pen and writes my combination on my palm, along with a series of circular arrows that indicate how to turn the lock. We are in the same homeroom, and Wanda leads the way as I follow behind her.

"How do you know where Room 204 is?" I ask her, looking wildly around at the room numbers.

"It will be on the second floor for a start," she says, heading towards the staircase.

My next class is English. It's only four doors down from where we were and easy to find. I stand by the door and watch Wanda walk away from me. She is swallowed up by the crowd of kids rushing to get to classes. When the teacher comes to unlock the door, I'm the only one who has arrived. I go in and find a desk, and feel self-conscious sitting alone waiting to see if I know anyone. The teacher does that thing where she stands writing stuff on the board and pretends we're invisible to each other until the class starts. Students trickle in, each one looking around for faces to latch onto. The only person I know is Damon. I think for a minute he might sit with me, and he does smile at me when he walks in. His rat tail is gone, and he has Sun In skater bangs. His skateboard is tucked under his arm. He doesn't sit with me. He sits with a blonde girl, not bleached but natural. She's skinny, the kind of girl who never has to lie on the bed to do up her jeans. "How's it going, Crystal?" he says, sitting beside her. They must have met over the summer because she didn't go to our school.

A girl comes in just as Ms. Chandra is about to shut the door of the class. There are only a few free seats left, three at the front of the class and one in between a couple of big guys. One is wearing a Black Hawks cap and sits with sprawling legs, and the other has a picture of Claudia Schiffer in a bathing suit stuck on the inside flap of his binder. I watch as he shows it to the guy in the ball cap. The girl is wearing a Smiths T-shirt. She glances around, sees me in my black outfit with my messed-up hair, and comes and sits beside me.

"Jude," she says, formally sticking her hand out.

"Daisy," I respond, shaking her hand.

Ms. Chandra does roll call. When she calls out Richard, the Claudia Schiffer guy says "right here," and when she looks down at her attendance sheet, he grabs his crotch and thrusts it towards her. The ball-cap guy shakes with mirth.

"Dumbasses," Jude whispers to me.

"Dicks," I whisper back.

"Probably dickless," Jude says, and when Ms. Chandra turns around, I'm giggling. Ms. Chandra smiles at me. When class ends Jude asks what's in my Walkman, and I show her the Sinead O'Connor tape inside. "I love her. I wish I was brave enough to shave my head," she says.

"Me too."

Richard overhears us. "Dykes!" he says to his friend, who glances over at us, and when we both stare at him, he does a repeat performance of his crotch grab and thrust.

Jude's locker is just down from mine and Wanda's. It is a shrine to Morrissey. She's obsessed. Wanda and I admire her collage of magazine pictures and the inserts from Smiths tapes, then we all head out and sit on the ledge that runs round the front of the school. From here I can see the parking lot, and I watch Damon's sister sitting on the hood of her car smoking. It's like she senses my eyes on her; she glances up, sees me, and tilts her chin up in greeting. Then she turns and continues to talk to the girl lying on the hood of the car beside her. Wanda drinks a Coke. Jude pulls out a sandwich and follows this up with an apple. I feel hungry seeing Jude's lunch, but I didn't pack anything. A packed lunch seemed not quite right for high school. I let hunger overwhelm me in almost pleasurable waves of light-headedness.

Jude's combat boots shine so much I can see my reflection in them.

"I can see myself in your boots," I tell her.

"It's because of Cadets. I had a meeting last night, and I always have to polish them beforehand."

"What's Cadets?" I ask Wanda when Jude goes to throw her apple core in a garbage bin.

"It's like fake army."

Cathy and I walk home together and talk about all the

homework we have and what we wished we'd done during the summer. Cathy is joining the Sunshine Club, which helps raise money for kids without arms and legs, and she wants me to come with her. I hate saying no, so I tell her I'll think about it, which we both know is a lie. I just can't be the girl who spends every Wednesday after school counting pop-can tabs.

"It comes to this, how much is twenty years of marriage worth?" I'm not supposed to overhear this, but I am coming through the door and Mum is on the phone; Olivia, I presume. I can tell Mum has been crying; there is the telltale red around her eyes. I know she had a meeting with her lawyer after work.

The dining-room table is littered with old bills and lists. There is a sheet of paper where Mum has tried to add up the cost of our life with the help of my old calculator.

"The lawyer says I should get the house, because of Daisy. There's no question of her living with him." She sees me now.

"Olivia, Daisy just got home. Talk tomorrow."

"How did it go?" I ask her.

"Not great. I've been thinking about something," she says to me.

"Umm," I shut the cupboard door that I just opened; my appetite is gone.

"It would be nice for you to have money, of your own," Mum says, when I face her.

"Umm hmmm."

"Carmen, who I work with, I've told you about her. We have lunch together sometimes."

"Yes, I remember. She's the one you like who helped you figure out parking permits."

"Yes, that's her. She needs a babysitter for her youngest,

she's six, and it isn't very far from here. She has other kids, but she wants someone for when they're not around. What do you think?"

"Okay," I agree.

"I'm sorry it's been so tight round here."

"That's okay, Mum. It's not your fault."

"Daisy…" she says, but doesn't finish her sentence, and all the things that are uncertain in our lives swirl in the air between us.

Carmen's house is on Mill Street. The street name means nothing to me, but when we pull up to the house I recognize it. This is Damon's house.

The world tilts left, and someone is breathing in and out very quickly. I worry if I stop thinking about breathing I might forget to breathe altogether. My knees feel like jelly, and I test the weight on my foot before standing, in case it has stopped working.

"Are you okay, Daisy?" Mum asks.

"I'm just nervous."

"I'll be home and you can call if there's a crisis. I'll come in and introduce you."

"No. Please, no. I'll look like an idiot."

Cora answers the door. "Hey, you must be here to look after Millicent. I wondered if you were the same Daisy," she says, as a small spectacled child emerges from behind her.

I wave back at Mum, who finally starts to pull away.

"Come play with my Barbies," Millie says to me, and I follow her into the living room. I don't have any experience looking after little kids, but I know how to play with Barbies. Elizabeth cut the hair off one of ours, and we used it as a substitute Ken and smushed her face, and sometimes body, against the other long-haired dolls.

It's not Barbies that Millie has, but Holograms dolls. "You can be Pizzazz. Cora is usually Pizzazz." I sit on the floor, and Millie hands me my doll. Her left eye has been markered over with a black eyepatch.

"Sometimes I play pirates with her," Millie explains.

Cora bends over and kisses Millie on the cheek. "Be good, Millicent," she says, as Millie pulls a face. Cora says to me, "Mom will be out soon; she's still getting ready. Damon is around somewhere."

"Is he going out with your mom?" I ask.

"He's not allowed to look after me," says Millie solemnly.

"He can't possibly do it. He's a *boy*," Cora tells me, rolling her eyes. Then she's gone.

I get my instructions from Mrs. Jones and hear the door close behind her. Millie and I play band battle on the living-room floor. For my song in the battle of the bands, I sing the chorus of "Metal Queen" a few times, and I get the Pizzazz doll to rock out on an imaginary guitar.

Damon comes in when Millie is singing. She is making up the words to a song that goes on for a considerably long time and ends on an impressively long, high note. We both applaud when she finishes.

"So, who won?" asks Damon.

"Well, Pizzazz was good," says Millie, "but Jem sang the best." She says this very seriously, then she makes Jem and Pizzazz stiffly shake hands.

"Daisy?" It's the first time she has used my name, and she tries it out. "I don't have to brush my teeth because it's

Friday. But you can read to me." Millie drags me off to her room, and I feel simultaneously relieved and disappointed to leave Damon behind.

When I come out of the bedroom, four long stories later, Damon is watching TV.

"Want some chips?" he says, handing me a bowl. The chip in my mouth seems unwieldy, and I can't seem to eat it without making loud crunching sounds. I try leaving it whole and letting the moisture in my mouth soften it. But then I'm aware that I keep swallowing as my mouth fills with saliva. I don't reach for another once it is finally gone.

Damon shoves handfuls into his mouth and then wipes grease and salt away with the long sleeve of his shirt pulled down over the back of his hand. He watches MuchMusic until a video he doesn't like comes on, then he groans and flips through the other channels until it is over. When "Papa Don't Preach" comes on, he starts to groan, but I say, "Hey, I like this one!"

"You and my sisters." But he doesn't change the channel. "Cora says it's romantic, but I just think it's stupid."

"How did it go?" Mr. Jones comes into the living room.

"Fine. Millie was really good," I tell him.

"Did she brush her teeth?" Cold creeps into my chest, and then I realize he is teasing me.

"Carmen's waiting for you at the front door. Didn't want to be bothered taking her shoes off, but she'll give you a lift home."

Cora is coming up the stairs to the house when I step outside. She looks like she might cry. Mrs. Jones asks her if she's alright, but Cora just pushes wordlessly past us. I see the car she just got out of pulling away. The driver is Mr. Dean.

ten

"Daisy, could you just try? He is your father. I'd like you to see him. I don't want him thinking I'm stopping you from going. Of course, it is up to you, dear."

He picks me up at the house. I feel queasy, like when I was younger and Mum made me go to the birthday party of a kid I didn't like. When the car pulls in, I'm ready and out the door before he's parked. I get in, and Dad gets out and heads up to the house. Mum steps outside, and they hug and he kisses her on the cheek. Watching this makes my stomach flip. Let's go, let's go, I think. His hair is shorter than it used to be, and he is wearing a pair of runners instead of his usual brown leather shoes that Mum used to polish for him every Sunday night.

I don't wait for him to come back and hug me. I strap myself into the passenger seat. As Dad backs out, I see Mum peeking at us leaving from behind the curtain in the front window. I imagine myself undoing my seatbelt, flinging open the door, rolling away from the car, and running.

"How's school?'

"Fine."

"How's your friend? Catherine?"

"Fine." I think about telling him I hardly see Cathy anymore. When we do, our conversations are like this one with Dad, awkward. It's like being in a dream when things look normal, but they aren't quite right. Your dead great-uncle is sitting at the table, and you're wearing a dress that hasn't fit you in three years.

Someone cuts Dad off at the intersection.

"Women drivers…" he mutters. He thinks this is funny. The news comes on the car radio, and we both pretend to listen.

Pat and Dad's apartment is in a small four-storey building. As we're walking up the inside stairs, a man is coming down.

"Hi, Dr. Radcliffe, how's it going?" he says, when we meet at the landing. He looks quizzically at me.

"Good. This is my daughter, Daisy. Daisy, this is Jeff, he lives upstairs."

"I didn't know you had a daughter, Dr. Radcliffe." This statement hits the shiny industrial tiles and echoes up to the tall ceiling of the stairwell. "So, are you a young biologist in the making?"

"No," I say. I don't elaborate.

"See ya." He hurries away, his attempt at lightening the mood having failed. I see his vision of me, Dr. Radcliffe's spoiled and rude teenage daughter dressed in ratty clothes with the roots showing in her rat's nest of dyed black hair. Dad opens the door to the second-floor hallway and leads me to the apartment.

"Pat, love, we're here."

I'm bent over trying to undo my boot laces in the tight

hallway when Pat comes to the door with a frilly apron on over her clothes. I look up from where I'm crouched over.

"Hi, Daisy, it's so nice to see you." I am glad I'm in this position as there will be no attempt at physical contact. No handshake or hug.

The rice is saturated with tasteless sauce. I am stirring pieces of translucent onion that look like the flaps of skin you pull from your feet once a blister has burst, along with pithy pieces of green pepper around my plate. I have eaten three strips of chicken, slowly putting the flavourless morsels in my mouth and chewing for a long time. Pat is talking about her sister who is getting married over Christmas. Dad and Pat are going to Vancouver. They don't ask me about my holiday plans.

"What do you think of the stir-fry?" Pat asks, noticing my still-full plate. "I'm trying to get your Dad to lose a few pounds," she says.

Dad rubs his stomach. "I think I'm fine how I am."

"Not according to your doctor."

"A few pounds. I could do with losing a few pounds, that's all he said."

It is so weird watching them joke around this way. It's just like when Dad used to tease Mum when she tried to serve us salad for dinner.

Pat gets up to clear the table, and when she comes behind Dad, she squeezes his shoulders with both of her hands. She stands behind him for a moment, her fingers working into his muscles. In response my own shoulders stiffen.

"Are you done, Daisy? You didn't eat very much."

"I'm not very hungry. Thanks."

"How about some ice cream?" She is holding a box of No Name vanilla in her hand, offering it to me like the congealed contents will somehow soothe this situation.

"How about a cup of tea?" Dad says. Pat puts the kettle on.

"So," Dad says. "How's school?"

We take our tea into the living room. It's a small room with a love seat and a rocking chair. I sit on one corner of the love seat and Dad sits on the other, forcing Pat into the uncomfortable-looking rocker. She has to move three teddy bears from it first. She has lots of cutesy little figurines up on shelves—ceramic things, girls wearing bonnets and carrying baskets of flowers. An angel mouse. What's weirder than Pat's girly ornaments is seeing things that I know so well in this strange room: a picture of my dad's parents, the mantel clock that he was given when he graduated and that used to be in our living room. There is a box of records that he packed up one day and took from the house. Leonard Cohen, Bob Dylan, he likes all those weird old men who can't actually sing.

At the door, as I'm leaving, Pat hands me a gift. It's a wooden bracelet.

"I got this for you in Africa. It's not much, but I thought you might like it."

I look in my hands. Dad has never got me anything like this from his trips. Sometimes he'd bring Mum perfume he purchased duty free on the airplane.

"Say thanks, Daisy," Dad says, while I'm still staring down at my hands.

"Thank you, Pat," I say quietly.

"No problem. See you soon." She glances up at Dad and

I see him shrug. I want to stamp my feet and scream.

At home as soon as I'm through the door, "How was it?" There is a glass of wine in her hand and an empty bottle next to the sink. No sign that Mum has eaten anything for dinner.

"Awful." I stomp up the stairs to my room, still wearing my boots.

I put the wooden bracelet on the floor and grind my heel into it, and it cracks with satisfying sounds. Then I brush my teeth for ten minutes trying to get the taste of undercooked onion out of my mouth.

I brush my hair in the morning so it hangs straight.

"Daisy? You alright?" Mum says suspiciously when she sees me.

"Mmmhmm." I grab my bag and I'm out the door.

At lunchtime, Wanda, Jude, and I meet at our lockers. Jude produces the shavers.

"Are you sure you know what you're doing?" I ask her.

Jude looks around, sees an outlet in between two sets of lockers, and heads over and plugs in the shavers.

"Here? We can't do it here," I say.

"Why not?" Jude says.

I sit cross-legged on the floor and Jude sits behind me. "How much?" she asks, conferring with Wanda.

"I'm here," I say.

"Shhh, I'm thinking," Wanda says. She comes over and grabs my hair into a ponytail. "Here." Wanda puts a finger on the back of my head. "Not over her ears, but level with them."

"Yep, I think you're right. Okay, Daisy, hold your hair up for me." I feel the trimmer buzzing against the back of my skull; a long wisp of hair falls down onto my lap, and then another.

I hear teacher footsteps coming down the hall. They have the click of authority.

"Girls." It's Ms. Chandra. I see one of her feet, shod in a brown, heeled ankle boot, stir the hair on the floor in front of me.

"We're just doing the back," Jude tells her.

"Just sweep up the hair when you're done. Okay?"

"Okay, thanks," we say in unison.

I can't stop rubbing the back of my head. It feels like the bristles on a soft brush. It's the haircut Cora had when I first saw her. If I put my hair up, it exposes the shaved back, but when it's down you can't see it. My head feels lighter.

I show Mum as soon as she comes home. She doesn't say anything, just rubs the back of my head with her hand.

eleven

I'm looking after Millie when the news comes on that a man has shot a bunch of women at a university in Montreal. Cora listens to the news in the kitchen, and I play with Millie in the living room, trying not to let her hear too many details. Mrs. Jones has already put up their tree. It's peach, like all the decorations on it. Mrs. Jones's Christmas village is set up on the coffee table.

Cora brings in hot chocolate and sits with Millie and me.

"I don't feel like being alone," she says.

When I get home, Mum is talking to Elizabeth on the phone. "I needed to hear your voice," I hear her say.

Ms. Chandra talks to our English class about what happened; she sits on top of her desk and tells us how upset she is. Richard whispers, "Fucking feminist," and Ms. Chandra calls him out.

"Why don't you share your thoughts with the whole class, Richard?"

"It's the feminists' fault. They take jobs that men should have got, because of equal-opportunity crap, and then guys like that get screwed. That's why he went crazy."

Ms. Chandra shakes her head, but the bell rings and the class ends. Jude and I are the last to leave, and Ms. Chandra puts her hands on each of our shoulders for a second as she ushers us out the door.

I walk over to Mum's office after school. "This is my daughter," she says, introducing me to the women in the office.

"You can tell that easily," one of the women says. A man comes out of another office.

"Grahame, this is my youngest daughter, Daisy."

"Hi," says Grahame, and he smiles at me. He's short and husky with a beard. He doesn't do anything weird like try and shake my hand, and his smile is nice.

"We're off to choose a Christmas tree," Mum says.

"Christmas-tree farming is a sign of the excesses of Western capitalism," Grahame says.

"Well, the only employment Roy Carter has all year is selling trees at the plaza, so at least I'm supporting him." Mum is flirting.

"Point taken, have fun."

He waves goodbye, and I catch him wink at Mum.

Roy's trees are all tied up. We can't see them, but we discuss options for a while; it's a tradition to consider a few. Roy wears fingerless gloves, and his nails are yellow and ridged. When he takes our money, he smiles, and I notice he only has a few teeth.

The tree stand is rusty. I hold it straight, and Mum tightens the stiff bolts. She crawls out; I shake it a few times, and it doesn't fall over. Decorated with lights, balls, and the toilet-paper-roll angel Elizabeth made in grade one, it doesn't look too bad. Underneath are presents from my aunts; they are wrapped in paper decorated with robins wearing Santa hats and plum puddings adorned with sprigs of holly. Mum puts three cylindrical packets from Dad under the tree, one for each of us. They look ominously like umbrellas. "They can't be. Can they?" I ask Mum, and she sighs.

"Hey, I have good news to tell you. I was going wait until Elizabeth gets home tomorrow, but we need some cheer, I think."

"What?"

"I am no longer the front-desk clerk, but an Assistant Administrative Officer. It's not much different. But I get a little raise, and my desk has a view. And no more dog licences."

I cheer.

"There's something else too. Grahame, the archeologist."

"With the beard."

"With the beard. He asked me out. I'm going to have dinner with him sometime next week."

"Mum!"

"It's just dinner."

Christmas Day is better than last year. It's the normal combination of eating, gift opening, and the phone being passed around so Elizabeth and I can thank relatives we hardly know for strange socks and mysterious Marks & Spencer bath products. Dad calls, but, luckily, it's just as we are taking the turkey out of the oven, so no one feels bad for getting off the phone with him. We saved half the present opening for after dinner; this way, we have something to occupy us in the evening.

I take the soft package Mum hands me and unwrap it. I'm determined to be grateful for whatever she has chosen for me.

It's a black roll-neck sweater made out of the softest wool I have ever felt, and it has sleeves that come down over my hands. I pull it on. I can hide my face in the neck and disappear into it.

"It's fantastic and it's even black."

"I thought you might like it." Mum smiles.

She hands out the last three gifts, the ones from Dad, and the three of us simultaneously unwrap our umbrellas. Mine is pink.

It's the end of January and cold. The trip to the Ontario Provincial Parliament is supposed to start at 7 a.m. The snow compacted on the sidewalk is squeaky. I haven't slept well. I'm waiting for Jude to show up. I don't want to get stuck next to Gary on the bus. He sits in front of me in class. Wanda says I'm too nice to Gary, and she's probably right. He's always telling me stories about the model airplanes he puts together on the weekend, and once suggested I could come over and look at them.

At seven the doors of the school are still locked. Mr. Jackman, our teacher, waves to me from the warmth of his car where he is drinking a coffee. I can't feel my feet. I'm wearing a pair of thin gloves that aren't doing anything to keep me warm, and I don't have a hat. Mum tried to get me to wear a toque this morning, but I blew her off. Now I regret it. The back of my head is particularly freezing. I bury my chin in the neck of my black sweater. Flakes of snow are either coming from the sky or being picked up by the wind from the roof of the school and swirling around me and the others waiting. I know my nose is red.

Jackie and Terry-Lee are jumping up and down with their arms wrapped around each other, trying to stay warm. I will myself to look unaffected by the elements, and simply curl and uncurl my toes inside my freezing boots. Jude is walking up the street towards me. When she is close enough to hear the music coming from Mr. Jackman's vehicle, she makes a gagging gesture, pretending to jam her finger down her throat.

A bus comes around the corner of the school. It emits smoke and a grinding noise as it turns, then shudders to a stop at the curb just in front of me.

The driver gets out and lights up a smoke. He and Mr. Jackman stand outside the bus and point up at the sky and the increasing number of snowflakes falling out of it as the students climb aboard.

I wedge myself into a window seat three back from the front, and Jude sits beside me. We both get out our Walkmans. It's too early to talk. The driver has a battery-operated portable radio playing at the front of the bus. He is playing the same station as Mr. Jackman. Ozzy Osbourne and a weather report that includes a lot of snowfall warnings leak in through my headphones. I stare out the window and put my backpack on my lap for warmth. It isn't much warmer in the bus than outside, and I can see my breath.

I slip my headphones down, irritated by the outside interference.

"Oh my God, it's cold," I say to Jude.

"Is there any heating on this bus?" She exposes her own ears.

"I heard the driver tell Mr. Jackman it's not working."

We can hear Mr. Jackman and the driver discussing the weather.

"No sign of snow yesterday," says Mr. Jackman.

"Well, I'm here now. And it's only an hour-long drive. But it's your call, buddy. I get paid either way." The driver smokes another cigarette leaning against the open door of the school bus, and the scent of cheap tobacco wafts in.

Every time the bus turns, the tires screech, and Jude and I slide back and forth across our seat. The driver keeps a running commentary with Mr. Jackman about the flaws of other drivers, interspersed with problems he is having with his girlfriend. She wants him to move out of his mother's house.

"I keep telling her, man, I got a good thing going. Housekeeper, cook, accommodation, and all I have to do is shovel in the winter and mow the lawn in the summer. Got the whole basement to myself, with a separate door. And Mom's deaf, it's not like she can hear when Michelle comes over."

Mr. Jackman is trying to steer him onto safer ground.

"You see the game last night? I'm an Oilers fan, myself."

Jude and I are eavesdropping.

"Ohhh, Michelle," Jude moans slowly.

"Don't worry, Mother can't hear."

"Ohhhh, ohhhh, ohhhh," Jude flutters her eyes. Mr. Jackman catches the drift of our conversation and shakes his head at us.

"How about them Oilers?" I say loudly to Jude, and I see the corners of Mr. Jackman's mouth twitch up.

The driver is oblivious and now telling Mr. Jackman about his preference for women who already have children.

"That way they just want some company. Not looking for commitment or wanting to get married. That costs a fortune. I have a buddy spent two thousand bucks on an engagement ring, and the girl dumped him the night before the wedding. Never gave the ring back either. You married?"

Jude and I nudge each other. Mr. Jackman is not as old as most of our other teachers, and he still has hair. He never talks about his personal life.

Smoke comes pouring from a vent at the front of the bus. Jude and I watch as the black stinking stuff streams out of the vent like a mushroom cloud. It engulfs us first and then travels back, filling the rest of the bus.

"Crap!" the driver shouts; the bus shudders, and we grip the back of the seat in front of us as he steers to the side of the highway and hammers on the brakes.

The doors of the bus are opened, and Jude and I are the first two in the cold air on the side of the highway. Mr. Jackman is making sure everyone is off. The driver has gotten out a stool from somewhere that he stands on while smoking over the smoking engine and shaking his head.

A police car pulls up after a few minutes, and Jude, to my surprise, walks right up to it and says, "Hello Officer."

She has clicked into Cadet mode, and I think for a minute she might salute, but she doesn't. She calmly explains our situation. By the time Mr. Jackman comes over, the police have all the details.

I just stand beside her, stamping my feet.

"Rough weather for a field trip?" the cop says in an accusatory manner to Mr. Jackman.

"Caught us by surprise, I'm afraid."

"Did you not hear the reports? We gotta get these kids off the road before the plow comes. Can they wait on the bus?" There is now about five centimetres of snow on the ground. And it is accumulating quickly. The officer looks toward the bus, and smoke slowly streams from the open door.

"Requesting Fire and Emergency," he says into his radio. "Get these kids on the other side of that ditch now! Away from the bus."

The snow is up to our ankles on the other side of the ditch, and we stand there for a good half hour getting colder. A fire truck and ambulance come, and despite the fact several guys from our class keeping yelling "She's gonna blow!" nothing happens. It's exciting, and then it is just cold.

Eventually, a second cop car comes and ferries us four at a time to the highway McDonald's five minutes down from where we are. Jude and I are in the first car, and Jude sits up front with the cop and asks him a million dorky questions. I keep expecting her to say, "Can I see your gun?"

"That was so cool." Jude is enjoying all of this. It turns out she has not one, but two extra pairs of woolly socks in her backpack, and I am so grateful to be able to pull one of these pairs on that I don't argue with her about the dangers of a police state.

"Have you ever read *1984*?" I ask.

"No, we do that in grade ten, don't we?"

We share a shake and fries, and make them last longer by dipping the salty fries into the sweet icy drink. It takes two hours for a new bus to come and take us back to school. Our field trip is officially cancelled.

There are advertisements for the Valentine's roses that the student council sells stuck to all of our lockers. I watch a couple of the grade thirteens walking hand in hand down the hallway. It's lunch, two days before Valentine's Day, and we are hanging out here in the hallway. None of us are eating, only sipping cans of warm coke we got from the machine. Its refrigeration system isn't working right.

"I'm so sick of being fourteen," I say.

"Even in all the books, if something happens to you before sixteen, really it happens to your parents—they die, or get in a car accident, or split up," Jude explains.

"What about *Romeo and Juliet*? Juliet's only thirteen."

"That's not a real book," says Jude. "That's Shakespeare."

Steve walks by us. He has a curly mass of hair on his head and wears plaid jackets and motorcycle boots. "Wanda," he says. "Wanda's friends." He nods at me and Jude. He continues down the hall. At the last locker before the corner, he pulls a pair of drum sticks out of his back pocket, plays a small drum roll on a metal locker, then disappears around the corner.

"There is no one at this school I find even vaguely attractive," says Wanda.

"I still think Damon is good-looking," I say.

"You're wasting your time with him. Rebel guys always date boring chicks. Have you seen *The Breakfast Club*? Cool chick gets boring guy; popular boring girl gets cool guy. It's how it goes. That's why I like Cadets. When everyone's in uniform, no one knows how rich your parents are or if you have cool clothes," Jude unhelpfully tells me.

"I don't think Morrissey is into the military?" I say.

"He just doesn't understand it. It's easy to say you're a pacifist until you're at war."

Wanda rolls her eyes.

Mum is getting ready for a date and I'm getting ready to babysit Millie. Mum borrows my lipstick, puts it on, takes it off.

"Where are you going?"

"Just to the movies. It's a documentary about sweat-shops."

"Romantic."

"It just happens that it's playing today. Grahame and I are too old for all this Cupid nonsense."

I open the door, and Grahame is wearing a suit and holding a red rose.

I bring a bag of milk-chocolate hearts to the Jones house. Millie hands me a card as soon as I get there. It is a large red heart with bits of cut-up paper doily stuck on with generous amounts of glue.

"That card is bigger than the one I got," Damon complains to Millie.

Millie is hyped up on candy, and when her mom sees the chocolate hearts, she tells me I shouldn't have. "Really, you shouldn't have." Millie is red lipped and cinnamon scented. She is spinning round and round until she falls on the floor, dizzy.

Mrs. Jones barks instructions. "Damon, home by nine, it's not the weekend—and Cora, not much later for you. Daisy, we won't be much after nine."

I'm in the kitchen trying to get ice cream out of a too-frozen container for Millie when the doorbell rings. I can see through to the front entrance from where I am. Mr. Jones answers it and shakes Crystal's hand.

"So nice to meet you," Crystal says.

"Likewise, I'm sure. I'll go find Damon for you. You'll look after him tonight?"

"Of course, Mr. Jones." Her laugh tinkles.

Crystal is wearing a pair of jeans and one of those one-pieces where the top is attached to flaps that you secure between your legs. You can tell by how seamlessly the fabric stretches flat and disappears into her waistband. She's probably not wearing underwear. Crystal hooks her thumb into one of her belt loops and leans her other hip and elbow against the wall while she waits for Damon. I feel my own jeans cutting into my stomach and become aware of the flesh hanging over my waistband. Crystal isn't wearing a belt, and her jeans look like they could slip right off.

Damon hands Crystal a heart-shaped box of chocolates, and she leans in and kisses him on the cheek. It hurts to watch this. They leave the house holding hands. I spoon some of the ice cream into my mouth. It is not satisfying.

Cora doesn't emerge from her bedroom until her parents have left.

She's wearing a red dress.

"I can see almost all your boobies!" Millie tells her.

"You look great," I say, imagining myself a few years in the future wearing something sexy.

Cora waits, watching *Be My Valentine, Charlie Brown* on the TV with me and Millie. Ten minutes in she moves to the window and stares outside. The phone rings at the end of the special. Cora runs to answer it in the kitchen. I hear her slam the phone down and retreat to her room.

Crystal's parents drop Damon off, and he comes in and blushes when Millie makes kissy faces at him. The phone rings and he picks it up and says, "Hello," but obviously no one answers at the other end. It rings again and he answers saying, "What do you want?"

"Is Cora home?" he asks me. Damon knocks on Cora's door and I hear muffled voices.

"She doesn't want to talk to you," he says into the phone.

twelve

It is the first weekend of March Break and I have no plans. It's one of those bad weekends. I feel the time I have to fill up like a weight pressing down on me. I am relieved when Mrs. Jones calls and asks if I can take Millie out for a few hours on Saturday afternoon. She asks me in those hushed tones that imply something very bad has happened, and I wonder if Mr. Jones has cancer. And then I wonder if he's moving out like my father.

Usually the Jones home is full of conflicting radios and shouted conversations. On the weekends it smells like sawdust as Mr. Jones hammers and saws in whichever room he is improving. Not today. I get to the house, and everyone says hello like everything is normal, but obviously it isn't. Mr. Jones and Damon are sitting at the kitchen table with separate sections of the newspaper in front of them. Neither of them speaks to me as Mrs. Jones goes to get Millie. Cora's jacket is slung over the back of a kitchen chair, but she doesn't come out to chat while I wait. When the whistle on the kettle goes, I jump at the loud intrusion.

"I don't want to go. I don't want to go."

"You'll have a good time," commands Mrs. Jones. "Back by three, okay, Daisy?" Mrs. Jones is all business. I have instructions to take Millie to the plaza where she can buy a treat from the toy store, and then we should get ice cream.

The weather's not bad, but it is still cold. Millie walks slowly. She is halfway through telling me a complicated story involving a class trip, on which they made bird feeders out of pine cones and peanut butter. She interjects, "I'm going to be an aunt."

"In a play at school?" I imagine her dressed in a costume made of three round, padded sections with a doodle bopper on her head, her and her grade three classmates carrying an enormous foam sandwich away from a checkered picnic blanket.

"A real aunt. It will be like having a little sister, only better. My Aunt Carol has a dog. Are you an aunt?"

"Who told you you were going to be an aunt?"

"Cora did. She's going to be a mommy and call her kid Wolfgang if it's a boy and Roxanne if it's a girl. Then it can be Roxie for short."

"You mean, when she's grown up?"

"No, next year sometime."

I'm walking to school the first day back after the break; there's been a thaw and the snow has all melted. I hear the familiar wheels of Damon coming up behind me. I'm preparing for our usual exchange of half waves, but instead I hear the click-clack of the board being flicked up, and Damon is walking beside me. My face flushes red; luckily, he doesn't actually look at me, just gets in step beside me.

"Did Millie tell you about Cora?"

"Sort of, is she really pregnant?"

"Yeah, she is."

"Is she going to keep the baby?"

"She says so."

"I think Cora's really brave."

"I think she's really fucking stupid." Damon puts down his board and zooms away. I feel like I'm going to cry. This was my chance and I've messed it up. As he hits the corner, Damon raises his hand and waves goodbye, and this, somehow, makes it okay again.

In May, Cora starts to show. I couldn't tell she was pregnant if I didn't know, but there is definitely a change in her shape.

On Friday at school, Wanda and I walk down the hall together. One of the senior girls is holding a paper bag of sugar dressed in overalls and wearing a white lace bonnet. The grade twelve Family Studies class is doing a project, where for three weeks, they pretend a bag of sugar is a baby.

"Take good care of Sweetie." The girl kisses the bag before handing it and a diaper bag over to her fake husband. Miss Cook, the Family Studies teacher, stops to admire the dressed-up bag. She is cooing at it when she catches sight of Cora just down the hall.

"So who's looking after your baby this morning?" she calls down to her. Cora doesn't turn, she pretends not to hear. Wanda and I stop when we get to Cora and lean against the opposite side of the hallway waiting for her to finish gathering her stuff. I see Cora's sugar baby suffocating inside a plastic bag up on the top shelf. Cora reaches up and shoves the bag back, but her locker is full, and instead of settling to the back of the shelf, the bag turns sideways. A trickle of sugar streams to the floor; she must have punctured the bag when she was trying to force it further back.

"Fuck," she mutters. She closes her locker door, but she doesn't get the lock on in time. When she turns to acknowledge me and Wanda, Miss Cook has descended and is standing between us, right behind Cora. She stands staring at the small pile of granules that have accumulated outside of Cora's locker. Then she reaches out and swings open the grey metallic door.

"I'm surprised at you, Cora. This is a serious project. A baby would be dead if you treated it like that."

"It's a bag of sugar."

"It's not just a bag of sugar. It's a baby. Your baby, and look how you're treating it."

"My baby is in my fucking womb," Cora says to her.

Miss Cook's eyes travel down to Cora's belly. "Office," she says. Cora slams her locker shut, but follows Miss Cook down the hall.

"Is she really pregnant?" Wanda asks me.

"I…" This doesn't feel like my news to tell.

"I can't believe you didn't tell me."

By the time my birthday arrives, everyone knows Cora is pregnant, even my mother. I didn't tell her, but Mrs. Jones did.

Mum pushes open my bedroom door, humming "Happy Birthday."

"You're sure it's okay if Grahame comes with us for dinner tonight?" she says.

"I'm sure." This must be the hundredth time she has asked me.

"Daise." I know this tone. I'm still wiping sleep from my eyes and sitting up.

"What?"

"I've been meaning to talk to you about Cora and…" I close my eyes and pull the covers over my face. "I brought you these." She places a box of condoms on the bed.

"You're too young to use them. Understand? Don't use them."

"It's too early for this. Can we talk about something else?"

"Daisy, I just need you to say you understand."

"I understand," I say, and she hands me a bunch of cards. The cardboard package of prophylactics remains lying on the bed, where I do my best to ignore it. There are cards from Mum, Elizabeth, my grandparents, and two of my aunts. Nothing from Dad.

"Who's coming on Friday for the sleepover?"

"It's not a sleepover. That makes me sound like I'm ten. We're just hanging out, and it's only Jude and Wanda."

"Did you invite Cathy?"

"No."

"I saw her mom at work the other day. She was asking after you. It is up to you, but you might regret it if you don't ask her. You don't want to hurt her feelings, do you?"

At school Wanda gives me a card she has made. There is a daisy with a yellow centre, with white petals around the outside; one of the petals is being pulled away and drips of red, like blood, fall from it. Around the outside of the card, she has written *he loves me, he loves me not*. And inside it says 15! *SEX, DRUGS, ROCK-N-ROLL.*

I'm telling her about the horror of being presented with a box of condoms at 7:30 a.m. when I see Cathy walking down the hall.

"Hang on," I tell Wanda, and I run down to catch up with her.

"You didn't invite her? Did you?" Wanda asks when I get back.

Grahame is a vegetarian. He eats a bean burrito and Mum and I get steak fajitas for two. Mum lets me take sips from her margarita. The salt around the rim of her glass doesn't last long. Grahame doesn't ask me about school; he asks about what books I'm reading and what I think of Joni Mitchell. Mum orders another margarita.

Grahame drops us off at home. Mum gives me her keys and sends me in the house first. I don't turn on the hall light as I sneak into the living room. From the window I see Grahame lean over and kiss Mum in the car.

Wanda bats an inflated condom in the air above her head. In honour of my birthday, Mum has absented herself from the house. Cathy can't stay the night because it's her youth group's day at the food bank tomorrow, but she has joined me, Jude, and Wanda for the early part of the evening.

"I'm just saying. She had options. She didn't have to decide to keep the baby. I'd have an abortion if I was her," Wanda says.

"Abortion is murder," Cathy interjects.

"Jesus, Cathy," says Wanda.

"Who's the father anyway?" Jude says, and Wanda cocks her eyebrow at me. I had told her about seeing Mr. Dean pulling out of the Joneses' driveway, but that was in the strictest confidence.

"No one knows," I say.

"I guess there's adoption. She could give it up for adoption, that's the only other moral thing she could do," Cathy persists.

I see the twitch in Wanda's eyebrow, and Jude must see it too because she gets up and snatches the condom out of the air above Wanda and then slams it down hard. It bounces off of Wanda's skull.

"Hey." Wanda gets up and grabs the condom, and they bat it back and forth. It comes my way, and I jump on my bed and hit it towards Cathy, who, still seated, hits it away from her. Wanda catches it and lobs it up. It hits my ceiling lamp and bursts.

"Condom failure," Jude says deadpan, and even Cathy laughs. "I brought my Ouija board, do you want to play?" Jude says.

"No, it's too dangerous," Cathy says. "I heard about a bunch of kids playing it at a sleepover in the States. It didn't seem like anything had happened when they were playing. They thought they were just fooling around. That night, one of the girls suffocated four girls to death with her pillow. The fifth woke up in time and managed to push her away. The one who killed them didn't remember any of it. They think she was possessed. Both her and the girl that survived ended up in a mental institution. The girl that survived the attack ended up killing herself. She hung herself with a bed sheet, and the murderer girl, she cut off her own tongue with a pair of scissors."

Wanda lies on the floor, grabs her pillow and puts it over her face and flails her arms, then slowly stops and lies still, her arm stretched out limp on either side of her.

"What about the falling game then?" Jude ignores Wanda's performance.

"That's not the same as Light as a Feather, when you pretend you're dead?" asks Cathy.

"No, it's just a trust exercise. We do it at Cadets."

"Okay," Cathy agrees.

We go downstairs; there's not enough room to play in my bedroom. We dim the lights and move the coffee table away from the middle of the room. I stand in front of Jude. I am supposed to keep myself stiff and fall backwards, and trust that Jude will catch me.

"Close your eyes, Daisy, I'll count to three, then you just fall back. I'll catch you. One, two, three," Jude says.

I am still standing. I can't do it. Every time I try, my body freezes to the spot.

"Daisy, just relax, it's easy," Jude encourages me. I try, but I as soon as I start to feel myself falling a sweep of panic travels up my spine, and I start taking steps and right myself.

"Wanda, come here and get behind me. I'll demonstrate." Jude takes my place in the centre of the room.

Wanda stands behind Jude, about four feet back. Jude closes her eyes, crosses her arms over her chest, and falls back. Wanda gently catches her shoulders and tilts Jude, who remains stiff, back up.

"Okay," says Jude, "now take a step back." Wanda takes a step back and Jude falls again. She has no hesitation, just drops into Wanda's waiting hands with complete trust. They do it until Jude is falling her full body length, and Wanda is catching her about a foot from the floor. There is elegance to this. Cathy and I watch in silence.

Wanda and Jude reverse rolls. Wanda takes a faltering step the first time she tries it, but the next time she falls gracefully.

"Okay," Jude says, "now try again, Daisy. I'll catch you. Cathy, stand beside Daisy and Wanda can catch you at the same time."

"I'll just watch," says Cathy.

"I'm not going to drop you," Wanda says to her. "Come on."

Cathy reluctantly gets up. It's quiet and dark in the room. We're all talking in hushed tones. Jude gets us into position. Cathy and I stand side by side. "Close your eyes, fold your hands over your chest, and on the count of three," Jude says quietly. I glance over at Cathy; she smiles at me, then I see her squeeze her eyes shut before I do the same. I hear Cathy gasp as I start to fall back, then we are both laughing as we have done it. It is like a synchronized dance routine. Cathy and I are tipped back up, Wanda and Jude take a step back, and we fall again. It is scary and exhilarating every time.

"You did good," Wanda says to Cathy, when we're done. "It looked like you were meditating or something."

"I was just praying you wouldn't drop me," Cathy says, and Wanda laughs.

I wake up that night at 3 a.m. from a nightmare. I can't remember the details, just the fear. Wanda is sitting on the side of my bed gently rubbing my arm to wake me. "Just a dream, Daisy. You're just having a dream."

"I'm okay. I'm okay," I whisper, now I am conscious. "Did I wake you?"

"No, I can't sleep. I kept thinking of that stupid story of Cathy's, about the girl cutting off her own tongue."

"Get in," I say, and Wanda gets under the covers with me and holds my hand until we both fall back asleep.

thirteen

When Steve walks towards Wanda on the last Wednesday of the school year, she hides her pack of smokes in her bag before he can ask for one.

"There's a party Friday."

"Where is it?" Wanda flicks through her notebook as she replies.

"Jimmy Hill's mom's going away. It's at his place. It backs onto the park, so we're going to have a fire in the yard."

"We might come by if we're around," Wanda gestures in the general direction of me and Jude, who has just walked up and joined us. Steve bobs his head. Wanda, Jude, and I head out to share a smoke before our next class.

"I don't know. I can't tell Mum I'm going to a big house party at Jimmy Hill's, and I feel so guilty when I lie to her."

"Guilt is a useless emotion," Jude says.

"We won't see each other all summer. You have to come," says Wanda.

Jude is going to Cadet camp all summer, where she will clean guns and polish her boots excessively. I am babysitting five days a week, while Cora takes summer-school courses. Wanda is leaving the first week after school ends and flying out to Newfoundland to stay with her grandparents. Her parents will drive down at the end of August with their tent trailer to pick her up.

When our family went camping, we all had to sleep in one tent on the hard ground, and then spend the day going for long, hot walks. Wanda's parents roast marshmallows, and her dad plays the acoustic guitar until the park rangers come by and tell him it is too late, time for bed. They are exactly the kind of campers who played the oldies station loudly on the radio and made my mum and dad mutter about peace and quiet as we all sat in silence waiting till it was dark enough to go to sleep.

"My parents are going be away that night with my little brothers. I'll tell them I'm sleeping at your house, Wanda, and then we can all crash at my place. If you tell your mom you're staying at mine, it won't even be a lie, Daisy," Jude says.

"Are you sure it's okay if we show up even though Jimmy didn't invite us personally? What if he doesn't let us in?"

"Daisy, you're making me nuts! It's a party. The whole point is that people come," Wanda says. I give her the finger when she turns her back to me.

One of Jude's Cadet friends has picked up a mickey of rum and six beers for us. We buy three small bottles of Coke. Wanda pours half the Coke out of each bottle, tops it with rum, then screws the caps back on so we can take these to the party.

It feels like we have forever to get ready. Jude gives the back of my head a fresh buzz with the clippers. I put on a plain black T-shirt and take it off and try on my ancient U2 shirt. I take the U2 shirt off and try on a black tank top. I put the original T-shirt back on. Wanda tells me the tank looks better, and I change again. I fix my makeup for the fourth time. We're outside sipping beers and smoking. Wanda notices the time, and we realize it's already eight and the party started at seven. We gulp down the last of the beer. After walking for two minutes, I have to pee.

It seems further to the Hill house than we realized.

"How much further is it, Wanda?" I ask.

"Ten minutes."

"I really have to have pee," I admit.

"Me too," Jude says.

This makes me laugh, and the laughter makes my bladder tighter. We hit the park, and it's about a five-minute walk still to get to the party. As soon as we are in the bushes, Jude crouches behind a tree and pulls down her pants.

"Me too," says Wanda.

"I don't know how to pee outdoors," I say, hopping from foot to foot.

"Pull your pants right down and hold them out away from you with one of your hands, stick your bum back and let go," Jude instructs me. I get behind a third bush and heave my pants and panties down to my ankles. Just as I'm starting to pee, a car swings down the road, and I panic and sit back on my bum fast. I sit on the ground and lift my ankles and pants in the air, and a puddle streams in front of me.

"I think I got pee on my shoes," I tell Wanda and Jude.

Now that we have made room in our bladders, we uncap our bottles and start sipping our rum and Cokes as we walk along the path that goes through the park to get to the back gate at Jimmy's house.

"Be quiet," Jude says, as a cop car pulls into the parking lot across the pond, and its headlights sweep over us.

We stop talking and focus on looking sober. I glance back to the parking lot. The cop is knocking on the window of a parked car, completely disinterested in us.

I am dishevelled and shiny eyed from the booze and the walk when we arrive at Jimmy's. Jimmy is dousing the fire with Zippo fluid when we walk into the yard. Flames shoot up. Raucous laughter and Pink Floyd are coming from inside the house. About fifteen kids mill in and out between the kitchen and the yard. It's impossible to imagine the end of the party, here at the beginning.

My rum and Coke is gone, and I'm sharing a bottle of beer with Jimmy Hill. I'm sitting next to him on a log around the fire, and he has his arm around me; occasionally, his hand lingers near my breast. I don't really care. There's a certain excitement about the proximity of Jimmy's body. He has a particular musty smell I associate with the rummage sale at church and my grandmother's curtains. He occasionally strokes my hair. I'm waiting for him to kiss me, and wondering vaguely where Jude and Wanda have got to.

Damon and Crystal appear across the fire pit. "Hey, Jimmy, Daisy, how's it going?" asks Damon.

I wave and laugh.

"That good, eh?" says Damon, as he swigs from the cooler he's sharing with Crystal.

"This one was loaded when she got here," says Jimmy. "I'm going to get us more beer."

Damon and Crystal sit across from me, and Crystal cuddles up next to Damon. I realize I'm staring at them.

Jude appears before me. "I've been looking for you everywhere. Come on, Wanda's really drunk. We need to get her home."

When I stand up, I stumble towards the fire. Damon is up steadying me by the shoulders before I know what has happened.

"Whoa, Daisy, take it easy."

"She's a mess," Crystal is saying.

I see Wanda, and propel myself out of Damon's hands. Wanda and I stand clutching at each other and laughing, and Jude stands beside us clucking like a mother hen and saying, "Come on, we need to go. We should go *now*."

About two minutes from Jimmy's house, Wanda vomits. She gets on her knees and vomits under a bush as Jude holds her hair back. The park is dark and empty. All I can hear is the lap of a light breeze over the pond, and Wanda retching. I hold out my hands and spin around, looking up at the dark branches of the trees.

"Go sit on that bench, Daisy, and do not move," Jude instructs me. I stagger to the bench and try and sit up straight.

"I'm okay. I'm fine. Get off me," I hear Wanda say to Jude.

She comes and slumps on the bench beside me. Jude urges us to get going, but Wanda and I stay sitting. Wanda hunches forward and pukes all over the ground. The smell hits me, and I find myself leaning with my head between legs as chunky vomit streams from my mouth.

I wake up in Jude's bed with my shoes off and my clothes

on. My arm is slung around Wanda, who is asleep and snoring. I'm not sure how Jude remained so sober or how she corralled us home. I have a vague memory of Wanda lying on the sidewalk and me trying to convince Jude we just needed a little rest and then we would be fine.

My mouth tastes of sweet, rum-flavoured vomit, and I feel like I am covered in Jimmy Hill's handprints. I go home and get straight in the shower, and then I go to bed at noon and sleep till five. When I come downstairs Mum asks what we were up to.

"We stayed up all night watching movies," I tell her.

"You crazy girls," she says.

fourteen

In the mornings Cora emerges from her bedroom after her parents leave for work. We nod, but don't talk. I make coffee and hand her one just like mine, black with one sugar. Millie erupts from her room. She practices karate chops down the hall. I sit her in front of the TV and get her cocoa puffs with chocolate milk. This is the only thing she will eat for breakfast.

I'm trying to convince Millie not to take her bike to the park, when Damon emerges from his room and dashes into the bathroom with nothing but a towel draped around his waist. Cora whistles at him, and I try and pretend I didn't see him.

Millie rides her bike for two minutes and then wants to walk. I carry the bike, the pedals bumping against my shins making them bruised and grease covered. Millie accosts the first kid she sees who's her age at the playground. "Let's play!" and they zoom around, poking sticks in the gravel and calling to each other from the top of the slide.

Two of the mothers sit on the bench I'm on and begin an intense conversation. They are discussing haemorrhoids and comparing brands of breast pumps. I open the book I brought with me and use it as a protective shield. Millie sings or hums almost constantly. I listen for her, and the moment I can't hear anything my head snaps up.

A group of older kids show up at the park and start hogging the swings. Most of the moms, nannies, and I watch, shaking our heads, but too afraid to confront the four twelve-year-old boys. One of the younger moms, Natasha, marches over and tells them to take a hike. The kids leave, yelling "Fuck off" at her as they jump on their BMX bikes.

"I know who your moms are, you little shits!" Natasha yells, and then she comes and sits on the bench beside me.

"Do you know their moms?" I ask.

"No, but they don't know that." Natasha has gravel in her voice. She offers me a cigarette, which I accept.

The other moms on the bench give us disapproving looks, get up, and push their strollers to the other side of the playground. I decide I won't care about what they think. Millie is pointed away from me on a swing and she won't notice.

Natasha tells me about her weekend. She went to the Gasworks, and this guy she is pretty sure is the drummer from Frozen Ghost bought her a drink.

"I'm always looking for someone to take the kids on Friday nights if you're interested?"

"I'll have to ask my mum." I feel like a loser as soon this comes out of my mouth.

"See what she says," says Natasha, and she goes and corrals her kids.

Millie and I go home and I get her a snack. We watch TV

until we hear the key in the door, and Cora comes in.

"Summer school sucks," Cora says. "You want some iced tea?" In the backyard, Millie runs through the sprinkler, and Cora talks to me about school as I look through the baby name book. Damon comes home. He sits on his skateboard and picks out really stupid names from the book. "Angel... Dick...Gaylord!"

When I get home there is a postcard from Wanda. There is a picture of a whale on the front, and on the back she has written:

The ocean is freezing.
I am tired of salt beef.
My Nan is driving me crazy!!!
I miss you.

I'm walking home from the park with Millie; it's humid hot. Millie and I are both sticky from an accidentally squeezed juice box that shot warm apple juice out of Millie's hands and all over her arms and mine. Jimmy Hill rides up beside us on his bicycle. He's wearing mirrored sunglasses and looks a little creepy. Millie grabs my hand and stares at him, her mouth set and her eyes wide. I can feel the dirt on her hand where the sand from the playground has stuck to it.

"Is that your little sister?"

"This is Millie. I'm her babysitter." Jimmy looks at Millie, or at least his sunglasses point in her direction, and she turns away and kicks at the dirt.

"We should do something sometime. Can I get your number?"

"Sure, that would be cool, but I don't have a pen."

"Oh." We both look around like a pen and paper are going to appear in mid-air.

Millie pulls on my hand.

"Let's go, Daisy. I need to go home." This means she has to pee, soon. Sometimes, very soon.

"It's under Donald Radcliffe in the phone book," I call over my shoulder, as Millie pulls me along, suddenly walking fast, which she only does when she's desperate for the bathroom.

"Radcliffe, Radcliffe, Radcliffe." He nods his head slowly up and down. "I'll be talking to you, D.," he calls out. As he rides away, he pops a wheelie.

"Do you like him?" says Millie. "He smells funny. How come he has long hair if he's a boy?"

Damon's home when we get in, and Millie yells to him as she runs to the bathroom, "Daisy has a boyfriend who has a ponytail."

"Are you seeing Jimmy Hill?" Damon asks, and I feel mortified.

"We were just talking. Millie's making things up."

"Daisy and Jimmy sitting in a tree, K-I-S-S-N-G. First comes love then comes BABIES." Millie is peeing with the door open and sings this accompanied by a loud stream of urine.

"I didn't think he was your type."

"What's that supposed to mean?"

"Nothing, nothing. Forget it, Daisy."

I wait for Jimmy Hill to call. I sit by the phone at home and check it's still working every five minutes. He doesn't call. There are two phones in the house: one in the kitchen and one in Mum's room. I wait by the one in her room until she comes home, then I mope around the kitchen. I insist on doing the washing up, even though I can tell Mum wants me out of her hair. The weekend comes and goes, and Jimmy does not call.

The next Wednesday, Natasha's at the park. I'm on a bench, using *Wuthering Heights* to protect me from the mothers.

"Is that for school?" she asks me.

"Not exactly," I say. Natasha just shrugs.

"Could you look after my kids on Friday night?" She doesn't say please or add a maybe to the question, and I don't know how to say no to such a direct request.

"Okay, but I have to be home by midnight, or my mum will freak out."

"Daisy, you're a lifesaver."

She takes out a pen and a piece of paper from her tasselled purse and scribbles down her address and phone number. "Come by for six, and I can settle you in before I go out."

It's an apartment about five minutes from my house. I can't decide what to tell Mum, but I figure I've already committed so she'll have to let me go.

Mum is not pleased.

"You agreed to babysit for a woman whom you met on a park bench."

"It's not like that, Mum. She's really nice and it's so close to here."

"Anything could happen to you there, there could be..."

"What? What could happen?"

"Daisy, I'm not happy, but I'll think about it."

Mum agrees I can babysit as long as she gets to talk to Natasha. When I call Natasha and ask her to call my mum, she is unsurprised.

"Of course I'll talk to her, Daisy. I'd do the same thing if it was my kid."

I listen from the top of the stairs when the phone rings. I hear Mum say, "Well, I am just a bit concerned about…" I plug my ears and rock back and forth. I am terrified of Mum being a snob or acting like I'm twelve. When I unplug my ears I hear laughing. The conversation goes on for longer than I can bear, and then I hear Mum say goodbye and I lunge down the stairs.

"Okay," she says. "But I want you to call when you're done. Otherwise Natasha will have to get the kids out of bed to bring you home."

I don't argue. There's no way Mum would let me walk home alone, but the thought of her meeting Natasha, who'll have been at a bar drinking Blow Jobs, worries me.

Thursday at eight forty-five in the evening the phone rings. This is too late for polite friends to call. I assume it's Elizabeth, Grahame, or Dad. Mum answers and calls me to the phone. I pick it up, and when I hear Jimmy's voice, my heart starts thudding. Mum lingers; I whoosh her away from me with both my hands as I cradle the phone against my shoulder. I hear when her footsteps stop on the stairs exactly where I eavesdrop on her.

The conversation is stilted; we don't really know each other, but Jimmy asks me if I want to hang out tomorrow. "I have to babysit," I say.

"Oh."

I realize it sounds like I am blowing him off, and I find myself saying, "What about Saturday?"

I want to talk to Wanda about my impending date. I start

letters that I don't finish. I'd like to ask Elizabeth for her advice, but there is no way to get a hold of her. She calls every Sunday from a payphone in Chapleau and can never talk long. There's always a line of quarter-laden tree planters behind her.

I promise Mum I'll call her and let her know how things are going at Natasha's. I'm nervous as I walk over. I'm stressed about finding the right apartment. I'll have to get buzzed in, and I've never done this before. I don't know Natasha's kids that well. Dwayne is six and Sara is three.

The inside of the building fascinates me. There are framed pictures of mountainscapes in the hallways, and all the doors have signs that indicate something about the residents' personalities. Someone has a Jamaican flag; someone else has a *Beware of Cat* sign with a picture of sleeping Garfield. Another door has an AC/DC bumper sticker. There's a slightly off-putting smell of smoke, other people's cooking, and air freshener.

Beside Natasha's door is a burnt-wood plaque that says *Jesus lives in this house*. She catches me looking at it and laughs. "My dad made it for me," she says, and ushers me in. The kids are happy to see me. Natasha has fed them dinner and got them in their PJs. They're sitting down in front of a huge colour TV. I talk to Natasha as she gets ready; I tell her about my date with Jimmy tomorrow.

Natasha looks fantastic when she leaves. Her hair is curled and piled on her head, and she has on red cowboy boots. She kisses the kids and leaves me three cigarettes to smoke while I'm babysitting.

"Don't tell your mom," she says.

"Sorry about all that," I say, feeling embarrassed again by

my mother's over-protectiveness.

"Don't be sorry, she's just looking out for you. She has such a cute accent. It was like talking to Lady Diana."

I shrug.

I put Sara to bed; she is sweet and easy. I read her a few stories, and then I play a game of Snakes and Ladders with Dwayne, who takes it very seriously. I put him to bed in the same room as Sara. I call Mum and assure her all is well, and then I go immerse myself in the television.

Natasha comes home at eleven o'clock. Before I go, she pays me ten bucks and gives me an almost new lipstick she thinks will suit me, for good luck on my date. I call Mum and then go wait for her in the lobby. No need for her to meet Natasha this evening.

I'm meeting Jimmy at the bus stop at 5:30. This is, conveniently, between our two houses, and I have suggested it. Mum offered to drive us up to the mall, but I declined. I apply the lipstick Natasha gave me. It's way too red. It has stained my lips and the skin around my mouth, and I have to use half a jar of face cream to get it off. There is still a red tinge underneath the burgundy colour I finally apply. I go heavy on the eye makeup and use pale powder. I settle on my usual jeans and black T-shirt; I wear a silver ring on each finger. I have the leather cord and half-heart pendant around my wrist; I always wear it. I "borrow" Elizabeth's black, high-heeled boots. Despite all these preparations, I'm still way too early. I have to time my arrival so I don't look overly anxious, but also so we don't miss the 5:33 bus, which is sometimes running ahead of schedule.

I'm ten minutes early at the bus stop. I am relieved to see Jimmy walking towards me, only a block away, down the main street. Jimmy sits in the middle of the back seat and I take one of the window seats. He takes up the rest of the bench, putting his jacket beside him and sprawling. I can hear Mum's voice saying, "How inconsiderate." But there are only five people on the bus, and two of them are old and at the front.

When we get to the mall, we head to the theatre. Jimmy buys two tickets. I stand behind him in line, in case he only buys one ticket and I have to get my own. We get inside and he buys an enormous bag of popcorn and a huge Coke. I buy a regular-sized pack of M&Ms. Jimmy offers me the Coke and I take a sip. We're sharing a straw.

In the theatre we choose seats away from the rest of the audience. The air conditioning is on and the theatre is freezing. Jimmy sees me shiver and puts his arm around my shoulders. I am on a date and a boy has his arm around my shoulders. I can't wait to describe this moment to Wanda.

The lights go out and Jimmy has to remove his arm to offer me popcorn. I am torn between watching Bruce Willis and angling my hand on my thigh in a way that says "Hold me." Then it happens: I feel Jimmy's long fingers take my hand and hold on to it. I smile. I sneak a look over at him, and he turns and grins. I am filled with zinging joy to be sitting here holding hands in the tiny mall theatre.

After the movie we disengage our hands and leave the darkness in that weird post-movie haze that is like waking up from a dream. We have twenty minutes till the bus comes; Jimmy plays the pinball machine at the mall entrance. He makes me play a ball, which I lose almost immediately. When

I tell him I've never played a pinball machine before he's shocked.

"No way! That's wild."

When the bus comes, we sit side by side and more hand-holding ensues. When we get off at the bus stop, I make to say goodbye, but Jimmy smiles at me and says, "Don't be crazy, D. I'm going to walk you home."

We share basic facts: siblings, parents split up (Jimmy too), grade school, favourite bands, favourite food, classes we hate, and movies we love. When we get to my driveway I say, "Well, here it is."

"I knew this was your house." He leans in and kisses me once on the lips. Then I lean into him and we are kissing. I feel his tongue slip between my lips and gently slip mine inside his. Our teeth click together, and we pull apart.

"I should go."

Jimmy waits till I'm in the house. Then I see him walk away. He does a little fist pump at the end of the drive. Mum has been waiting at the front window. I know she can't see the end of the driveway, but she can see Jimmy as he walks down the street in front of the house.

"He sure has long hair. How did it go?" she asks me.

"It was good. I'm going to bed now," I tell her in a rush. I am anxious to retell myself the events of the evening, shining the highlights and letting the memory of Jimmy sprawling at the back of the bus fade into the background.

It's one of those summer Sundays when you can hear the buzz of the fridge and the click of the numbers turning on the stove clock.

Mum and I both wait in the heat and silence for the phone

to ring. I'm hoping to hear from Jimmy, and Mum is hoping to hear from Grahame. He's on a canoe trip with friends. Mum sits on the back deck with an open book. I can see her from my bedroom. She has not turned the page in a long time. I stare down at Mum for a while, then roam around listlessly. I look in the fridge, walk around the yard, and then walk down to the end of the driveway. All I can think is, "Call me, call me, call me." In my head I replay our date round and round— everything Jimmy said, everything I said. I'm pretty sure he likes me, and yet he does not call. I crouch down at the end of the driveway and watch a line of ants carry a dead beetle. I hear a skateboard approaching.

Damon does the stop-and-flip-the-board-up thing.

"Hey, what's up?" he says.

"Not much," I reply.

He crouches down and looks at the ants.

"Cool."

"I hate Sundays. They're so damn boring."

"Me too. Mom and Cora had another big fight, and Dad is trying to fix the kitchen sink. I had to get out of there."

"What was the fight about?" I know it's rude to ask, but the heat makes me petulant.

"You know, my parents want to know who the father is."

"Cora hasn't told your parents?"

"No, she keeps saying it doesn't matter. She doesn't want him involved."

"She's probably right. Millie keeps showing me how big the baby is on a ruler. She's obsessed with the pictures in Cora's baby books."

The noise of a lawnmower starting up next door breaks

into our conversation. Damon's board goes down. "My mom thinks you're great," he says, and then he turns and pushes off the ground and rides down the street.

Jimmy finally calls me Sunday night. We talk for two hours on the phone, right up until Mum starts harrumphing around the kitchen in her dressing gown, making tea and turning off the lights in the living room.

Millie and I dance in the kitchen on Monday morning, and Cora eyes me with suspicion. "Beware of love," she says, rubbing her belly and wiping sleep from her eyes.

fifteen

Elizabeth calls two weeks before Labour Day and announces she is not returning to finish her fourth year of university. She arrives home two days after the call. I can't wait to tell her all about Jimmy.

Dad picks her up at the airport. He has been sent to try to get her to return to school. When Dad's car pulls up outside the house, a skinny, tanned woman with a rat's nest of hair gets out, along with a skinny guy who looks like he could do with a wash. Dad pulls out of the driveway and does not come inside for the family reunion Mum has been working herself up to all day.

Elizabeth puts both her and Eric, the boyfriend's, bags in her room when they arrive and that's where they stay. Eric speaks with a slow syncopation that makes him frustrating to listen to. I feel like yelling at him to get to the point. He has eyes that seem to look right through you while he holds you in his long gaze. He smells. After he showers, his scent still lingers. He uses strange sandalwood soap for both his hair and body, and judging from her hair, Elizabeth has been using it too.

We've never been skinny girls, but Elizabeth has morphed into a muscle-armed lean creature. Her cheek bones are pronounced, and she's tanned the colour of cardboard. Mum has been trying to extricate her from Eric, but she simply doesn't respond to Mum's subtle hints of "Why don't you help me in the kitchen?" She just ignores us both and gazes at Eric like the constellations are circling around his head. Even Mum's pathetic sigh and sad voice don't seem to rouse much empathy from Elizabeth. She just brusquely smiles and continues folding laundry or mixing up textured vegetable protein meatloaf.

They stay for two weeks and I never get to have an actual conversation with Elizabeth. When we spend time together, Eric is always there, and she is constantly performing for him. We don't giggle like we would if he wasn't in the room. She goes through her old clothes and gives them almost all to me. When I tell her I have been wearing her boots, she just laughs. When she does ask me about Jimmy and what I think of Grahame, Eric is in the room, so I can't tell her anything that I really want to. Jimmy's at his dad's cottage for the end of the summer, and I'm almost relieved. Jimmy and Eric together would be an odd meeting, like watching a poodle and a bulldog sniffing each other on the sidewalk.

Eric and Elizabeth are vegans. Eric makes lentil soups; he burns the bottom of the pan and then inadequately scrubs it out. Mum is starting to develop a twitch in her eyebrow.

Mum orchestrates one big discussion about Elizabeth dropping out of university. Dad comes over and stands awkwardly by the window holding a glass of wine. Mum sits on a chair, and Elizabeth and Eric lounge on the couch. Eric's legs are flopped open, and it's almost impossible not to stare in between them. He doesn't contribute to the conversation. He sits and watches the words go back and forth as if he is at a tennis match. He is unmoved by the proceedings and weirdly comfortable in the midst of our family's domestic turmoil. I am not technically supposed to be here, but no one tells me to leave so I sit on the stairs and keep quiet.

My parents both express why they think Elizabeth should head back to school rather than travel around Europe with Eric. She keeps very calm and says, "I hear what you're saying but I need to do this." She says it over and over again like a mantra.

Dad doesn't want to be here. He tells Elizabeth, "I have more important things to do than waste my time telling you not to waste your own. This is exactly why women should stay out of academics; they can't stick to anything."

"What about Pat?" Elizabeth asks, and Dad feigns deafness. He's distracted and only half with us. You can almost see the rats running around in his brain.

Elizabeth and Eric pack big backpacks, and she converts her tree-planting money into traveller's cheques. Then they go.

"It's just us now," says Mum, after they leave for the airport.

When the phone rings, the day after Elizabeth goes, I expect it to be Jimmy or Wanda or Jude. Grahame is over. There is a map on the kitchen table. Grahame is planning an afternoon of touring antique markets. He is trying to cheer Mum up, but she is distant and just keeps agreeing with everything he suggests.

Cora is on the phone. She needs me to look after Millie

for an hour. Her mom's out, and so is Damon. When I arrive, Cora is not in her usual pregnancy uniform of track-pant shorts, but in full-on Cora black. Her breasts have gotten enormous, and I find it hard not to stare at them stretching out a black undershirt. She puts on a thick layer of lipstick. She inserts her middle finger between her lips and draws it out of her mouth slowly while gently sucking on it. She makes her eyes wide and wiggles her eyebrows at me. "If you give your finger head, it stops you from getting lipstick on your teeth," she explains.

"No one else knows, well except for Damon, but I know you saw Mark drop me off that time. You can't tell anyone, okay, Daisy?"

"Mark?"

"Mr. Dean, he's probably the father. He keeps calling and freaking out at me. He's worried I'm going to tell his wife, but I never want to see him again. I don't want him to have anything to do with my baby. I need to tell him in person."

When she's gone, I reapply my lipstick in the Joneses' bathroom. I draw my finger out from my lips, and I wonder how Jimmy would react if I tried this trick in front of him.

Millie and I play in the backyard. The sun is hot, and I'm almost dozing when I hear the door open and Mrs. Jones and Damon walk into the house.

Millie runs inside. "Mom, Daisy's here!"

Mrs. Jones flops into a deckchair looking pale. Damon's arm is in a sling, and I see him flinch when Millie runs up and touches it.

"I fell off my board. It's just a bad sprain, not broken."

Mrs. Jones is looking at me intently. "Is Cora here?"

I can feel my palms get sweaty.

"She had to go out, so I said I'd watch Millie."

"That girl! She shouldn't have asked you to look after Millie without telling me first. Millie, do you know where Cora went?"

"Daisy's here," Millie replies unhelpfully.

"Daisy, did Cora say where she was going or if she was meeting anyone?" Mrs. Jones is giving me an authoritarian stare.

"No, she just asked me to look after Millie for a bit."

I am trying to figure out how to leave politely when Cora comes home. I see her before anyone else, looking out at us all in the backyard from the kitchen window. She looks hot and tired, and like she cannot take another thing.

I head home. No one pays me for babysitting, and Mrs. Jones is cold with me. She doesn't get angry; she just isn't friendly when she sees Cora and says, "Daisy, you should go now."

When Cora calls me later, we don't mention my awkward departure.

"How did it go?" I ask her.

"He tried to give me money, like a hundred bucks was going to solve all my problems. I told Mom. At least she understands now why I don't want to involve the father. Daisy, do you want to hang out here on Friday night? I need a break from my family."

When Jimmy gets back from his dad's on Friday, we have our first fight. "I haven't seen you in two weeks. Can't you just cancel on Cora?"

"I promised her, Jimmy, and she's having a tough time."

"I had a tough time at my dad's."

"I'm sorry. We can hang out Saturday."

"I guess. I have to go, Daisy," he says and hangs up the phone.

Natasha asks if I can babysit for her on Saturday. I tell her I have a date with Jimmy, and she tells me to bring him over. "Then you can have the place to yourselves once the kids are in bed." I tell Natasha I'll have to ask Jimmy first. I don't want him to be disappointed in me again.

Jimmy likes the idea. "I'm sorry I was mad earlier. It's just I missed you."

My ears ring with excitement.

"I'm sorry too," I say. We are generous with our apologies and our forgiveness.

"I wish you were here," I whisper into the phone.

"I wish I were there too, babe."

Wanda is less forgiving. "Jesus, Daisy, I've been away all summer and you're ditching me to babysit." I don't tell her Jimmy is coming with me.

"There's going be a big party in the parking lot behind the arena. My cousin picked up a bottle of Lambs for me and I snuck it home in my backpack. Jude's coming too. You're going to miss out big time."

Cora's is wearing an oversized Depeche Mode shirt with her usual shorts when I arrive at the Joneses'. Damon is playing video games in the living room. He keeps swearing in frustration. He can only use one hand and keeps losing lives. I hear bleeping sounds that signify his player's repeated death. There's no sign of Crystal. Cora ushers me past Damon and into her room. He gives me a two-fingered wave when we go past.

"He's sulking. Crystal dumped him, and Mom won't let him go out with his friends. She's worried he'll fuck up his arm."

"When did Crystal dump him?"

"Oh…about a week ago. Officially, anyway, but they've hardly seen each other for the past month." It's nothing to do with me I keep telling myself. Jimmy, Jimmy, Jimmy. I can't help but have a brief Damon-and-Daisy fantasy. But Damon is not the one who holds my hand and calls me "babe." Also, I have found out recently from Cora that Damon watches *Star Trek*.

Cora has her parents' old record player in her room, and we listen to her dad's Nazareth album recording of "Love Hurts" over and over again. She has glow-in-the-dark stickers on her ceiling just like I wanted, but wasn't allowed in case they wrecked the paint. She has candles and incense she's allowed to burn in her room. She even has an old black-and-white TV. Her bedspread is black, and she has a futon instead of a bed. It used to be on the floor, but when she got pregnant her mom insisted she use a frame. She has an old-fashioned dresser covered in makeup and perfume bottles. We have a cigarette out the window, but she only has a drag because of the baby.

"Don't your parents get mad?"

"My dad smokes down there," she says, pointing at an old coffee can. "We all pretend we don't know when he sneaks out every night after dinner. They've never caught me smoking in here. They just think the smell is the smoke drifting up."

Cora shows me a picture of her parents when they were first married. Mr. Jones has long hair and is standing in front of a motorbike. Mrs. Jones is sitting on the motorbike looking like Sandy from *Grease*. "Your parents are so cool," I tell her, and she laughs at me. I tell her about Mum and Donald and Pat Rat.

"Men are bastards," Cora says.

"Except Jimmy," I say, protectively.

Cora shows me the baby clothes her friends have given her at her baby shower. They're all black, except for one tie-dyed babygrow.

"They all got together one night and dyed them. Belinda's mom had a fit because they used her washing machine," Cora tells me. I wonder where all her friends are tonight, but I don't ask. Instead, I ask if she's scared about having the baby.

"I am not scared of anything," she says, but she looks so young in this moment it is hard to believe her.

Mrs. Jones drives me home at ten. Cora doesn't come in the car because her back is hurting.

"It's nice of you to spend time with Cora," Mrs. Jones says to me. I cringe. "Her friends haven't been around so much this summer." How does it happen, that people get old and forget the embarrassment they cause when talking about their children like this?

"You're a good girl," Mrs. Jones says, and I feel like a five-year-old being congratulated for playing with the retarded kid. Mrs. Jones looks tired.

Olivia is over when I get in. There are already two empty wine bottles on the kitchen counter. Grahame is white-water rafting this weekend, and I know Mum is feeling hurt he didn't invite her. "Not that I'd have gone." I overhear this refrain several times before I fall asleep. I hear the doorbell ring at around one in the morning and Olivia leaving loudly. At 2 a.m. I hear Mum in the bathroom repeatedly flushing the toilet.

It is 7 a.m. and Mum is vacuuming. She is pretending she is not hungover. She makes us both scrambled eggs for breakfast, but can't eat hers, and admitting defeat, retreats to her bedroom with a cold cloth for her head.

On days like this, the thing to do is just *tell* her what I'm doing. Instead of saying, "Is it okay if Natasha's friend brings me home?" I say, "Natasha's got a drive home for me," then I run around getting ready so there's no time for an argument. I blare CFNY on my radio until I hear Mum's quaking voice. "For God's sake, turn it down, Daisy." I do not tell Mum I'm bringing Jimmy to Natasha's with me.

Jimmy meets me on the corner. He pulls me into a huge hug right there on the street, and I inhale the musty Jimmy smell. It turns out Jimmy and Natasha recognize each other. They've gone to the same softball games, and Natasha knows Jimmy's aunt a little. Jimmy is surprisingly charming. He plays snap with Dwayne, as I sit on the edge of the bathtub and watch Natasha spray in hair product.

"He's nice," she mouths to me. Then, more audibly, "How's your mom doing?"

"Hungover and grumpy today. It's her own fault."

Natasha looks at me.

"Give her a break, Daisy."

I turn my head from Natasha, riding a wave of self-pity that I worry will make me cry. Natasha doesn't let me escape her gaze. She reaches out, grabs the side of my chin, and turns my face and eyes towards to her.

"Cheer up. I just meant being an adult can be hard. And don't have sex on my couch."

She leaves us saying, "Don't do anything I'd do!" and laughing. I put Sara to bed and Jimmy puts on the TV. Dwayne sits beside Jimmy in the middle of the couch.

"Jimmy said I could watch for half an hour." He gazes at Jimmy with adoration. I sit on the other side of Dwayne, and Jimmy puts his arm across the back of the couch and places his hand on my neck. Dwayne starts yawning, and I bring him into the bedroom and check on Sara, who is sleeping soundly. When I come back out Jimmy has turned out the lights and put on MuchMusic. I sit down beside him.

Jimmy and I make out until Jimmy says he has to stop for a minute to get himself together. I know he has a hard-on but I pretend not to notice. Natasha comes home when Jimmy's in the bathroom; she has a guy with her. She's a little drunk and kisses me dramatically on the cheek before we leave. "Wish me luck," she whispers. She hands me five bucks and half a pack of smokes, and tells me she will make up for her lack of cash next time.

On the way home, Jimmy holds my hand and makes me stop to look up at the stars. We are holding hands and looking at them when he asks me to be his girlfriend. "Before we go back to school, I thought we should make it official." We kiss some more, and because we are standing up, I can feel him harden against my thigh. I can't help but think of Wanda and her sound effects. *Bloop.*

When I get home, Mum calls to me from her bed.

"Daisy, I didn't hear a car. You didn't walk home by yourself, did you?"

"No, Mum, one of Natasha's friends and her boyfriend walked me home." I cross my fingers and pretend to myself that this is the truth.

"Come in here so I can talk to you."

"I have to pee. I'll be right in."

My lipstick is smeared and my hair is dishevelled. I'm worried Mum will see the way my body is still vibrating from Jimmy's attention. I fix my hair and lips, and hover at the edge of her doorway.

"I thought you'd be asleep."

"Of course I couldn't sleep until you were home."

"Mum, I was babysitting around the corner."

"Anything could happen, Daisy. I'm not comfortable with strangers bringing you home."

"They weren't strangers; they were Natasha's friends. Why do you always have to overreact to everything?"

"We'll have to talk about this in the morning."

"Fine."

When I go to bed, I can hear her crying. I am guessing she hasn't heard from Grahame. I want to go back and say I'm sorry. But I'm not sure what I'm sorry about. The electrical tingle flowing inside of me has been swept away, and I lie down and listen to her until I start to cry myself.

sixteen

Jimmy kisses me, pressing my back against my locker, and I see, when I open my eyes, a bunch of niners walking by averting their eyes. I push him away. I've got to get to class. At lunch, I'm sitting between his legs and I can feel him hardening against the small of my back. He keeps kissing my neck. It's embarrassing in front of Jude and Wanda. I suggest to Jimmy that we go for a walk. We wait until his erection goes down before we walk through the school. Jimmy takes me back into the short hallway by the seldom-used newspaper darkroom, and we make out. One of the grade thirteen guys walks by and whistles, but this doesn't faze Jimmy at all. A part of my mind is on the making out; I am definitely responding to Jimmy's probing kissing and starting to feel hot and sticky, but part of me is starting to worry about my math test. Did I remember my protractor? The bell goes, and I literally unstick myself from Jimmy. Sweat has made our arms meld together.

After school, his mom is out and his older brother Dan is too. As soon as we get to his basement, Jimmy's hands are on me. He starts creeping up inside my shirt and under the elastic of my bra. It is like a fire breaks out in my body, and I want to be touched everywhere. Jimmy sits on the couch, and I sit on top of him. He takes off my top, and then I take off my bra. Sitting astride him, I feel exposed but powerful. I can feel him hard underneath me, and he kisses my breasts. My body is greedy, and I find I'm grinding against him. When I open my eyes, Jimmy is smiling. He takes my hand and gently guides it to the front of his pants.

Jimmy zips himself up and gets me some toilet paper to wipe my hands on. He pushes me back on the couch, undoes my jeans, and slips his hand inside of them. It feels so good with his hand touching me. He doesn't have a lot of room to move inside of my clothes, but all of a sudden his fingers find the right place, and I'm moving against his hand. I cry out when I come. I feel self-conscious now we're finished, and aware of the fact that I'm half naked. I gather my shirt and head into the bathroom to get dressed. I can hear the upstairs door being unlocked and cupboards being opened in the kitchen. When Jimmy's mom comes downstairs, I am drawing a triangle with my geometry set and Jimmy is playing Super Mario.

"Nice to meet you, Mrs. Hill," I say as she looks me over.

Every chance Jimmy and I get to be alone, we explore each other's bodies. I'm less embarrassed when I'm naked. Jimmy goes slower and learns how to touch me gently and make me more desperate for his touch.

A month goes by and I've hardly seen Wanda. I tell Jimmy I'm going to her house because I need to study without distraction. I'm supposed to be doing homework, but our text books lie abandoned beside us.

"Are you having sex with Jimmy?"

"Not yet, but we're serious. We've done other stuff, just not gone all the way."

"What's it like?"

"It feels good. I was worried I'd feel guilty, like I was stealing candy or something, but it just feels great. Natural."

"I gave a guy a hand job over the summer. Allen, a friend of one of my cousins. I was going to have sex with him just to get rid of my virginity, but he came too fast. All that stuff all over my hands, and I couldn't face going through the whole thing all over again. He kept apologizing and that made it worse."

"No one tells you how much stuff actually comes out, or what a penis is really like. The top of Jimmy's penis is so soft, it almost feels like velvet."

"Do you get off when you're with him?"

"Sometimes."

"What does he do?"

I'm starting to feel hot between my legs, talking about this with Wanda.

"Girls," Wanda's mom calls out, and we both sit up quickly like we've been caught at something.

When I get home, Mum is on her way out. She's headed to Grahame's. "Don't wait up, I might be late," she says. "I left his number on the fridge." I call Jimmy.

Mr. Kleinberg asks Damon and me to stay after English class. He tells us that he thinks we should try out for the school play.

He makes everyone read out loud at the beginning of every class, and the two of us are better than most of our classmates. Damon folds up the flyer and sticks it in his back pocket. I hand Wanda the paper with the tryout date and instructions on preparing for an audition when I meet her and Jude for lunch.

Wanda laughs. "No way, who would want to spend more time in this hell hole than they have to?" and then returns to examining her eyebrows in her compact.

Jude, on the other hand, is drawn in. Despite her struggle to be non-conformist, the lure of organized fun is too much for her, and she agrees to come to the tryouts with me.

Jimmy and I are at the arcade after school. Both of our mothers are expected home early. I stand at Jimmy's side as he plays Street Fighter II. He karate chops the limbs off his animated opponents. I now know the minute details of the Street Fighter gaming console, each cigarette burn, the *Led Zeppelin* someone has scraped into it in jagged lines, and the *SUCKS* etched in in larger letters.

"I'm going to try out for the play," I tell him.

"Uhh huh. Shit. Take that, motherfucker. Did you see that?"

I go and buy a single cigarette from Mr. Linn, the owner of the arcade. He doesn't sell them during school hours. I hand over my dollar, and he passes me a cigarette from under the counter and lends me his lighter.

I return to Jimmy's side. "So the play."

"Yeah?" Jimmy takes a drag from my cigarette and then puts another quarter in the machine.

"I'll have to try out."

"Shit…see that?"

"Jimmy? The play?"

"Yeah, go for it if you want to. Now watch this."

I steal a copy of *Streetcar Named Desire* from the back of the English classroom. I pick out a speech by Blanche DuBois and say the lines again and again. Then I pose in front of the bathroom mirror and practice. I produce tears by staring at the same spot on the wall without blinking. The morning of the auditions, I wake up early and go for a walk around the block, pretending I am Blanche. Jimmy isn't at school. At lunch I reread my lines again and again, sitting with Wanda and Jude. Jude hasn't memorized anything new; she plans to recite "In Flanders Fields," which she memorized for a school assembly in grade eight.

Jude stands on the staircase landing and looks down at Wanda and me sitting on the stairs below her. She stands at attention and salutes before she begins. She rhymes off the poem perfectly, but with almost no emotion. I take my place up on the landing. I put the back of one hand to my forehead and my other hand on my thrust-out hip. I concentrate on making my eyes well up, but as soon as I start with my southern accent Wanda and Jude start to giggle. A grade nine boy comes into the stairwell and looks at me and my dramatic pose like he's worried I'm having some kind of palsy. I drop my hand and try to look natural. Other students start using the stairs. Jude and Wanda stand up to get out of the way, and I never finish my piece for them.

Gerry is in charge; he teaches English and Drama. The only person who calls Gerry Mr. McDonald is the principal. I thought Mr. Kleinberg would be running things, but he's just organizing the stagehands. He sits on the sidelines.

Gerry talks for thirty minutes. He likes to use the names of the kids he knows and addresses parts of his introductory talk to them. He says "damn" a lot, and "groovy." He swings his arms around. He throws a piece of chalk at Kleinberg, who reacts too late and doesn't catch it. Since he doesn't know me or Jude or Damon, we aren't favoured with his special glance or his hand on our shoulders as he wanders around the class-room telling us how glad he is we're here, and that we're going to create something awesome. Gerry has chosen three plays and wants us to vote on which one we want to perform.

"I want you to think of this play as a gift. When we choose a play, we are picking out a present to give to our school. I want you to think hard about what you are going to give to your community. What would they like, and more importantly, what do they *need*?"

Mr. Kleinberg stares at his shoes during this speech, and I recite my lines over and over in my head and breathe deeply getting in the right frame of mind for my performance. The grade twelves and thirteens watch Gerry and hang on his every word.

"An updated version of *Romeo and Juliet*, *Hair*, and *Arsenic and Old Lace*, these are your choices. *Arsenic and Old Lace* is in there because my pal Carl felt we should have one classic option." Gerry smiles patronizingly at Mr. Kleinberg as he says this.

I write down *Arsenic and Old Lace* solely out of loyalty to Kleinberg. I shove my piece of paper in a yellow envelope Gerry has circulating the classroom. Gerry assures us he will carefully tally our slips and report the winner of our dramatic election at the meeting next week. Gerry takes the envelope and puts it in his bulging brown leather briefcase. He grabs his coat, and then Jana from grade eleven bravely asks when we are going to perform our soliloquies. She's wearing a brown-and-cream Indian-print cotton caftan over a pair of faded jeans. I know her from the smoking area. When the weather is good, she spends lunch playing Cat Stevens songs on her acoustic guitar while sitting cross-legged on the lawn of the school.

Gerry smiles. "If you're here in this room you have a part in this play. Asking you to prepare a piece was my way of finding out that you were serious about this production. You know you did it and I know you did it. There's no need to waste our time listening to them. When we choose our play, then we'll start figuring out who's the best player for each part."

Gerry leaves first, and Kleinberg waits for the students to leave, fiddling with a bunch of keys so he can lock the door behind us.

Jimmy's waiting outside the rehearsal for me.

"What are you doing here?"

"Principal's office, I got called in with my mom. She just left."

"What happened?"

"If I skip any more classes I'll be suspended. The principal thinks I should transfer to the tech school like I'm some kind of dumbass."

"I'm so sorry, Jimmy." I reach up and hug him, but he is stiff in my arms.

"I'm okay, Daisy; it's no big deal. Jesus, suspending me would be great. A whole week off school. Come on, let's get out of here. I'm sick of this place."

"I can't, Jimmy. I've got homework."

"Just come with me for half an hour."

"I can't, I have to get home. Mum's expecting me."

"Whatever, Daisy." He turns and walks away from me.

"It's just tonight. Tomorrow we can hang out," I call after him.

"Maybe," he says, but he doesn't stop walking or turn around.

I don't get any studying done. I lie in bed and worry that he doesn't like me anymore. When I get to my locker the next day, Jimmy is there closing it. He grabs me and pulls me in. "The best part of fighting is making up," he whispers in my ear. He leaves me to get to class, but when I open the locker I find flowers and a note folded up like a fortune teller. At the bottom of the note it says *I LOVE YOU, DAISY RADCLIFFE.* When I read this, in my English homeroom, I feel a little sick with excitement. Damon tries to grab the note from me.

"Fuck off, Damon." It comes out louder than I intend.

"First warning, Daisy. Another word and you are out of here," Mr. Kleinberg says, almost yelling. I never get in trouble, so the class snickers. Damon sticks his tongue out at me. I pretend not to notice.

At the next Drama meeting, Jude, Damon, and I sit together. We're the only grade tens to show up, and Kleinberg tells us he's glad to see us all again. Gerry comes in and sits on a desk at the front of the class. Outside the wind has picked up, and wet leaves keep hitting the window. The school takes on new sounds as the other students empty out of it. The last of the locker doors shutting echo in the hollow hallways.

"I have some good news and some bad news." Gerry looks at us seriously. "The play you have chosen is *Hair*. The play you will be performing is *Romeo and Juliet*." He sighs. "The *oppressive hierarchy* has ruled that *Hair* is not appropriate for a school production. I argued that students of your maturity could handle it, but I was shot down." He looks around, making eye contact with each of us. "We are going to stand up to this oppression."

No one says anything.

"This is what we're going to do. We are going to make our version of *Romeo and Juliet* a *Hair* for your generation. We are going to take this play and tailor it to tell the story of being young now. This is going to be about the Berlin Wall, AIDS, and growing up in the cultural shadow of the sixties. This is going to be your story."

A few of the grade thirteens applaud this.

"My senior classes have already been workshopping the play so it reflects our times. This is your chance to stick it to the Man."

He announces that Roseanne will play Juliet and Nathan will play Romeo. He reads a list of the Capulets and the Montagues, both lists are made up entirely of his senior Drama classes.

"Don't worry if you don't have a part," he says, smiling out at us all. "There is a place for everyone in this play."

Jana raises her hand.

"No need to raise your hand." Gerry smiles, and the front row titters.

"All the good parts are gone and the rest of us"—Jana waves in the direction of a few grade elevens and then me,

Jude, and Damon— "didn't get a chance to try out."

"I think what you will find, what's your name again?"

"Jana."

"Well, Janis, the thing to remember is that there are no small parts, only small actors."

"Is he high?" Damon whispers to me.

"High on himself," I whisper back.

seventeen

Our P.A. beeps, and for a moment everyone is still. Often direct class messages mean trouble, a death in the family, or that a student is being picked up by the police or social services.

"Mr. Kleinberg, can you please send Damon Jones down here to the office and ask him to collect his books?" the secretary's disembodied voice says. I know this means Cora must have gone into labour. Damon fist bumps me as he heads out.

We have a test, and I'm trying to concentrate when we hear a whoop outside the room. I look up and Damon has shoved a piece of paper against the small square of glass at the top of the door. IT'S A GIRL is scrawled across it. Even Mr. Kleinberg smiles and shakes his head. Cora liked his classes.

Mum and I arrive at the hospital to visit the day-old baby. To get to the entrance, we walk through a cloud of smoke. Patients stand outside the hospital holding onto metal posts on wheels with IV bags hanging off them. Inside the hospital there is the smell of disinfectant and sick bodies.

I am nervous and feel like crying for no particular reason. We're waiting for the elevator, and two porters wheel a gurney with someone lying on it beside us. The patient is heavily bandaged and unmoving. The porters wheel the gurney silently into the staff elevator, and Mum and I politely avert our gaze.

"Okay, Daisy?" Mum says, as we get into the visitors' elevator. I nod. "Babies make everyone emotional," she reassures me. The maternity ward is less desolate than the first floor of the hospital. There are balloons on the front desk, and you can hear people laughing. Mrs. Jones is standing outside a door chatting with a nurse; she waves us over.

"Go in, Daisy. Go on."

Cora is propped up in bed, her face clean of makeup. She is holding a tiny white bundle in her arms. She looks up, sees me, and starts crying.

"Sorry, sorry, it's the hormones, they say. I'm so happy. Come see. She's amazing." I gaze down at the baby in Cora's arms. Her face is red and squished up. She has little whiteheads all over her skin, but still asleep, she reaches out a tiny arm towards Cora, and I am taken with the miniature fingers.

"Look at her hands," I say.

"I know."

"How are you?" I ask.

"I don't know," says Cora, crying again. "But look at her."

I look up and see Mum hugging Mrs. Jones. She squeezes Mrs. Jones's arm, and a look passes between them. They both come in, Mrs. Jones wiping away tears.

"Babies make everyone cry," Mum says. The baby, Sinead we learn her name is, opens her eyes and appears to look around at us before starting to wail.

Grahame comes for dinner that night. He brings a book to show me. The cover is a green-moss colour and made of very soft paper, almost like construction paper, but stronger and velvety. There's no picture on the front, only the title *Standing Still in the River*, but down the thin spine is the author's name, Carl Kleinberg. "Isn't this your English teacher? Your mum mentioned you liked him, and the name sounded familiar. I bought this a few years ago after hearing him read."

I flip open the book; it is all poetry. At the back is a black-and-white photo of Mr. Kleinberg, the picture is ten years old, and he is younger but unmistakeable.

"It *is* my teacher. He never told us he was a poet."

"Maybe best keep that to yourself, Daisy?" Mum says. "He might not want everyone to know."

"You can borrow it if you like," Grahame says.

The poems are beautiful. There is poem about a boy who drowns on a canoe trip and a poem about a night spent contemplating suicide.

I call Wanda and describe Sinead to her. I read Wanda one of Kleinberg's poems. It's about a swallow stuck in a house searching for an open window.

"Read it again," she says, and by the end of the second time, we are both crying.

The classrooms are decorated with tinsel, and the teachers are all laid back. In French we play French charades. In Math we work out the total area of a reindeer made up of triangles, rectangles and a perfectly round red nose. In English we watch a crackling black-and-white version of *A Christmas Carol*. By the time I get to the gym for rehearsal, I'm looking forward to the holiday.

Kleinberg's wearing a Santa hat and is handing out candy canes to all the kids as they come in the door of the gym.

"In five you have to flash, 1, 2, 3, 4, now." I give Damon the cue. Damon flickers the lights up and down. This represents the bad trip Romeo and Juliet have after taking acid. Damon and I are lighting crew, although this is secondary to my role as understudy to Jana, who Gerry gave the nurse's role.

"Cora's boobs are huge. And it cries the whole time. How can something so small make such disgusting smells?" Damon tells me.

"Come on, it can't be that bad. And don't talk about your sister's breasts. That's just wrong."

"I can't help it. They're everywhere I go, popping out in the living room and the kitchen. And when it's not boobs, it's nursing pads lying around on the coffee table or on the bathroom counter."

Jude comes in to join us. She's sewing one of the costumes.

"Hey, Jude!" Gerry yells. He's been barking instructions since the start of rehearsal.

"Gerry!" Jude yells back from the lighting booth.

"Black pants and a flowing white shirt for Mercutio. I see him in three-hole Docs. No, scratch that, Converse."

"Got it!" Jude jots down these notes.

Jude gets me to hold a hem in place. She has run out of pins. I follow her down the stairs, holding one end of a dress as she holds the other. We cut across the back of the stage into the equipment room where baseball bats and pylons are stored. Jude is the costume and prop mistress. Carefully labelled garment bags hang above the sacks of balls. Jude is supplying most of the character Romeo, the child of a military family, with bits of discarded Cadet uniforms she gathers from her troop. Juliet's wardrobe comes from students pillaging the backs of their mother's closets for castoffs from the sixties.

Jana joins us in the cupboard and shakes her fist at Gerry when he isn't looking in our direction. Gerry keeps changing her lines and making her nurse outfit less and less attractive. Jude is trying to source a nun's habit, but in the meantime is experimenting with an old pillow case slit down one side. Jana sits with her face shrouded like a druid as Jude tries different methods of securing the pillow case.

"I can't stand Gerry. It's like he thinks he's so cool, but he's just a loser."

"No, no, no, not like that!" Gerry shouts at Mercutio. "Off the stage."

Gerry is not in a festive mood. Jude, Jana, and I watch him staring at the empty stage, muttering inaudibly to himself.

"I want you all out here. Everyone in front of the stage now."

Damon sprawls on the floor next to Jude, Jana, and me, as we sit at centre court in the gym and wait for Gerry to start talking. Kleinberg places a chair behind the students seated on the ground.

Gerry turns from the stage and stares out at us. There are dark shadows under his eyes. He walks in a circle around all of us seated on the ground, and as he passes by us, I catch a whiff of whiskey on top of his usual cigarette smell.

"Is he drunk?" Jude whispers to me.

"He can't be, it's only 4:30 in the afternoon," I say.

"It's five o'clock somewhere," says Damon.

"His girlfriend left him for a guy she's in the chorus of

Phantom with. He told us in class today," I overhear a girl behind me saying.

Gerry has completed his tour and stands in front of us again. Everyone is silent.

"The play is the thing!" he shouts. I don't know if we're supposed to laugh or not. Jana, foolishly, grins.

"Funny? You think this is funny? We have only a few months before this theatre," he gestures around the empty gym, "is going to be full."

"Do you know what it's going to be full of?" He takes a long dramatic pause. "It's going to be full of shit!"

I have an awful urge to giggle; it's nerves. I'm working on being inconspicuous, lips neither smiling nor frowning. My hands are clasped together like they are posed for a formal photograph that is meant to look unstaged.

"Here you all are thinking because of some overly commercialized holiday you can sit back and have a laidback little read through. Well, you are wrong. Theatre is work. Art is work. You need to be eating, drinking, and shitting this play. I need you to believe in this play the same way that the Pope believes in Jesus."

Gerry stops. He pauses for breath, and Kleinberg walks past us holding his Santa hat in his hands and seizes the moment.

"What Gerry is saying is that just because you are on holiday doesn't mean you shouldn't still be working your lines and thinking about your characters. Now go. Practice hard and enjoy your vacation. Get out of here."

We grab our stuff and leave.

"What the fuck?" Damon says, when we get outside.

"He must be having a really hard time," says Jude.

"He's right, you know. I haven't been putting my soul into my part," Roseanne says, and Damon smirks at me. Damon, Jude, and I dawdle outside the gym doors. I can hear Kleinberg raise his voice. But his words are undecipherable. When footsteps start heading towards the door, the three of us get out of the school fast.

Jude heads off to the bus stop. "You going to the arcade to meet Jimmy?" Damon asks me.

"Actually, I'm going to your house. I'm visiting Cora."

He jerks his head in the direction of his house, and we start walking together.

"Do you think Gerry really was drunk?" Damon asks me.

"I don't know. People go crazy when they break up. He could be drunk or just depressed or maybe both."

Damon nods and we walk in silence for a while.

"When Cora got pregnant, I caught Mom smoking. She was out where Dad hides his butts, smoking and crying all alone."

"What did you say to her?"

"Nothing. I just backed up slowly and went around to the front of the house. You're the only person I've told."

"Mum does crazy stuff. She gets drunk sometimes, then she pretends like it never happened. She's more fun now, though, not always so worried about what other people are going to think."

"It's cool you're coming to see Cora. She gets kind of down sometimes. I think it's pretty boring being stuck at home all day with Sinead."

"This town is boring, even if you get to leave the house."

"Jimmy not exciting enough for you?"

I give Damon a look. "I'm just kidding," he says.

When we arrive at the house, Millie and Mrs. Jones are making cookies in the kitchen. Millie is icing the cookies and then adding sprinkles. She is incapable of keeping her hands dry, and the rainbow sprinkles are running in the white icing making all the sugar cookies appear as if someone has licked the top.

"Can you give me a hand? Girls? Damon?" Mrs. Jones asks when I arrive, and Cora comes to meet me.

There are six dozen cookies; we form an assembly line. Two hours later Mrs. Jones goes to pick up pizza for us. Cora takes Sinead to change her, and Damon, Millie, and I remain in the kitchen.

Damon starts chasing Millie around with the icing tube. He draws a blue moustache on her. Then he turns towards me. Millie is shrieking around us, and Damon grabs me from behind and pulls me close to him. It feels strange. He leaves his arm around me for what must only be five seconds, but it feels like time has stopped. Mrs. Jones comes in holding pizza, and Damon lets go.

When I get home, Mum is wrapping up presents. "Jimmy called. Actually, he called three times. Daisy, you know this thing with Jimmy? It's just…"

"Just what?"

"Nothing, nothing. It's just you're both so young." She leans down and kisses the top of my head.

eighteen

I am going to Wanda's for her family's big Christmas party, and Grahame is coming over to our house to spend the night.

"You know I was with your father for a long time, but I have very strong feelings for Grahame, and I miss the physical side of being married." Images of Mum and Grahame performing aerobics form in my mind. Grahame wears a Richard Simmons headband, and Mum is in leggings and one of those weird high-cut swimsuit things that Jane Fonda wears. A smile forms on my lips.

"Daisy, this is serious. I need to know you are okay with this. Having Grahame stay in the house is important to me. It's not something I've decided lightly. Since your father left…" she trails off.

"I know, Mum," I say.

Jude and I show up at Wanda's, and her parents are already a bit drunk and being all kissy-kissy in the kitchen. Wanda drags us into her room where we change into our festive outfits and abandon our sleeping bags. We all wear sparkly eye shadow. I wear my hair down, and let Wanda go at it with her mom's ancient crimper.

Her parents are blasting Steve Miller and Lynyrd Skynyrd. Her mom has said we can each have three glasses of her Pepsi punch, but no more. "I don't want to have to deal with a bunch of puking teenagers tonight, okay, girls?"

Wanda smokes in front of her parents; it feels weird to be standing in the kitchen sharing an ashtray with them. I can hardly taste any booze in the first glass of Wanda's mom's punch. Wanda waits until her mom is greeting guests, then pours us a second glass with an extra glug of rum from the bottle her dad has been mixing his drinks with. I'm sitting on the couch between Wanda's mom and her friend Wanita. Wanita hands me her smoke and I take a drag.

"Men," Wanita says, leaning in close. "The thing is, the most important thing to remember…" She points her finger and the burning cigarette at me. Then she stops mid-sentence and bounces up off the couch, patting my knee. She rushes over and throws her arms around a couple of women who have just walked into the room. The house is shaking with music and full of smoke. A couple of men have guitars and are competing with the songs Wanda's dad is playing on the stereo. Wanda, Jude, and I escape the heat of the house and head out into the backyard for a smoke. Wanda's cousins Bill and Craig are already outside smoking a joint.

"Little cousin Wanda!" Bill pulls her in for a hug. "Who are these lovely ladies? Your babysitters?" he says, teasing her.

"Give us a hit, Craig." Wanda pouts at him.

"Too late," Craig says, and pinches out the end of the joint and sticks the remnant in a small tin he takes from his pocket.

"Here, kid," says Bill, when Craig heads inside first.

Bill's not that much older than Wanda. He hands Wanda a thin white joint. "Merry Christmas!"

Wanda ceremoniously wets the joint. She puts it in her mouth, then gently draws it out between pursed lips. "So it doesn't canoe," she tells us sagely.

"Are you sure this is a good idea?" Jude asks.

"It will be fine. I've smoked up loads of times before." The lie floats from her lips without any hesitation.

I don't feel anything. I stand around not feeling anything. Then I start giggling. I giggle at everything. I look at Jude, and I'm going to tell her something really funny, then I forget what it is, and I think this is hilarious. I laugh so hard I can't tell her that I forgot what I was going to tell her anyhow.

Wanita pokes her head out of the back door.

"Shhhh! Act normal," hisses Wanda.

"You okay, girls?" Wanita observes us. She is swaying slightly in the door, and everyone is singing to Meat Loaf in the background. She looks angelic. The glow of the house lights illuminates the smoke pooling in the doorway behind her.

"You look like an angel," I tell her.

Jude and Wanda are laughing so hard that snot is bubbling out of Wanda's nose. Wanita laughs. "You fucking kids! Get your shit together before your mom sees you, Wanda. Your eyes are like fucking saucers."

The music inside is calming down, and we can hear Chris de Burgh mellowing out the party. When we go in, couples are shuffling together in the middle of the living room, and intense conversations are taking place in the kitchen. I have no idea what time it is. Wanda grabs a bowl of Cheezies and a bag of chips, and we head to her room. Jude goes looking for dip for us and returns with a jar of mayonnaise. We use a spoon we find in a bowl under Wanda's bed to smear mayo on our chips. The party continues outside Wanda's door. Her mom pokes her head in to make sure we are all accounted for, then we hear her laughing in the kitchen. The conversation ebbs and flows, and eventually the stereo goes off, and there is the sound of one acoustic guitar and a few earnest voices singing "Blowin' in the Wind" and "Sonny's Dream."

In the morning I wake up stiff on Wanda's floor with my head resting on a stuffed pink hippopotamus. Jude and Wanda are both snoring away. I look at the clock radio on Wanda's bedside table and see it's already ten. Everything smells like smoke, including Hippy, who has been holding my delicate head. I am vaguely concerned that movement might make me puke. My mouth is oily with mayo residue. I slowly raise my head.

When I come out of Wanda's room, I can hear voices in the kitchen. Wanda's dad and a couple of his buddies are drinking beer at the table.

"Hair of the dog," he says, grinning at me through blood-shot eyes.

"You need a ride, Daisy? Billy here is about to head off." Billy raises his head from where he's been resting it on the table.

"No, I'm all right. Thanks. The walk will do me good. Thanks for having me." I fumble getting my boots laced up and then step into the cool, clean air.

"Daisy, Natasha called."

"I'll call her later. I need to have a shower." I crave the feeling of cleanliness. I am going up the stairs pulling off my socks, preparing for my arrival in the bathroom.

Mum puts her hand on my arm, stopping me from my ascent. "Her dad's in the hospital. It's bad. Her mom's with him. Natasha needs someone to look after the kids so she can go to the hospital too. She's upset, and she said she didn't have anyone else to call."

Mum comes up with me to the apartment. There's an empty glass on the counter. Natasha has been drinking. Mum ignores the overflowing ashtray, the vodka vapors, and the kids still in their pajamas; she bosses Natasha into clean clothes and insists on driving her to the hospital.

I get the kids changed and stick them in front of the TV. I can't stand the smell of sweat and smoke on my body so I use Natasha's shower. Her Coconut and Flower shampoo swirls around me. I come out of the bathroom dressed, but still drying my hair with a thin and dirty Sesame Street towel I found on the floor. Sara says I smell like her mom. I empty the ashtray and do dishes. I make the kids pancakes. Dwayne eats his with peanut butter. Sara pours sugar on hers with nothing to soften it. She coughs when she takes the first bite, and I convince her to shake some of the sugar off and try a little syrup. I call Jimmy. I can hear the bleeping music of his video game over the phone.

"That sucks, Daisy," Jimmy says.

"It's really sad about her father," I say.

"Uh huh." I can hear shooting lasers and Danny in the background. "Pay fucking attention, man!"

"I'll let you know when I know more."

"Okay. Bye, Daise."

"Love you," I say.

"Me too." Click.

The kids ask when their mom is coming home. I give Dwayne an orange-juice box instead of an apple one, and he throws it on the floor. Sara starts crying. The apartment is smaller than I remember it being when I arrived. At 6 p.m. there is a knock on the door, and I put my eye to the peephole. It's Mum.

"I've been at the hospital," she explains. "I'm not sure when Natasha is going to make it back, so I thought we'd take the kids out for dinner."

It's good to get out of the apartment. Mum gets burgers for us all at the drive-through, and we eat them in the parking lot of Mr. Burger Giant. There is a sign for Mr. Burger Giant on a tall pole. We watch it as we eat. It is a huge lit-up burger face wearing sunglasses and a top hat. It flickers a little, and then while we are watching, the left side burns out like it's had a stroke.

The kids are in bed. I find teabags in a tin with a rusty lid on Natasha's counter. Mum and I sit on either end of Natasha's couch drinking the stale tea with our feet on Natasha's coffee table. My head lolls back and I close my eyes. The phone finally rings and Mum answers it.

"Okay, okay," she says. "I'm so sorry to hear that. No rush, dear. You stay with your mum. We'll wait as long as you need us to."

"At least it's over," she says when she gets off the phone.

On Christmas Eve, looking out from the dirty bus windows, the scene is like the beginning of a Christmas movie. The rundown motels on the edge of town and the empty fields all look softer and cleaner under the dusting of fresh snow. Jimmy holds my hand on the bus and puts his jacket over his lap and tries to convince me to touch him underneath it.

"People will see!"

"Come on, Daisy, it'll be fun." I cross my arms and stare out the window as we head downtown.

At Nathan Phillips Square, the skaters laugh and couples hold hands. I see two women going around holding hands. One of them pecks the other on the cheek; I get caught staring, and she smiles at me. I don't think I've ever seen a lesbian in real life before, only TV. Once my parents were watching the news about a pro-choice rally; one of the women they interviewed was wearing a necklace of plastic fetuses and her hair was cut really short. Behind her another bald woman yelled and held up a bunch of coat hangers. "Lesbians," Dad had muttered.

"Look, Jimmy," I nudge him.

"What is it?"

"Those women, holding hands."

"Kinky. You don't really want to skate, do you? The skates are so expensive to rent. It's a waste of money."

"I do kind of."

"Well, you can get some and I'll watch."

"Never mind." We watch the other skaters go around. On Queen West, we find a café where the menu is written on a chalkboard behind the counter and all the spoons are old mismatched silver patterns. The waitress has a tattoo of a snake running up her arm. I order coffee, black with sugar. Jimmy orders hot chocolate. It comes in a bowl, and he complains it has no handles.

I look through dresses in a second-hand store. Jimmy says the shop smells weird and is giving him a headache. We leave and I walk past stores full of unknown treasures as we abandon Queen Street and head to the really big Sam the Record Man's at Yonge and Dundas. Jimmy flicks through CDs.

There's a clerk, around twenty, with short black hair, black jeans, and a T-shirt. He's helping an older bald man in a suit. The bald man waves his hands around.

"It's a love song. About a guy on a bus who sees this girl. And her name is in the song. Heather or Claudette or Fran...something like that? And the tune goes kind of like this." The customer starts humming in an off-key manner. The clerk sees me watching, shoots me a smile, and shakes his head. I smile back, then look away.

"What?" says Jimmy. He's holding up a disc by Queen and telling me something about why Freddie Mercury is a genius.

"What's so funny?"

"Nothing, I was just thinking of something else."

"Let's get out of here." Jimmy grabs my hand, and we walk down Yonge past strip bars and tiny restaurants that smell of curry and smoke. An endless stream of "Jingle Bell Rock" and "Frosty the Snowman" pours out of open doorways. We end up at an arcade. The clientele is different in this place, not like the teenagers at the arcade by the school. It's full of men who are too old to be here, with long hair and leather jackets and younger girlfriends. They hang around smoking. The place feels dirty, despite the old man with a greasy grey pony tail pushing around a bleach-filled bucket and an industrial mop. Jimmy plays Street Fighter II. I start to shuffle from foot to foot and sigh.

"Why don't you go play Tetris? I saw a machine when we came in."

"I'm okay." There aren't many women here, and none of them are alone. There's a girl about my age teetering on high heels. She has bare legs, despite the snow, and is wearing one of those jackets made up of a patchwork of little pieces of rabbit fur. She's laughing and hanging off a guy who mostly ignores her. Every once in a while, she casts a glance towards the door of the arcade and her face hardens.

"I'm bored, Jimmy. And it's cold in here too."

"Just let me finish this game." I stand beside Jimmy, acting, as the other women do in this place, as a living accessory.

Jimmy types his name into the game at place number 27 and seems satisfied. In the headshop next door, I buy Jimmy a black-light Led Zeppelin poster as an early Christmas present. The store sells pussy-scented incense, concert tees, glass bongs, and those Mexican ponchos you see kids at school wearing when they come back from March Break trips. This place smells sweet, a little like overripe strawberries, and mustier than the second-hand store we were in earlier. On the subway home, we get one of the two-seaters at the front of the train. Jimmy's hand creeps onto my thigh, but I keep pushing it back. Jimmy walks me home from the bus stop, and on the front porch we say goodbye. He kisses me long and hard, and then guides my hand to his front pocket.

"Jimmy, my mum's inside," I hiss at him.

"Come on, Daisy," he says. I slip my hand in his pocket and find a small box. I pull it out and open it. Inside is a silver charm bracelet with a daisy hanging from it. Jimmy puts the bracelet on my left wrist where it gets tangled with my leather cord and the half heart Wanda gave me in grade eight.

"You can cut off that later," Jimmy says.

He walks backwards down the driveway, and I blow him kisses until I can't see him anymore.

I untangle my new bracelet from the half-heart pendant. I take off the silver bracelet and put it back in its box. I wash my hands, rubbing the grime of the city and the sticky surfaces of the arcade off my fingers.

nineteen

It is the last week of January. The snow that was romantic in December has taken on an ominous persona. Everything is white and bleached of colour, the ground and the sky. My nostrils are sticking together in the cold, and the exposed tips of my ears burn with pain. I scrape up the snow that has accumulated overnight and pile it on the dirty ridges of the stuff on either side of the driveway. Mum is busy brushing snow off the car.

"Put your hood up, for heaven's sake, Daisy."

I'm walking to school, and the air is so cold it cuts into my lungs with each breath. I find Wanda and Jude before classes start, and they are in the usual place at the top of the stairs. Jimmy has yet to arrive, and as it gets closer to the start of classes, I realize he's not going to make it in time for first period.

"Do you guys want to do something?" Wanda asks.

"What do you mean?" Jude asks.

"I don't know, get out of here. Do something. Anything but be stuck in here all day."

"I can't skip, Wanda, you know that. My parents would ground me for two months if I got caught," Jude says.

"Daisy?"

"I don't know. Jimmy might show up later, and he'll be pissy if I skipped without him."

"Really, Daisy? Because Jimmy always consults with you before he doesn't show up to school?" Wanda says.

"I've got to go to my locker. You should just go to class; it's not worth the hassle if you get caught." Jude leaves us.

"Goody two-shoes," Wanda says mildly as Jude leaves.

At first the sound of kids going to class is like a herd of elephants, then there is only the sound of a few late kids running. The national anthem plays, and I stay sitting beside Wanda. All the other kids will be standing by their desks. The low tone of droning teacher voices starts seeping through the closed doors of classrooms.

Wanda leans her head on my shoulder, and I stroke her head twice.

"Okay, so we're skipping? Now what?" I ask her.

"Shouldn't you be in class?" Mr. Hunter spies us heading towards our lockers as he leaves the shop room. He is holding a Maple Leafs toque and a pack of smokes in his hand, sounds of sawing and male laughter come from his room as the door swings shut.

"Doctor's appointment," says Wanda, and Mr. Hunter nods, accepting that doctor's appointments are something teenage girls do together. At our lockers, I start to sort out what books I'll need for homework tonight.

"Just leave them, Daisy. Let's just leave it all behind for the day." Wanda gestures around us at the dented lockers and the metal water fountain with a piece of gum stuck at the drain.

Outside the cold claws at us as soon as we exit the school. We're not really headed anywhere, just away, when we see the bus travelling south on Yonge Street, and we both run to catch it.

Taking the route to the city is instinctual. At Finch Station, we head to the automatic entrance furthest from the ticket booth. Wanda shoves me in ahead and slips in the token then grinds her body into mine. The turnstile goes forward, then stops for a second. I think we're going to get stuck, the two of us jammed here red faced and squeezed together as passersby stare. Then it starts moving and we push through. I stumble when I get spit out on the other side.

A train is pulling out when we hit the platform, and we just make it through the closing doors. We slump in seats next to each other. It takes five stations until Wanda convinces me the transit cops are not hunting us down after seeing us on their security camera. It's cold even on the train, and I have my hands shoved between my thighs to keep them warm.

It is Wanda's idea to go to the museum. The wind whips us as we walk down the street from the subway towards it. The city dwellers are wrapped in scarves and hats with only their eyes and nostrils poking out. My fingers in their black stretch gloves are so cold they feel hot, and I try to remember how long it takes to get frostbite. We push through tall front doors into a foyer blasting hot air; the change in temperature hits me with a little wave of nausea.

I'm busy checking my fingers and tentatively rubbing my earlobes. "Shit." Wanda's eyes are up roaming over the admissions prices. "I had no idea it would be so expensive."

We are standing contemplating the impossible price when

a flood of teenagers comes through the entrance. Through the doors we see three yellow school buses issuing forth kids our age, an unmistakable suburban homogeny, and we are soon lost among them. A parent helper hands us two worksheets and then two of the little plastic things you attach to your lapels that gives you permission to enter a place like this. A guard takes down a velvet rope to let the massive group through. We both merge with the crowd as it goes past the ticket booth into the museum. The school groups swerve towards the geology exhibitions. Afraid of being recognized as interlopers, we dip into a washroom and hide for a few minutes before heading out to explore.

"This is amazing," Wanda whispers as we climb a massive staircase. Away from the school groups, we have the place mostly to ourselves. A few guards eye us, but with little interest, as we peer at different displays.

We find the mummies. A gnarled fossilized toe pokes out of the ancient wrap in one mummy's open casket. We stand staring at it for a long time.

The dinosaur area is hushed; we ignore the informational signs and stare up at the antlers on an enormous prehistoric elk.

"I've never been here before, you know," Wanda says.

"I came when I was little. But it wasn't as fun. Dad was measuring specimens in the basement, and we didn't see much because it only took him an hour. We skipped the dinosaurs completely. This is way better."

"Better than skipping to get finger fucked by Jimmy Hill in a public bathroom?"

"Shit, Wanda." One of the security guards looks up when I swear.

"Sorry, it sounded funny in my head. Really, I'm sorry."

In the natural history section, Wanda shows me birds she has seen in Newfoundland, gannets and kittiwakes. I pull out a drawer below the display and gasp when I see what's inside: a dozen tiny songbird corpses, all neatly labelled.

"Poor things," says Wanda. She places her hand over the Plexiglas where the birds lie, one by one by one. We stand in silent vigil for each tiny body.

"Where were you?" Jimmy asks me later on the phone.

"With Wanda, I skipped," I whisper. I'm in the kitchen, and I'm not sure of my mother's location.

"I looked all over for you. I only missed first. You could have called me; we could have spent the whole day together. Both our moms were at work."

"Do you want to come with me to Carly's party on Saturday? I need to let her know if we're coming. She's collecting cash, and her sisters are going to pick up beer. Everyone is going, Wanda, Jude, Steve, Damon…"

"I'd rather just be with you alone. My mom's got a date; let's just hang out here," Jimmy says.

It's true, everyone is going to Carly's party. Wanda keeps trying to get me to change my mind, but I keep telling her I have plans with Jimmy.

"What plans? Rutting in his basement like you already do three times a week?"

Jude and Wanda already have everything organized so they can stay out late and get a ride home with Wanda's cousin Craig. Jude even made up a fake permission slip for a school trip to the planetarium.

On Saturday night, I am not at Jimmy's. I'm moping

around the house. Jimmy applied for a job at Mr. Burger Giant, and they called him for a trial run. Grahame and Mum weren't expecting my company. Mum has spent all day making tofu bourguignon. "Why don't you go see Cora?" Mum firmly suggests as I come into the kitchen and prod it with a wooden spoon.

"If he can hardly manage to make it to school on time, I don't know how he's going to manage to show up to work." I tell this to Cora in confessional tones.

"Maybe it will be different when he's getting paid?"

"Maybe. I just don't know when I'm going to get to see him."

"Damon's going to a party tonight."

"It's at Carly's."

"You didn't want to go?"

I shrug. Cora is sorting through her closet. "Here it is." She hauls out a green silk dress. "Try it on. It doesn't fit. My boobs got too big for it."

I turn away from Cora, pull my T-shirt off, and pull the green dress over my head. I pull my jeans down. They have no knees and a hole in the crotch that forces me to keep my legs together. I have a pair of grey wool tights underneath that Jimmy told me reminded him of his great aunt; she's dead. I step out of my jeans and turn around to show Cora.

"That looks great on you. It never fit me right. Take that one for sure. Now try the other one."

The dress is purple with puffed sleeves.

"Seriously?"

"Just try it on, then go show Millie."

The dress is ridiculous. Cora laughs from her bed when I

have it on. She kisses the top of Sinead's head and leaves a lipstick mark. I walk into the living room and curtsey in front of Millie.

"You look so pretty!" Millie exclaims. "Just like Madonna."

"How do you put your arms down?" I call out to Cora, flapping my arms for Millie. The sleeves look like those inflatable arm bands little kids use for swimming.

"You don't," Cora calls out to me. "You keep them up holding flowers in front of you, and during dinner you make loud rustling sounds every time you raise your fork to your mouth. It's my bridesmaid dress from Joanie's wedding."

Cora flings the red dress I saw her wear on Valentine's Day at me. "Go on, humour me."

I put in on with my bra still on and Cora laughs at me. "You can't wear a bra with it. It doesn't work." I turn around, take the dress and my bra off, and put the dress on again. Cora smiles. "That looks great," she says. She stops me before I go to look in the mirror. "Wait, let me put your hair up first."

Cora sweeps my hair up and sticks in a bunch of bobby pins. Then she comes at me with a lipstick and makes me pout my lips as she applies it. "Finger," she says, and I draw my finger out between my lips. She grabs a pair of black pumps from her closet and I put them on my feet.

I hardly recognize my reflection. I look like a woman, not like a teenager. My boobs seem enormous and my cleavage is a deep valley. The dress holds me in, but lets my breasts swing slightly free, and I feel embarrassed by how sexy I feel. The only thing that doesn't look quite right is the charm bracelet Jimmy gave me.

"You look awesome. Go show Millie again."

I walk into the living room pretending to be a super model, and Millie laughs. Then I notice Damon standing in the kitchen doorway looking at me. Cora has followed me out and notices too. I catch her winking at him; Damon blushes and withdraws into the kitchen.

"That dress I'm keeping, but the next time you and Jimmy have a big date, let me know and you can borrow it."

"Jimmy never wants to go anywhere," I say.

twenty

"Jana, you are a deeply caring person."

"Damon, you have a fantastic sense of humour."

"Jude, your attention to detail is superb."

"Roseanne, the beauty of your soul shines through your eyes."

"Nathan, your dramatic spirit is strong like an ox."

"Daisy, I admire your loyalty to this production."

Gerry starts rehearsal with personal affirmations. We sit in a circle and meditate. I close my eyes and hope my stomach doesn't make any noise. Gerry gives us breathing instructions, in through your nose, out through your mouth. Most of us are battling winter colds and can't get air through our clogged nostrils. Sucking in dry lips, we sniff as we pat our noses with damp and disintegrating tissues.

Jana and I are together at the back of the gym, far from the stage, running lines together. Jana keeps shooting glances at Gerry, who's laughing with Roseanne on stage. The scene is at an anti-Vietnam rally, and Roseanne sticks a fake flower into a plastic pistol that Nathan holds.

"That was great, Roseanne, really great. I get a real sense of Juliet's free spirit in the way you dance around Romeo. It was perfect how you brushed his hair behind his ear. And Nathan, you were good too, but I need you to memorize those lines," Gerry says.

Jana ignores the prompt I read to her. "If that was anyone else, he'd be losing his shit because they forgot their lines. And as for Roseanne, she looks like she's dancing at a ballet recital, not a protest."

I make a non-committal sound and shake my papers ready to keep going.

"Her parents paid for the new stage curtains. That's how she got the part; they bought it for her."

I look at the red velvet curtains hanging from the stage. They replaced brown ones that emanated an odor of dust and mildew.

"Nathan is good. He's just bad at memorizing his lines," I say, watching him on stage.

"Good looking, you mean." Jana and I watch as he stands up stretching, confident and comfortable with all the parts of his body, up on the stage.

They start up again, and Nathan fumbles and looks to Jude who is acting as prompt.

Jana whispers, "This is why we should have had tryouts."

I notice Kleinberg. He's sitting in a chair pushed against one of the long walls of the gym. A newspaper sits in his lap. He rustles it and looks up the third time Nathan can't finish the same line.

Elizabeth is coming home. Grahame stocks the fridge with vegetarian delicacies he unpacks from a paper bag with rope handles. Mum and I can't stop smiling. Eric isn't coming with her.

Grahame drives Mum and me to meet Elizabeth's plane. Donald is off rat catching and unable to do the airport run. Mum and I are bubbling with joy as we stand looking through the sliding security doors, hoping to catch a glimpse of Elizabeth at the baggage carousel. Grahame, nervous at meeting the prodigal daughter, stands to the side twiddling his thumbs. We see her and wave and smile madly, but she isn't looking for us; she's staring at the suitcases and backpacks going round and round. She's even skinnier than when she came back from tree planting. She looks really tired. When she finally comes out to meet us, Mum and I both hug her ferociously; she just stands there and lets us, but keeps her arms by her sides. She doesn't even put down her bag. When we let go of her, she kisses us both on the cheek in a weird European way and bestows an absent-minded smile on Grahame, to whom she relinquishes her enormous backpack. She's wearing ripped jeans and a plain white T-shirt. She has on hiking boots and no jewellery, except a braided piece of dirty string around her wrist. When I turn to look at her as we pull from the airport parking garage, she is asleep.

"Travelling can be exhausting," Grahame says, placating Mum and I. He distracts us from our disappointment, telling stories of his drunken youth spent hitchhiking in Germany. The car pulls into our drive, Elizabeth wakes up and staggers into the house straight to bed. Grahame leaves her bag just inside the front door, then drives away.

For the past forty-eight hours, Elizabeth has hardly left her room. Mum stands outside Elizabeth's door, listening to the silence. We know she's alive; there's evidence of a late night shower, and although the tofu remains intact, three pieces of cold Kentucky Fried Chicken have evaporated from the fridge.

When she does finally emerge, it's like a backwards butterfly. She left all winged and colourful, and now she is a strange Elizabeth caterpillar who moves slowly and follows us around rooms with her eyes. She is polite, but evasive.

Dad is here for dinner. It's strange sitting around the kitchen table with Mum, Dad, and Elizabeth. Just like old times. Dad looks confused sitting in his old place at the head of the table. He looks like he can't figure out why he doesn't belong here anymore. "Are those curtains new?" he asks.

"No," says Mum, "we bought those from Sears just after we moved to Canada."

"Oh, did we? This chicken is nice. I don't remember having it before."

"I made it that time you had the beaver expert come to talk to your students."

"Ken Ferguson. I remember now."

I roll my eyes at Elizabeth, but she passively eats the veggie stir-fry Mum has made for her and ignores me.

"Was there trouble with the boyfriend?" I overhear Dad saying to Mum before he leaves.

"I think she's just having trouble adjusting to regular life."

There is no regular life for Elizabeth. She gets up at strange times and eats strange meals. She rarely leaves her room. In the old days, she used to nag at me to help out around the house more. She hasn't done a single dish since she's gotten back. After watching her wear the same dirty jeans for a week,

Mum does her laundry. She folds Elizabeth's underwear on the kitchen table, worn cotton with the elastic starting to come through the seams at the waistband.

"Can you try talking to her? See what happened? If she's okay?" Mum whispers to me when I come into the kitchen to make tea.

I make two mugs and knock on Elizabeth's door.

"Yes?"

I gingerly use one hand to hold the two mugs by their handles and use my other hand to open the door.

She is sitting on the bed writing in a thick notebook. "Do you want something?" She's smiling, but I can sense irritation.

"Tea?" I say, as all the things I want from her run through my head. The list is long.

"Are you busy?" I persist, putting the mug beside her. I sit on the edge of the bed.

She takes the tea and blows small waves meditatively across the surface, but remains coolly uncommunicative.

"What happened with Eric?" I blurt it out. The words push out of my mouth before I can shape them into something that might inspire intimacy.

"Oh, Eric, we split up ages ago. I didn't want Mum to worry about me being alone, so I never said anything."

"Weren't you lonely?"

"Sometimes, but I travelled with lots of people."

"Boys?"

"Men, sometimes with men. Did Mum put you up to this?" For a moment I see Elizabeth back there, somewhere beneath the Elizabeth-doppelganger's eyes.

Jimmy and Grahame are here for dinner. Mum's vegetarian lasagna is soupy. Grahame, Jimmy, and I all manage to spoon it in, but Elizabeth only eats the layer of cheese that floats on top of red tomato sauce and overcooked noodles.

Grahame is wearing his elbow-patched donkey jacket and is talking intently about a pottery shard he recently found in a field, the site of a proposed new baseball diamond. He is self-effacingly describing himself huffing and puffing and falling over in the mud. There is an endearing Eeyore-like quality to Grahame, but Elizabeth eyes him coolly. She laughs only when he describes dropping his car keys in the middle of a mud puddle.

Grahame asks Jimmy about his job, and Jimmy tells him about finding a dead rat in the deep fryer. Elizabeth fixes Jimmy with studied concentration during his brief telling and shakes her head. "Sounds a lot like an urban myth to me."

Jimmy shrugs, and I hope he doesn't tell the story of the friend of his dad who found an alligator in his hotel toilet in Florida.

"So, Elizabeth," Grahame says, "any plans now you're back from Europe?" He is either naïve to the vitriolic mood bubbling inside Elizabeth or foolish enough to think he can diffuse it.

"No," Elizabeth says. Mum pours herself more wine, and I estimate how many more mouthfuls it will take to finish my lasagna.

In the morning Grahame tapes plastic bags around the heavy woollen socks he is wearing before sticking his feet in rubber boots.

"You're welcome to come with us, Daisy," Mum says, sounding mildly panicked, as Grahame tapes bags on her feet. They are going to visit Grahame's site, in hopes of finding more bits of broken plate.

"No thanks."

Elizabeth is in the kitchen and looks mildly irritated at my intrusion.

"Do you want to come see Cora and the baby with me?" I ask out of politeness.

"Okay," she says.

All the Jones women are home. Mrs. Jones goes on about how much we look alike, a conversation which leaves me adding up all the ways we look different. Mrs. Jones asks Elizabeth about her trip. We sit around the table listening to Mrs. Jones—"Call me Carm!" —and Elizabeth exchange stories about travelling through Europe. They talk about missing trains and sleeping on beaches, shopping in markets and beggar children in Istanbul. My ignorance about Istanbul's presence in Europe, as well as Elizabeth's trip there, feels like failing a test I thought I'd aced. Mrs. Jones makes us mint tea. I learn more about Elizabeth's trip over a cup of tea at the Jones household than over days at home. Millie and Cora gaze at Elizabeth in adoration.

"I'm so jealous you got to do all that travelling," says Cora.

"You're taking a journey too," Elizabeth says, stroking Sinead's head.

Millie is sitting next to Elizabeth, making her a friendship bracelet out of scratchy coloured plastic.

"Come back anytime," Mrs. Jones yells out as we leave.

For the past three weeks, Elizabeth has gone to the Joneses' almost every day. Millie gives her drawings. Twice Elizabeth babysits Sinead, something I have never been asked to do.

Going to the Joneses' seems to have reminded Elizabeth that a world exists outside of her bedroom, and she's seeing an old friend tonight, spending the night in Teresa's dorm room at U of T. Knowing Elizabeth won't be at the Joneses', I drop by to visit. I want to hear someone complain about Elizabeth's weirdness. I long to hear how she gets on Cora's nerves with her constant presence, and stories of Paris cafés and night trains to Portugal. "I'm going to miss your sister when she goes," Cora muses to me.

"If she ever goes."

"I thought it was all set."

"What was set?"

"The tree planting in the spring." Elizabeth's impending absence hits me, a hard ball in my throat.

She's gone quickly, before we can fix our broken communication lines. Her flight is mid-day. I sit in class looking out the window and imagine Elizabeth up in the air above me. When I get home from school, I go snoop in her room. I walk in and look around. It feels good to be in here; I feel closer to her standing in amongst her remnants than I did when she was occupying the space. Her bed isn't made, which is unlike Elizabeth. Everything else looks the same. She's taken her backpack full of dirty jeans and her tree planting equipment, which has spent the winter like a shrouded corpse in a corner of her room. I don't know what I am looking for, a crack pipe or bag of mysterious white powder, maybe pamphlets from the Jehovah's Witnesses. I open the drawers in her dresser and nothing has changed. Clothes that both of us have rejected lie undisturbed. When I open her desk drawer, I find a folded piece of scrap paper with my name on it and a folded-up tissue underneath.

Daisy,
I figured you'd be in here. XXX
Elizabeth

I pick up the tissue: inside it is something hard. I shake it and a silver ring falls into my hand. It's a silver snake. The head curls up towards my knuckle and the tail points back at my hand. It fits me perfectly.

twenty-one

April rain courses down on the outside of the windows at the top of the high gymnasium walls.

"Six weeks left, people!" Gerry reminds us.

Friday after school, this is an extra rehearsal. All day long I have itched to burst from the doors of the school and become my weekend self. Grabbing a quick smoke after classes, Jana stays behind as I head in.

"Are you coming?" I yell at her, holding open the door.

"One minute." She waves me on.

We all wait for Jana; she's in the first scene. She shows up twenty minutes after I left her with some cockamamie story about being held up by Ms. Chandra. I'm pretty sure she's stoned.

It's the best scene in the play. Romeo and Juliet end up in the hospital after a bad acid trip. The Capulets and the Montagues are thrown together; one mother dressed in a twin-set, the other still clutching an anti-war protest sign. Jana is the nurse who comes to tell them of their children's fate. Jude has managed to find an actual nun's veil and puts it on Jana now.

Jana walks dramatically on stage and then stops. She looks eerie with her hair draped in black and her face outlined by a white frame of material. She doesn't say anything. At first I think she's trying out a dramatic pause, but then I realize she's distracted by the swirling dust illuminated by her spotlight. She gazes at it, lifts her hand to fan the air and then smiles as the tiny particles move frenetically around her.

"Jana," Kleinberg says. He rarely attempts to intervene, but Gerry seems unsure what to do.

"Mmmm," she says, smiling beatifically down at us all.

"Your line, Jana." I hope the serious tone of Kleinberg's voice will snap her out of her reverie.

"I forgot," says Jana. Then she starts singing, "I forgot, I forgot, I forgot."

It sounds just like Millie, who sings her thoughts out loud when she's concentrating.

Kleinberg, not unkindly, steps on stage and says, "Come on, Jana, let's go have a chat in my office." He takes her gently by the upper arm and guides her from the stage. Jana, her head still covered, glides along like a ghost beside him.

The rest of us sit quietly. When Kleinberg opens the heavy gym fire door, you can feel the gossip sweeping out and around the school, ready to fill Monday with whispers and rumour.

"Well," says Gerry, "let's take five, and then we'll come back and go through the scene again."

I know the lines by heart; I've even run them with Millie and Cora a few times. I'm also pretty confident about the blocking. I've practiced in my bedroom and had fantasies about Jana breaking a leg (literally), or her parents' car breaking down and of me having to go on stage at the last minute and save the day.

I always feel guilty afterwards, as if imagining some harm befalling her could actually make it happen. When we get back from break, I am ready.

"Okay, for now I'll read Jana's lines, and the rest of you just pretend she's onstage," Gerry announces.

Jude sees me looking deflated and pipes up, her voice confident with reason.

"Daisy is Jana's understudy. Shouldn't she run the lines?"

"No. We don't need to put Daisy on the spot." Gerry glances over at me, and I'm mortified. Everyone in the room seems to be staring. He turns back and starts bossing the Capulets around. Jude shrugs her shoulders at me.

No one has seen Jana at school this week. Everyone sits outside at lunch. It's the first warm day of the year. You can lie back and close your eyes in the sun. The schoolyard is full of the usual detritus of the winter, the matted remains of lost mittens, cigarette butts, and faded chocolate-bar wrappers.

Jimmy's encouraging me to skip my rehearsal tonight and hang out with him after school. He's kissing the back of my neck and making innuendo-filled comments about rolling in hay. I am tempted. I feel shackled to the school gymnasium. While not going home used to feel like an escape, now it feels like a chore. I think about quitting the play.

In English, Kleinberg asks me to stay for a minute after class. I think I'm going to get in trouble for missing one of his classes last week. Damon makes "You're in trouble" sounds and faces as he heads into the hall.

Kleinberg is not like Gerry. No one calls Mr. Kleinberg by his first name. He has the non-committal hair and clothes of the average teacher, but when I'm here alone in class with him, I think about him standing in the corner of a smoky bar, reading his poetry.

"So," he says, "about last week…"

I don't hear him. I'm busy worrying he'll call Mum about my absence, and then I realize what he's wittering on about is Jana. "It just seems she isn't in a place right now where she can really commit to the play. So, Daisy, what do you think?"

"Well," I say. I am not really sure what he's asked me.

"You've done the work. You've gone to every practice, and Jana seems confident you know the lines just as well as she does. Why not?"

"Just for a few rehearsals?" I need to be clear about what Kleinberg is telling me.

"No, we need you to do the part. We can't afford to take someone on who isn't up to it at this stage of the game. Gerry asked me to talk to you since I know you better." Kleinberg's voice raises slightly at this last line. I can see Gerry with his list of grade twelve darlings, and Kleinberg tapping him on the shoulder and reminding him Jana has an understudy.

"Okay," I say.

"Good. Congratulations. I have no doubt you won't disappoint us."

"Thanks, Mr. Kleinberg."

"And Daisy, skip my class again, and I'll have you in the office so fast your head will spin." Kleinberg doesn't smile as he says this.

When I turn around to thank him once more, I notice he is smirking, presumably at his own authoritarianism.

I am holding the birthday card from Wanda when Nathan

walks by our locker.

"Hey, happy birthday, Nurse Daisy!" He high fives me, but his eyes linger towards Wanda. "Hey, Wanda, what's up?"

"The ceiling," she says dryly, tilting her head back.

"You should come to the play's afterparty with Daisy. You can amaze us all with your sense of humour."

"Fuck off. I'll think about it."

"Don't think about it, come," he says, walking away.

"The guys from his band are going to be at the party too," I tell Wanda. The Delinquent Penguins play at school assemblies and have recently started playing bars. The other members are a little older than Nathan.

"His band sucks," Wanda says.

"He's good looking."

"I guess."

To celebrate my birthday, Mum, Grahame, Jimmy, and I go to a Vietnamese restaurant Grahame has chosen. Jimmy only likes the appetizers. Grahame tries to teach us all to use chopsticks, but our food starts to get cold and he lets us fork up our noodles. Jimmy gave me an enormous white teddy bear carrying a pink heart. "Something for you to sleep with until you start sleeping with me," Jimmy whispers to me when I lean in to kiss him after opening it. Its fur has a strange plastic feel to it. It sits in an empty chair beside me throughout the meal at the restaurant. I try taking the bear to bed with me, but the fur makes me itchy and turns my skin red and bumpy.

On the Saturday following my birthday, Jimmy's working. I thought he might take me out for a romantic birthday date, but instead Wanda and I roam the aisles of the video store. In the cult-classic section, we pick out a movie called *The Rocky Horror Picture Show*. Neither of us has heard of it, but the guy at the store who always comments on our picks does not make any snide remarks this time, which means he approves of our selection. In my bag is a mickey of vodka Wanda gave me for my birthday.

"Happy birthday, Daisy! Sweet sixteen, I can't believe it." Wanda's mom envelopes me in a perfume, smoke, and rum-scented hug.

"Happy birthday, kiddo!" says Wanda's dad, who is sitting at the kitchen table with the rolling machine, getting cigarettes ready.

"Since it's your birthday, you girls come have one drink with us, before we head out."

"Mom..."

"Don't Mom me, Wanda,"

Wanda's dad hands us each a glass of rum and Pepsi.

"Now, you made them light, didn't you?" Wanda's mom says.

"Just a half shot." Wanda's dad winks at me.

When I take my first sip, I almost splutter, it's strong enough it burns.

At the table Wanda's parents reminisce. Her dad pours another round of drinks, and Wanda's mom starts telling the story of Wanda's birth, but Wanda cuts her off. "Enough, you'll be late for your party."

"Alright, alright, but your head was huge!" Her mom kisses us both goodbye.

"Be good, girls."

Wanda mixes vodka and Wink. It is sweet, but thinner than the thick drink her dad gave us and slips down easily. We take our drinks and the movie into the living room.

Wanda fast forwards through the trailers, then once the video is cued up, she switches off the overhead light. I blink in the darkness and Wanda complains, "I can't see a fucking thing," as she stumbles on her way back to me. We sit on the floor with our backs against the couch and our legs sticking out in front of us.

The TV is a big old one with a wooden case, and occasionally I squint my eyes and think I can see the individual pixels on it. I can't see Wanda, but am aware of where our arms touch, the bare parts just above our elbows that the arms of our T-shirts don't cover.

At first, the movie just seems like some hokey horror film, almost like a grown-up version of *Scooby-Doo*. The Wink and vodka are on the coffee table, and Wanda and I have sloshed more into our glasses a couple of times. Brad and Janet end up at a creepy house after their car breaks down. The music sounds a little tinny coming out of the TV speaker, but it's flowing straight into me and making me move my feet in time. The movie starts getting weird. A man dressed in lingerie, with perfect red lips and a muscled body, appears on screen. I have a pang of desire. There is warmth spreading across my thighs; I'm relieved that we're in the dark and Wanda can't see my flushed cheeks. I take a big sip from my drink.

I'm having a hard time keeping track of the plot. Brad and Janet are in their underwear. Janet is exposed to the world in her plain bra and slip. I cross my arms over my own breasts. A new song starts, and Wanda's body moves with the music. She hasn't said anything for ages. She chugs back her drink, then stands up, grabbing my hand and pulling my to me feet. I feel dizzy with the sudden movement. Wanda turns the music up. The vase of fake flowers on top of the TV set vibrates. The dancing means I don't have time to feel self-conscious watching so much naked skin and sex on screen. Dr. Frank N. Furter, the guy in the lingerie, has sex with Janet, and then with Brad. There are women kissing women. No one is fully dressed. When we aren't dancing, we slump back on the couch and reach for our drinks.

When Susan Sarandon, who plays Janet, starts singing "Touch-a, Touch-a, Touch-a, Touch Me," Wanda dances close to me. I close my eyes. She runs her finger slowly down the centre of my face right down over my nose, down my throat, to my breast bone. Her finger makes me shiver. She pulls it away and laughs. We are just acting, I remember, stumbling back to sit down and refilling my glass with the last of the vodka.

In the end Frank N. Furter gets shot, and I find I'm wiping away tears. His makeup is running and I want to fix it for him. He looks like a broken clown. I look over at Wanda and see her eyes are glossy when they catch the light from the TV. The credits roll. My ears buzz still from the volume we played the soundtrack at. With the lights turned on, we clear away the sticky glasses that held our drinks, and the room seems different. We are formal with each other. We set up our sleeping bags and pillows on the floor. Our heads are a few feet away from the TV. The movie has finished rewinding, and Wanda restarts it with the sound turned down. I can just hear it if I concentrate on listening. Wanda turns off the light. The dark comes as a comfort. We've hardly talked in the light. Wanda wiggles into her sleeping bag. I feel her playing with my hair, and I fall asleep.

The play opens tonight. Everything is surreal. Every time I run into someone else in the cast we clasp our hands together and whisper, "Break a leg." Energy swirls around us, and the other kids' drab demeanors are the only thing reminding us we are still here at school. I feel like I'm going to puke when I peek in the gym and see just how many chairs have been set up.

The numbers swirl on my page. This math test feels inconsequential. I try and concentrate, imagining the numbers as individual actors jumping around and on top of each other like they are on stage. I draw a cape on a number five. Time isn't behaving properly, and the end of the day seems to come at first slowly and then very fast.

Mum and Grahame are coming tonight. Wanda and Jimmy have tickets for Saturday, the night of the cast party.

Roseanne's dad has a huge bouquet of flowers delivered right to the school, and you can see some of the parents clutching roses to present to their daughters post-performance. On stage I hesitate for just a second, take a breath, and then I'm in. Nathan flubs one line back to me, but I gloss it over like Gerry told me to if this happens, and Nathan winks, picking up my cue, and recovers the scene. I watch the last scene from the side of the stage with Jude. We clap and cheer when the curtains go down before we step on stage to bow as part of the group.

Mum and Grahame wait for me to get changed. There are no bouquets of flowers, but Mum hugs me and Grahame shakes my hand and tells me it was a "no *nun*sense" performance.

Closing night, we're all exhausted and jittery from running on three days of overdrive, too much caffeine, and not enough sleep. Girls are tearful in the dressing room.

"This is it, gang. You have put on two great shows. This one, this one, is the one that will stay with you. Tonight is the night to go to *that* place in your performance. You are not Roseanne or Nathan tonight. You are Juliet. You are Romeo. I need you to leave the part of your brain that's whispering to you about the woman in the front row, or that's worried about getting your lines right, behind you. Leave that voice in the dressing room. Tonight we are all magic, and that magic is going to fill the stage." Gerry is incandescent. Parents and friends think this play is a diversion, an extra-curricular entertainment, but Gerry believes, and makes us believe, this is real.

I look into the gym from behind the curtain. I catch a glimpse of Wanda and her mom, but I don't see Jimmy.

"Go get ready! You need to think about your performance and nothing else. Remember, you're not Daisy right now." Jude ushers me away.

I feel all the practices, all Jude's hemming, and Damon's lists of lighting cues underneath me and holding me up when I walk onto the stage. It is magic tonight. When I hold Juliet's hand and mop her brow in her hospital bed, a tear forms in my eye. For a second I believe she's in real trauma. We were good before, but tonight we are great.

Everyone is hugging and congratulating each other. Gerry and Kleinberg are toasting us with real wine. Gerry raises his glass towards me. "To Daisy, for stepping in to save the day in the play's hour of need." I'm coasting on adrenaline, remembering the audience laughing at my funny lines and the intensity of the moment when I told Juliet's parents she might have brain damage.

Wanda comes over and grabs me up in her arms. "You were wonderful!" When she lets go, I catch a glance shared between her and Jude. I look around expecting Jimmy to arrive, a bunch of flowers and pride in his face. I spin around happy with anticipation, and then I see Jude's face.

"Daisy." Her voice is soft, meant to dull the sting of her news, but really just making it more of a prolonged agony.

"He's not here," I say, coming to the end of my ride on the joyous wave of creation.

"I just want to go home." I am crying in the girl's bathroom. Jude and Wanda have followed me in, and Damon, seeing me dash from the festivities, has come in to give moral support.

"Come on, you'll have fun at Nathan's party," Damon says.

"What a shit, you should dump his ass. You were so good, Daisy. You don't need him; he doesn't appreciate you." Wanda is twisting her Xeroxed program in her hand.

Jude holds wet brown paper towel to my eyes to stop them from swelling. It smells like damp cardboard.

"Maybe you should call his house and just make sure he's okay?" Jude suggests. All the ways Jimmy could have died in the past three hours run through my mind.

Danny answers the phone.

"Is Jimmy okay?" I ask, trying to keep the quiver out of my voice.

"I don't know. He's at work. Try him there." Danny hangs up.

Outside the school, Wanda wordlessly hands me a smoke.

It settles my nerves. I abandon my hysterical self and take on a new persona. I exude reason and create excuses for Jimmy that sound acceptable until I say one out loud.

"Maybe he mixed up the time?"

"He's known about this for weeks, Daisy," Damon says.

"Fuck it," says Wanda. "Let's get drunk."

"How am I going to get home from the party? Jimmy was supposed to walk me."

"Daisy, we'll make sure you get home okay. We're hardly going to leave you passed out on the couch at Nathan's house," Wanda points out.

"I'll walk you. Your place is on my way home," says Damon.

Wanda gives me a look.

Damon produces a joint and lights it up as we walk to the party. I take a long draw and hold it in. I take another hit, and another. There is no feeling in my knees, and I keep looking down to make sure they are still there.

Entering Nathan's house, we pass Roseanne and her maidservants in the living room where they are drinking coolers.

"Daisy, you were awesome," Roseanne says.

I beam. "You too, Roseanne." I'm so high my head feels empty. My brain has developed a strange weightlessness. I try not to act stoned, which makes me feel more stoned. In the kitchen, Nathan and his band drink beer and strum guitars. They argue over whether the Doors suck or not, in the way that boys seem to need to do at every party.

Damon pulls a beer from his bag and drinks it warm. He joins the Doors conversation. Wanda raids Nathan's freezer for ice, takes a lemon out of the fridge, and cuts three thin slices, which she puts in tall glasses. I pass her the vodka and she pours. Jude, Wanda, and I each have a glass containing one third of the vodka bottle. Jude disappears into the living room, but Wanda and I hover, resting our drinks on the kitchen counter.

Wanda observes the party with a bemused look on her face. The guys from Nathan's band covertly look at her as they raise beer bottles to their mouths. I see how much effort she has made tonight for the first time. She towers above most of us in her high-heeled white boots; her hair is a cascading mass of loose curls. Her lipstick is just slightly smudged, and she catches me staring at this imperfection and puts her finger up to the corner of her mouth. I reach out to fix it for her, but Nathan calls her name and she turns her head.

My drink slides down my throat easily. The band boys offer tequila. Wanda and I do shooters together, licking salt from our fingers and sucking on lemons without flinching. The lemon tastes clean and cuts through the slick of tequila on my teeth.

At 12:30, Jude comes to get us. I'm sitting on a chair trying to determine if I'm moving, or if it is the tiles on the kitchen floor. Wanda's standing and leaning against Nathan with the full length of her body. Jude ushers me to the front door. Jude, Damon, and I stand outside and wait as Nathan walks a swaying Wanda to the door. He turns her towards him and plants his lips on to her mouth. Wanda doesn't pull away, but her eyes are open and she looks like she needs a gulp of air. I hear my name and look around to see Jimmy walking towards me.

I see him and I smile. Then, through the vodka and the tequila and the dope, I remember my disappointment. Damon and Jude watch me watch Jimmy. Nathan releases Wanda, and she stumbles towards us.

She sees Jimmy and pauses, then her brain catches up with her eyes. "*You*," she points at Jimmy. Jimmy ignores her.

"Daisy, can we talk?"

"No, you cannot fucking talk to her, you motherfucker!" Wanda yells. The Capulets are watching us through the curtains.

Jimmy walks towards me, and I burst into tears and shout, "Leave me alone!" I weave down the driveway, and as I go, I realize that a straight line is surprisingly hard to walk.

"See what you've done?" Wanda snaps at Jimmy.

"Shut the fuck up, Wanda," Jimmy says.

"Motherfuckingbastardsonofabitchstupidfucking…"

Jude cuts in, sounding sober and clear. "Damon, go look after Daisy. Wanda, we're going."

Wanda keeps swearing. Jude physically moves her away. Wanda is drunk enough that her limbs are ragdoll-like, and she can't fight against the direction Jude is taking her. Wanda turns her head around; she yells "Jimmy!" then spits in his direction as a parting shot.

Crying and walking slowly down the sidewalk in the direction of my house, I am flanked on either side by Damon and Jimmy. When Jimmy tries to put his arm around me, I push him away and yell hysterically, "Don't touch me!" Jimmy backs off a little.

"Daisy, you have to calm down. Seriously, or someone's gonna call the police," Damon says.

I sob and refuse to talk to Jimmy. My house is blazing with light when we arrive.

"You okay if I take off now?" Damon says.

"Yeah," says Jimmy. "Thanks."

"What about you, Daisy?" Damon waits until I raise my head a little and look him in the eye. I don't say anything, just nod my head.

Grahame pokes his head out of the door.

"Daisy, are you going to come in now? Your mum has been really worried."

"I'm fine." My voice veers up and out of my control. "I'll be in in a minute."

"Five minutes, then you need to be in the door. You hear me, Jimmy?"

"Yes," says Jimmy, and the door closes.

"Daisy, you're really drunk."

"I know I'm fucking drunk."

"I'm sorry. I wanted to come to the play, but I had to stay at work."

"You don't care."

"Someone quit and they needed me."

"You didn't come."

"Daisy, don't be mad."

I say nothing.

"Daisy, I'm sorry. I love you. How did the play go?"

I shake my head. There are things I want to say, but I can't formulate the words. It's hard to remember why I am so angry, but I know that I should be, even if I can't remember why.

"Can I at least kiss you?"

I don't say anything. Jimmy hugs me, and I let my body

relax momentarily into his, then I pull away and march to the front door.

"I'll phone you tomorrow," he calls after me.

Emerging out of the mellow darkness and into the unforgiving light of the house, I want more than anything to sleep. I know I am hurt and upset and having a fight with Jimmy, and that tomorrow I will be filled with sorrow, but now the alcohol coursing through me has created only one desire: I must lie down. Mum is wearing her dressing gown, and her face, although difficult to focus on, is clearly distraught.

"Daisy, do you know what time it is? I was so worried. You can't ever do this again."

"I have to go to bed." I propel myself up the stairs. As soon as I think Mum isn't watching, I use my hands as extra support.

"We will talk in the morning," she shouts ominously after me.

When I am lying down, the bed betrays me. It appears to pitch and fall just like a boat at sea, and my ceiling light is swirling around. I sit up and puke on the floor.

Mum comes in. She cleans up the puke and gets me a bucket. I puke and puke and puke. Mum empties the bucket and wipes my forehead with a damp cloth. I am too hot, then I am too cold. She brings me water. I drink it, then puke it up. I apologize throughout. "I am so sorry," puke. "Sorry, Mum," puke.

My eyes open, and the light in the room indicates that it is past morning. As I turn my head back to the pillow, the most unbelievable pain shoots through my brain. My mouth tastes like my stomach has moved into it. The pain veers upwards.

I sit up and grab the bucket just in time. All that is left is clear liquid, and my gut aches from contracting. Mum opens the door; she is holding a tray bearing a cup of tea and toast with Marmite. I wave her away, but she doesn't understand the urgency, and I retch some more. I lie down. I cannot bear to be awake, but my mind starts whirling over the events of yesterday. I think of the play, of the lack of Jimmy, of Wanda pouring the vodka and her face sucked into Nathan's. I think of Damon looking me in the eye and of Roseanne hugging me. Then I think about all the kids watching me cry on Nathan's doorstep and Wanda losing it at Jimmy and Jimmy not showing up. I think of Mum and the inevitable conversation we will have to have. I want to sleep, but it is impossible.

Mum tries with the toast again. My clock reads three o'clock in the afternoon. I experimentally nibble a corner of the bread. Mum sits down and pats my leg through the covers.

"I was so worried. You were an hour late. Why did you drink so much, Daisy? Do you need to see a therapist?"

I roll over in bed. "I was stupid. Too much beer on an empty stomach. That's all. I'm really, really sorry."

"Daisy." Her voice is different now, the colour muted out of it.

"What is it, Mum?" I sit up to look at her.

"Grahame's leaving Ontario. He told me last night. His contract's over in two weeks, and he just found out he got another one in Quebec."

"When will he come back?"

"It's a two-year contract, and after that who knows where he'll go."

The phone rings. Mum answers it, then brings it to me,

heaving the long trail of telephone cable across the hall from her room into mine. I sit up in bed, the base of the phone resting heavily on my lap. If I jiggle, the bell makes a slight jingle.

"I don't know what more you want from me. I'm sorry, Daisy. I should have been at the stupid play."

I breathe deeply. I can feel irrational sentences bubbling up and trying to push their way out of my mouth.

"Daisy, aren't you going to say anything?"

"I don't know if there is anything to say."

Silence, silence, silence. This telephone call is made up of so much blank space.

"You remember the party last year. When we sat by the fire."

"Of course I remember."

"I knew you from school a little bit, and I always thought you and Wanda were kind of snobs."

"Thanks."

"Wait, I'm not finished. Then you were at my party, this cute, smart girl, and you were hanging out with me. I couldn't figure out if it was just because you were drunk or if I really had a shot with you. I saw you a couple of times in the distance, but I was too nervous to go talk to you. When I finally asked for your number, I'd been working up to it for weeks."

"I didn't know that," I say. "I waited and waited for you to call after I gave you my number," I confess.

"Danny always says you should wait at least three days before you call a girl. How are you feeling, anyhow?"

We don't talk about the play and Jimmy's absence after this.

After the phone call my body relaxes; by eight o'clock I'm in bed asleep clutching my prickly teddy bear, with the word "cute" occasionally rankling at the back of my mind.

twenty-two

Kleinberg is talking. It's stuffy in the class, and he has propped the door open to let in some air. I stare out into the hall. Wanda wasn't at her locker this morning, and I half expect to see her running past on her way to first period, clutching a yellow late slip. Cathy walks by, a clipboard in her hand; she must be on student-council business of some sort. She sees me and hesitates for a moment, then walks up to the open classroom door and knocks on it gently to get Kleinberg's attention. "One minute," he says, and completes what he is writing. *Is Lady Macbeth the true villain or hero in this play? Discuss!* He gives a flourish with his arm after dotting the exclamation point.

"Sorry to interrupt, Mr. Kleinberg. May I speak to Daisy for a minute?"

Kleinberg eyes her clipboard, nods, and waves at me to go. Cathy pulls me away from the classroom door.

"Wanda and Jude are yelling at each other in the girls' bathroom, the one by the music room. I thought you might be able to calm them down before they get caught."

"Thanks, thanks, Cathy." I glance back at the classroom. Kleinberg is tapping the board with a piece of chalk; my books are still open on my desk. I walk as fast as I can down the hall and around the corner to the washroom.

I can hear a raised voice, loud but not shouting, words making a slight boom as they reverberate against the hard surfaces of the room. I push through the first door into the bathroom; my hand is about to swing the second door open, but I stop. I stay standing in the small space in between the two doors. I can hear Jude clearly now.

"Saying you're sorry isn't always enough, Wanda."

"I was drunk. I was upset."

"And you needed your ego boosted. Do you even remember what you said to me, that you'd do me a favour? I don't like you like that, Wanda. And even if I did, I wouldn't lower myself to be some kind of experiment for you."

"I didn't mean it to come across like that. I thought you'd want to try it."

"You think you know so much, but you don't know anything about me. I know who I am. I don't need to try anything out."

"I thought I was helping you."

"I don't need your help. I'm tired of being your substitute friend every time Daisy goes off with Jimmy."

"This has nothing to do with Daisy."

"Really?"

"You're putting this on me, but if you weren't such a coward."

"Coward? You think I'm a coward. I have two more years at this school. Two more years of living with my family. And

I'm not going to make that any fucking harder than it already is. And you, you were making out with Nathan and you don't even like him."

"Fuck you, Jude!"

Jude pushes open the door fast. I back out of the way in time to avoid getting hit with it. She sees me; it's obvious I've been eavesdropping. I follow her out into the hallway and put my hand on her arm. She shakes it off.

"Not now, Daisy." I turn to go back in and talk to Wanda. I hear the sound of her kicking a stall door, and I wait outside instead, sitting on the window ledge just down from the bathroom door. Wanda comes out a few minutes later. She doesn't see me and marches down the hall with such determination that I decide not to waylay her.

I've missed half the class. "Okay?" Kleinberg asks when I return. I nod and take my seat.

I can't find Wanda at lunch, but I find Jude in the library reading *National Geographic*s at one of the tables in the back corner of the room.

"What's going on?" I ask.

"What did Wanda say?"

I shrug.

"She can be so selfish," Jude says.

"Do you want to talk about it?"

Jude shakes her head. I sit beside her flipping through magazines. Jude shows me a picture of a surfer going through a tunnel of water made by an enormous wave.

"Did he make it out?" I ask her.

"I don't know," she says, turning the page.

Wanda and Jude have not spoken for two weeks. Wanda is determined to ace her exams; she has spoken to a guidance counsellor. If she gets good enough grades, she can graduate after grade twelve and go to university a year early.

"You should try and graduate early too, Daisy."

"I didn't take the right classes this year."

"You could catch up at summer school."

"I don't even know if I want to go to university."

I see a car pull up in the driveway below Wanda's bedroom.

"Is that…?" I ask.

Nathan gets out and waves up at Wanda.

"I'm studying. After exams. I told you. No distractions," Wanda yells down to him. He bows and leaves a paper bag under her window and then departs back to his car.

"What's in the bag?" I ask her.

"Weed, I hope. But it's probably something stupid like gummy worms."

"Aren't you going to go look?" I am pretty curious.

"I'll look later. He comes by every day. I wish he wouldn't."

"Do you like him?"

"I don't really know. How do you know anyway? I feel like I might like him, if I give him a chance."

"The fight you and Jude are having?"

"We're not fighting. Just not talking. Which is different."

"Wanda, it's been a while."

"I can't fix it. If I could I would, but I can't."

With summer arrives the construction of the ball field on the plot of land that Grahame deemed to have no archaeological significance. At first he called every day, then every week, and now not so often.

One day Cora brings Millie and Sinead to the park and meets me and Natasha's kids. Natasha is taking classes this summer, and I am babysitting for her four mornings a week. Millie plays pirate queen with Dwayne and Sara. Sara wants to pet the ducks, and I pull her away from the pond and place her on a swing. Millie teaches Dwayne how to climb up the slide. Sinead is mobile now, and Cora is constantly redirecting her or removing dirt or rocks from her hands and mouth.

At home, Mum is sitting on the porch drinking white wine spritzers and listening to Ella Fitzgerald through the open screen door. There are tiny webbed cracks running through the plastic arm of her deck chair. Inside the house I notice the carpet on the stairs is looking threadbare. I open the fridge to look for milk and discover the fridge light has stopped working.

I'm relieved when I come outside and see Olivia's car in the driveway. Ella has finished playing, and Mum doesn't ask me to turn the record over.

"Just come, it will do you good. We can go swimming, and wash away all, all this…" Olivia spins around on the porch.

"I can't leave Daisy."

"She's sixteen! And it's just for a weekend, and the cottage is only two hours away."

"Go!" I say. "I'll be fine for a weekend. It will be good for you. When was the last time you went to a cottage?" Our last family vacation springs to mind. Dad spent the entire time demanding we stay silent as he worked on a paper regarding the effects of underground drilling on mole rat populations.

Or insisting we went on long hikes through mosquito-infested forest when all we wanted to do was hang out on the beach and take occasional swims out to the diving dock.

"It would be nice to get out of here for a few days," Mum says.

Olivia's car is packed high. I carry Mum's bag out and hear chinking bottles as Olivia closes the back hatch of the car.

I have a long bath and listen to the stereo, turned way up in the living room. I can hear it all through the house. I burn incense in my room and change my sheets. Tomorrow, I'm going to have sex with Jimmy. I vacuum my floor. Wanda calls at midnight. "I had such a boring night. I wish you had been with me."

"Well, you should have invited me."

"I figured you'd be with Jimmy. Nathan said it would be fun, but the girls just sit around watching the band play with their guitars. They were all drinking beer, and the more they drank, the worse they sounded. The other girls there were twenty and snobby. One of them, Tasha, kept saying 'That was awesome' after every single song. They only play covers, and it's not like they wrote 'Midnight Rambler,' and anyway it's a song about a rapist. Why are they singing it? I asked Nathan and he said, 'Everyone loves the Stones.'"

"Why are you going out with him, Wanda? You complain whenever you spend time with him."

"I'm not going out with him. I'm just hanging out with him. And because I'm bored. You're with Jimmy. Jude's not speaking to me, and even if she was, she's off playing Sergeant Major in some dusty field in Alberta."

When I get off the phone with Wanda, I worry about men

lurking the streets, trying door handles, and looking in windows. It takes me a while to fall asleep listening to the empty house.

I wake up to the sound of someone knocking on the door. It's only six in the morning. I'm wearing an old T-shirt and pink cotton undies. I wrap a sheet from the laundry basket in the hall around my waist and grab a carved stone bear from the shelf in the hall to use as a weapon. The knock comes again, and I look through the peephole: Jimmy is standing on the threshold looking sheepish.

I can still taste the cup of tea I drank in bed last night on my tongue. There's a crust of sleep uncomfortably glued into the corner of my eye. When I open the door Jimmy comes in and kisses me. He kisses me on the mouth, and he covers my neck with kisses. I'm not wearing a bra, and I'm aware of my nipples straining against my shirt. Jimmy must feel them too, because he pulls back and brushes them lightly with his palm. I take his hand and lead him up to my room.

We don't speak at all. Jimmy fumbles a little, but he gets the condom on. He lies on top of me, and I feel him pushing against me, but his angle isn't quite right. His penis prods against my pubic hair. I take my hand and guide him inside of me. It hurts a little bit, in an oddly good way, and then it starts to feel quite good. *This is it, this is it—there's a penis inside me,* I think. Jimmy shudders, and it's over. We lie in bed. Jimmy strokes my hair, and then I go to the bathroom to see if I'm bleeding. I'm not. When I get back, Jimmy is already hard, and we do it again.

Jimmy is slower the third time. I move against him, and he follows the rhythm of my hips. I have an orgasm, and Jimmy comes seconds afterwards.

Sitting outside in the afternoon, we lie back and watch clouds run across the sky, and point ones out where we can see faces. I'm a little sore, but I feel accomplished. Every once in a while, Jimmy reaches over and brushes my lips with his hand. Everything seems in sharp focus—the grass, the blue sky, the taste of our cold glasses of Coke with lemon.

Jimmy's spending the night, and the luxury of this is spread out in front of us. Walking to the plaza to buy popsicles, Jimmy holds my hand. We run into Steve, and he tells us about a big bush party on the edge of town.

"We have better plans," Jimmy says, and winks at me.

The summer goes on. Mum sits on the porch and switches from Ella to Billie Holiday. Wanda and I go downtown and buy earrings from the vendors by Nathan Phillips Square. Jimmy and I make love and fuck in backyards (mine) and basements (his) all over town. Sinead gets faster, and Cora looks older. I don't see much of Damon. I catch only fleeting glimpses of him skating by as I push Sara's third-hand stroller and encourage Dwayne to walk slightly faster than standing still.

twenty-three

"I just want to relax and hang out here. Dan's away and my mom's going to be out," Jimmy says.

"We haven't done anything in ages. And I promised Wanda."

"Anything?" Jimmy jokes.

"Anything else," I say.

Jimmy agrees to come with me to see Nathan's band play and watch the fireworks at the Labour Day party the town puts on every year. The event takes place at one of the big soccer fields behind the tech school. It's on the edge of town, surrounded by concrete strip malls. There are no old churches or tall trees that might accidently catch fire. I catch sight of Cora and Mrs. Jones, and head towards them. They have deck chairs set up in the middle of the field and sit observing Millie running around blowing dandelion seeds. One drifts by Jimmy, and he sneezes dramatically, waking Sinead who was asleep in her carry cot.

"We made Damon carry the chairs. He's around somewhere," Cora says as she picks up Sinead and comforts her.

Jimmy stands a little apart from us. He doesn't say anything, but I can hear him snuffling. I see Natasha in the distance and wave across the crowds.

"We're going to go find Wanda," I tell the Joneses.

"Are you okay?" I ask Jimmy, now we are out of Cora's earshot.

"I have a headache. It might be allergies. Too much grass and stuff." He sniffs.

I hear my name and turn. Wanda is up at the stage with Nathan and the band. She's sitting on an enormous speaker swinging her legs back and forth. Nathan plugs things in and out of guitars.

"So great you came, Daisy," Nathan says to me, jumping down from the stage to greet us.

"It's the highlight of her summer," Wanda says dryly, clambering down from her perch.

"Are you nervous?" I ask Nathan.

"Just excited."

Jimmy rubs his temples.

"What's up with Jimmy?" Wanda says to me.

"He's not feeling well."

"Clearly."

Jimmy remains silent.

"You okay, Jimmy?" Wanda asks, observing him.

"I have a headache."

"Too bad."

"Do you want me to see if Cora has any painkillers?" I ask.

"Don't bother," Jimmy says, and I flinch.

"If you feel that bad you should just go home," Wanda says.

"Maybe you should go home," I say to Jimmy.

"I do feel pretty bad." He looks at me with doleful eyes. "I don't want to wreck your evening. I know you were looking forward to this."

"Why don't you go, and Daisy can stay with me?" Wanda interjects.

"I could stay with Wanda?" I say to Jimmy.

"Do what you want, Daisy." Jimmy departs, scuffing his feet on the grass.

"You okay?" Wanda asks me.

"Yeah, he gets like this when he has a headache. He'll get over it later."

Wanda snorts.

The speakers crackle, and Nathan strums his guitar once. There are a couple of women standing up in front of the bandstand. Wanda nods her head at them in a brief non-committal greeting. The crowd hasn't hushed. Most people are still walking around and greeting friends, chasing children, or tying helium balloons around their wrists. About a dozen kids gather around the stage waiting to see what happens.

Nathan starts up with a cover of "My Sharona." He stares at Wanda and dances, pointing his finger in her direction. She averts her eyes, but he keeps doing it, hamming it up, and clutching at his heart.

"I told him not to do that. I hate it. It's embarrassing."

Nathan continues despite Wanda's discomfort. And there are so few people gathered around the stage it is obvious his attention is meant for her. The kids, most of them are around nine years old, are up dancing and jumping around. They point at Wanda too, imitating Nathan.

"This next song is dedicated to the coolest girl I know."

Nathan sings the opening line to "Wild Thing."

"Come on, Daisy. We're going." Wanda turns and marches away from the stage. She doesn't look back. I follow her. Nathan's voice trails behind us, still going but less exuberant. Past the crowds, we keep going through the parking lot. People are still streaming towards us, heading towards the music, and we thread our way through in the opposite direction. The sidewalk is crowded with latecomers, and we walk for three blocks until we're alone. At the empty parking lot outside the closed AAA Mechanics, Wanda sits down on the curb. She puts her head in her hands for a moment. I sit down beside her.

"I have to break up with him."

"I thought you weren't going out."

"Nathan thinks we are. I slept with him."

"I slept with Jimmy too."

"Did you like it?"

"Yes."

"Honestly?"

"It's the thing that we do best together. How was it with Nathan?"

"To be honest, it was kind of like riding a mechanical bull, and I kept looking down at his face, and it was all contorted, and I just kept thinking, really? Why does everyone make such a big deal about this?"

"Oh Wanda, I'm sorry."

"His lips taste like cold cabbage."

Wanda pulls out a pack of smokes, and we watch the fireworks from a distance. At first we are silent, but as the fireworks get bigger, we start cheering along with the crowds in the distance. The grand finale comes, with a cacophony of loud bangs, and we start walking home. The street gets busy with cars coming from the park passing us. A van pulls up beside us, and we both ignore it out of instinct, then I realize Nathan is driving it.

"Hey! Hey, where did you go? Let's go somewhere," Nathan calls from his window, his elbow resting on its frame.

Wanda looks at me. "Can you drive us to my house? Daisy's not feeling well." I try and look sickly. Wanda gets in the passenger seat, and I climb in the back with bits of drum and guitar cases.

"Why don't I drop Daisy off at home, and then we can go somewhere?"

"No, her mom's away, and she's going to call to check Daisy's at my place later." Lies coming out of Wanda's mouth start to sound like the truth. When we get to her house, Wanda opens the passenger door of the van, but stays seated.

"I'll just be a minute," she says to me. I head up to the house and linger at the front steps.

I can see Wanda and Nathan illuminated inside the van. Wanda's open door keeps the inside lights on. Nathan puts his hands on Wanda's shoulders to draw her near, but she plants her hand against his chest and pushes him away. I see her lips moving and her head shaking. I see Nathan throwing up his hands. Wanda gets out of the van. Nathan reaches over and grabs Wanda's arm, but she shakes him off and shuts the door. The interior light goes off in the van; Nathan reverses out too fast and speeds away.

When school starts, the cable from the phone jack in Mum's room is permanently stretched across the hall and into my room. I'm lying on my bed, my homework strewn around me. I doodle in the corner of my English notebook as I talk to Jimmy.

"I'm working all week. Two of the guys are gone; they only wanted to work for the summer," Jimmy tells me.

"When are you going to do your homework?"

"You're not my mom, Daisy. It's not like we learn much the first week of school anyway."

"I guess."

I flick through my textbooks. I have twenty Math questions assigned, but instead of that I've read three quarters of *Hamlet*. I call Wanda at exactly 10 p.m. It's prearranged, and she snatches up the phone as soon as it starts, so there is only a tiny second of it ringing, and we don't disturb her parents.

"Did you see Jude at school?" she asks me.

"Yes."

"And?"

"And nothing. She said hi, asked how my summer was, then walked off with Cathy."

"She didn't say anything else?"

"No, Wanda. Nothing."

"Nathan left me a poem."

"Where?"

"In an envelope shoved under the front door."

"Isn't he gone? Didn't his parents drive him up to university?"

"I thought so. But I guess he's still here."

"What was the poem like?"

"I didn't read it; I just threw it away."

It's midnight. We keep saying we should get off the phone, but then one of us has something to say.

"I don't see why Ophelia has to die?" I'm telling Wanda. "It's not like Hamlet's all that great. He's obsessed with his dead father and wants to screw his mother, according to Kleinberg anyway."

Then I hear something in the background at Wanda's end of the line.

"Can you hear that?" she says to me.

"Yes, what is it? A cat or something?"

"I hope so. I'm going to look."

I hear Wanda get up. I know the route she pads from her bed to the window.

"Fuck, Daisy, he's out there."

The sound of Wanda's window getting pushed wider comes to me through the phone. It squeaks in its aluminum track.

"Get out of here, Nathan. You'll wake up my parents."

"Wanda, I miss you."

"Don't go out there," I say into the phone.

"Go home, Nathan."

"Why are you so mean to me, Wanda? I didn't deserve this. All I did was love you, and you broke my heart." He sounds angry.

"It's late, Nathan. Go home."

"Why are you being such a bitch?" This is loud.

"I'll take care of this, Wanda." Wanda's dad. His voice is distant—he must be outside.

"Call the cops, I don't care," Nathan screeches. I realize he's drunk.

"I don't need the cops to handle my problems, b'y," Wanda's dad says.

I hear Wanda slide her window shut.

Nathan doesn't show up again. I phone Wanda every night and do my homework with the phone wedged under my ear. Jimmy is always working.

twenty-four

Wanda insists we will get into a club if we dress right.

"Jimmy says there's no way they'll let us in without ID."

"I went to see Nathan's band twice; no one ever carded me."

Wanda picks out my outfit. She hands me the green shift dress Cora gave me and digs Elizabeth's cast-off high-heel boots from the back of my closet. I wear my usual half heart from Wanda and my snake ring. I'm redoing my ponytail, but Wanda shakes her head. "You look too young. You have to wear it down." She takes my brush from my hand and scours it roughly through my hair. She twists bits of it around her finger and sprays them with hairspray. Wanda wears tight jeans and a tight red velvet top with her leather jacket.

"How come you get to wear jeans?" I complain to her.

"Because I don't write song lyrics all over the thighs of my pants," Wanda says.

It's 6:30 when we catch the bus downtown. We'll have time to kill, but we have to get out of the house before Mum comes home and figures we're up to something because of our outfits. I told her I was going to watch movies and sleep over at Wanda's. I feel very conspicuous in my finery. Everyone stares as we get on the bus, and, to my horror, Jude is sitting with Cathy at the front.

"Hi," I say to them when they see us. Wanda doesn't say a word, just sweeps by. I stumble in my heels down the narrow aisle after her.

"I don't look like a hooker, do I?"

"Of course not, hookers don't carry handbags," says Wanda, pointing out the leather purse she has made me take instead of my backpack.

Jude and Cathy get off at the mall. Cathy waves goodbye to me, but Jude just stares out the bus doors and completely ignores us. I think Wanda hasn't noticed until she says, "Well, fuck her." She delves into her purse and pulls out her newest purchase, a stainless-steel hip flask, which she takes a sip from right here on the bus. Then she passes it to me.

The first bar cards us and we don't get in. I'm mortified, but Wanda just shrugs her shoulders at the bouncer, and we head down the street. The next club is called Dead Flowers. There's a short line of goths and punks and we join the back. While we wait, we finish off Wanda's flask. She drinks without trying to hide what she's doing. I can see a couple of older guys checking her out. This time the bouncer cards two guys at the front of the line and then waves the rest of us in.

It's dark, loud, and smoky. I'm desperate to pee and Wanda makes me go alone. The ladies' room is full of goth chicks with eye makeup like artwork and black clothes that cling across cleavage and float around hips. They are smoking up and sitting on the radiators. "Nice dress," one of them says to me as I wash my hands. I meet her eyes in the mirror. I can see she's not being sarcastic, and I say thanks. She nods back at me.

I locate Wanda through the dark and the flashing lights: she has acquired two drinks and is having her smoke lit by a guy with a Mohawk and home tattoos running down his arms. He lingers around but she ignores him, and after she hands me my drink, we shuffle towards a less populated area of the bar. When Home Tattoo approaches again, Wanda slugs back her vodka and tonic, and abandons her jacket on the chair. I find myself doing the same, and follow her to the dance floor. For the first time in my life, all my adolescent bedroom dance practice comes in handy. I surrender myself to the music and forget to be self-conscious. We drink and dance, and I am unconcerned about what time it is or potential police raids or what Jimmy is doing, and just enjoy this: being here, now, on this dance floor with Wanda.

The last bus home leaves Finch Station at 12:30. Getting off the subway at the end of the line, we run down the underground hallway, checking the clocks that hang from the ceiling. Bursting out into the bus station, I see the tail lights of our bus already disappearing around the corner.

My sweat cools from the running. The bus station lights start to turn off, and it's like we are standing on a film set. Everything is in black and white. It feels unreal to be here with all the buses gone and a security guard padlocking the doors shut with a chain behind us.

"Come on," Wanda says, and we go. As we start walking, the distance home becomes more tangible.

"We could hitch," says Wanda.

"What kind of person is going to pick us up at one in the morning looking like this?"

Wanda looks at me and shrugs. I'm coming down from the booze, and the September air is much colder at night than in the day. It will take us about three hours to walk home from here. We don't have enough money for a cab, and neither of us even considers calling our parents. We are walking north down Yonge Street, and by the end of the first block, I deeply regret my choice of footwear. The traffic starts to decrease the further it gets from last call; we hide in the shadows when we see a police car approaching in the distance. A car comes barrelling by; a bunch of men yell something indistinguishable out the window, and I start to cry.

"Come on, Daisy, it's not so bad." Wanda lights one of our last three cigarettes, and we share it as we stumble along. For half an hour we walk until we're in one of those weird wastelands between towns. There's a golf course on one side of the road and a cemetery on the other. It's such a familiar place, one I've seen so many times through the grey-streaked bus windows, but outside the bus at night, it feels like the enchanted forest from a fairy tale.

Our progress gets slower and slower, and Wanda finally says, "Let's take a break." The fence of the golf course is really high, so Wanda and I go through the stone pillars that mark the entrance to the cemetery. It looks empty but we're still cautious. I'm afraid. I pee in a place with no actual headstones and apologize silently to the dead people around me.

"I'm so tired, Daisy," says Wanda, and she looks sixteen now, not twenty-six like she did earlier.

"If we stay here we could get the first bus in the morning.

That's only about five hours," I say.

I glance around, looking for bad men in the shadows. It's like the beginning of a horror film, two drunk sixteen-year-old girls alone in a cemetery. I'm cold and tired, and I have blisters burning on my heels. Wanda and I stick to the older edges of the space, where there are faded headstones and it is dark and dense with trees. This is probably the most dangerous place, but the shadows feel safer than open ground. At the back end of the cemetery is a garden shed, and when I check the door, miraculously, it isn't locked. Wanda flicks on her lighter, and we cautiously look in. It's clean-smelling, dry, and occupied only by a lawn mower, a weed whacker, and some garden tools.

I find some twine inside the shed and use it to tie the door closed behind us. Nothing else seems to matter, except that we are inside and sheltered. Huddling together in the far back corner of the shed, we push our bodies close and hold hands. Wanda flicks on her lighter again and illuminates some burlap for wrapping trees, and we use it like a blanket; eventually I start to warm up. Neither of us speaks much as our voices sound loud and unnatural in the silence.

Wanda falls asleep. I sit up with her head on my lap and try to control my thoughts. Despite the vodka and the dancing, I am awake. I can't tell what sounds I'm hearing and what sounds I'm imagining. I stay awake listening. I cover Wanda up as best as I can with the blanket of burlap and her jacket. I stroke her hair and feel her relax. I worry about the morning and trying to explain my state of dress and early arrival to Mum. I push this out of my mind; the main thing now is getting through this night. We should have called someone, I think. Wanda's parents, Mum, Cora—even Donald—would have had to make an attempt to collect us. It's too late now. I have no idea where a phone booth is and Wanda's out, too asleep to be afraid.

The sky lightens, and through the small high window in the shed, the night turns from inky black to a bruised mauve. Wanda is still sleeping. I gently move her, untie the twine, and step out of the shed in my nylons onto the dewy cemetery grass. I look around. A crow caws behind me, and I jump a little.

I wake Wanda, anxious to get out of here. My feet are a mess. When I put my boots back on, I can hardly walk. Blood has congealed through my nylons and formed a scab that sticks the fabric to me; each step is like a flame being held to my flesh. As we exit the cemetery, an early jogger comes by and stares at us. I'm thankful when I see we're not completely alone with this man. A homeless guy with a long friendly beard is sleeping on a stone bench nearby. There are condoms by the side of the entrance, but neither of us mentions them as we stagger to the nearest bus stop. The few people on the bus with us are early shift workers who survey our last night's clothes with speculation. It's Wanda's turn to be vigilant, and she wakes me and gets off at my stop with me. It's still so early that our voices seem sacrilegious cutting through the air.

My house is closer. We sneak in quietly, but Mum hears us anyway.

"Daisy?" she calls down.

"It's just me," I yell in my brightest I-have-not-been-drinking-or-smoking-or-sleeping-in-a-cemetery voice.

"Is everything all right? Why are you home so early?"

I usher Wanda into my room, throw a sweater over my dress, and poke my head round Mum's bedroom door.

"We stayed up all night watching movies and decided to come here and make breakfast, but now we're both tired. Wanda and I are going to take a nap for a while."

Mum raises her head to survey me, and I yawn and rub my eyes, the picture of post-sleepover innocence.

Wanda's in my bed, and her jeans and bra are on the floor. I take off my dress and painfully detach my nylons from my feet. I put on a T-shirt and snuggle up next to Wanda. I'm too tired to make up a bed on the floor, and want to be close to her.

I wake up hours later, too hot, and I think I'm in bed with Jimmy. When I open my eyes, I realize I'm on my side, and it is Wanda's hair, not Jimmy's, that is tangled with mine. She's spooning me, and in her sleep, nuzzling my shoulder.

I feel a little breathless, and I remove myself slowly so Wanda doesn't wake up. I can hear Mum downstairs. When I look at the clock, I see it's two in the afternoon. I'm supposed to meet Jimmy at four, and I know Wanda has to be home for dinner.

"You guys have certainly wasted the day," Mum says, in one of those crushing tones.

"I'm meeting Jimmy in a couple of hours."

"Another night alone for me, I guess." Her voice quivers.

"You should call Olivia." I can't help suggesting practical responses to her misery, even though I know how irritating these helpful ideas are.

"She gets tired of me, Daisy. Everyone gets tired of me. No one loves a woman over forty."

"Mum," I say, and hug her.

"I need a change, Daisy. I need something to change."

Wanda is bright-eyed when I wake her up.

"Last night was so cool," she says.

It becomes even better as we retell each other the story of how we slept with the dead.

twenty-five

Jimmy saunters up to me at the end of the day. It's Friday, and he hasn't been at school all week. One of the guidance counsellors catches sight of him, and he is swept along to the principal. I wait for a long time. I'm sitting with my back against the wall in the hallway just outside of the main office. When Jimmy reappears, he can't look me in the eye and covers up all his other emotions with rage. "That guy is a fucking dickwad." He doesn't wait for me to stand, and instead marches towards the closest exit. I catch up just in time to see him kick the brick wall of the school. I attempt comforting words, and Jimmy snaps at me.

"Don't say anything. You can't fix this."

We walk in sombre silence, and I hope Jimmy will eventually start talking. His mom is watching TV and smoking in the kitchen when we come into the house.

"Jimmy, the school phoned," she calls out to him.

"Can we talk about it later?"

Up in his room, Jimmy packs beer in a backpack for Steve's house. I don't want to go to Steve's, but Jimmy isn't in

226

the mood for discussing other options.

"That boy is useless. You should get yourself a real boyfriend," Mrs. Hill says to me as I come back downstairs. As I head out the door, she yells after me, "You should dump him, Daisy. He's just going to bring you down in this world."

"Fuck you, Mom," Jimmy says, shutting the door with a thud.

I am perched on the arm of the couch next to where Jimmy is sitting. He is playing a new fighting game. I sip a warm beer and observe the screen filled with blood, swords, and women with tiny waists and huge breasts. The only other girl is Alicia Cole who is dating Trevor, one of Steve's friends. Alicia sits on Trevor's knee, and when it's not his turn to play, they make out.

"Grab me another beer." This is the first thing Jimmy has said to me in half an hour.

I fetch his beer and return. I'm bored and drunk. The arm of the chair is uncomfortable, and my buzz is less prominent than the sense of swilling liquid in my gut.

"Jimmy?"

"What!"

He is absorbed by screen and controller. His player is decapitated. Her head bounces gorily across the TV screen. For a moment she remains standing, her neck bleeding, the top of her white spinal cord visible.

"Fuck, Daisy, look what you made me do."

Everyone, even lip-locked Alicia and Trevor, look at him and then me.

"I'm leaving," I say.

Jimmy says nothing and continues to stare at the screen.

I get up and go up from the gloom of the basement to the lit front entrance and put on my shoes. I turn, hearing someone follow. It's Steve.

"Are you okay?"

"Uh huh. Thanks for having me." Politeness during this interaction fills my mouth, so no embarrassing display of emotion can.

I focus my gaze on the corner at the end of Steve's street. I will go that far before looking back. I listen for Jimmy's feet coming after me. I get to the corner and turn around, but there is nothing, only the dark and empty street, illuminated by the occasional puddle of light from a streetlamp. The dark and quiet are different than usual. A car goes by, and I feel the eyes of the driver on me, a teenage girl, out late, alone. I hear something behind me and expect my name to be called through the night or the sound of sneaker on pavement. It's just a voice coming from one of the houses; a moment of conversation slipping out from a cracked-open window as I walk by.

"Daisy, you're home early." At the sound of Mum's voice, tears come.

"What happened?"

I shake my head. I walk through the house and lie down on my bed. Mum stands looking at me from my still open bedroom door. "Oh, Daisy."

I roll over and stare at the ceiling; tears fall down my cheeks, and I let them trickle.

I wait for the phone to ring all through Saturday. Through the evening and the night, I watch each hour on the clock roll over: 6:00, 7:00, 8:00, 9:00, 10:00, 11:00, 12:00, 1:00, 2:00, 3:00, 4:00, and 5:00. No phone call.

I fall asleep at some point, and when I open my eyes again, I'm okay for a moment; then I remember the waiting and the absence of Jimmy, and I want to go back to the blissful ignorance of sleep. I lie in bed wondering how I'll get through this day and the next. I make up excuses for Jimmy in my head. The phone rings, and the spring of hope that has been coiled inside of me bursts open.

"Wanda's on the phone," Mum yells up to me, and I think for a moment she is mistaken and really it's Jimmy.

I pick up the phone from the floor beside my bed.

"Why didn't you call me? I ran into Alicia, and she said Jimmy was being an asshole to you and you walked out on him."

"It wasn't like that," I tell Wanda.

"Did you break up?"

"I don't know."

"I'm coming over."

I hear Wanda and Mum conferring downstairs. After a while, I hear their footsteps on the stairs; they come into my bedroom carrying cups of tea. Mum leans in the door, and Wanda sits on the end of the bed.

"What happened?" they ask in unison.

I close my eyes and pull the covers over my head. Mum and Wanda talk about how shitty men are.

"Okay, Daisy. Time to get up. Wanda and I have made arrangements. You need to be downstairs in half an hour," Mum says.

"I'm not getting up."

"Yes, you are," says Wanda.

I don't know where we are going, and I don't ask. I get in the back of the car and curl into the corner. I rest my head against the glass, bits of music from the radio and snatches of the conversation between Mum and Wanda float back to me. Wanda's university plans, the residences at Queens, and how nice a city Ottawa is, but far away. I seethe at them for making me leave the phone. I imagine Jimmy sitting at our front door. I picture it like a music video, in brief melodramatic snatches, with pouring rain, fist shaking, and snaking tears.

I don't know where Mum is taking us. We're down in the Don Valley; its treed sides are like autumn in a calendar. The colours are sharp and threaten to break through my ugly mood.

Mum drives west and down a series of side streets. Wanda is map reading and peering at numbers on a street. Mum stops the car outside a house. Two storeys, covered in cedar shingles, and attached to a mirror image in drooping beige vinyl siding. There is a square real-estate sign on the small lawn with an open house notice hanging down from it on short chains. Mum and Wanda stare at the house. Mum cranes forward, her hand still on the keys in the ignition.

"It's a bit…" Mum says.

"Woodsy," I say. My first word since the journey started. Mum turns to look at me.

"Do you want to look? I've been thinking you and I need a change."

I don't say anything, just stare out the window.

"We're here. It doesn't hurt to look. My mom loves open houses; she's always dragging Dad to them on the weekends." Wanda fills in my unkind silence.

We get out. Mum goes first. Wanda loops her arm through my elbow, like I'm infirm and need supporting, and we follow behind.

The real-estate agent hands us flyers. "Call me Trent. Any questions just ask. Real character this one has." There is so much paneling, cheap basement paneling, through the entire house, made of laminate with scratchy black stuff in between. Walking across wall-to-wall shag carpeting in beige, brown, and something in between, I can smell damp dog. Up in one of the bedrooms there is relief from the compressed wood—one wall is taken up with a full-size wallpaper mural of a canoe pulled into the edge of a lake. There are curtains with geese flying across them.

"At least the curtains would be easy to change?" says Wanda. And Mum stifles a laugh.

"I think we've seen enough," Mum says.

In the car, Mum exhales. Across the city, we park in front of another house, detached. In its tiny front garden we follow a winding path to the front door. Instead of grass, the little bit of green on either side of the path is lush clover. There is a porch on this house with tasteful vases of dried grasses on display on the stairs. It feels hopeful, until we enter and everything is pink. The walls are pink, the carpets are pink; the swags across the windows, the couch, the chairs, the toilet, and bath are all pink. You can see the house is old, but the ceilings have been lowered and no original woodwork remains. In the master bedroom, there is a mirrored ceiling. The three of us stand staring up at our reflection. Wanda waves and I watch a reluctant smile break across my face.

Mum drops Wanda off first. Jimmy is not waiting for me at our house.

"Ready?" Mum asks before unlocking the front door, and I nod. Mum checks the answering machine.

"Well," I say.

"I'm sorry, no messages."

I walk over and look at the red zero flashing on the display of the machine.

"You will be okay," she tells me, as my tears start again.

My eyes are too sore from crying to put on makeup. I have not finished my homework. I don't care. I want to stay home, but Mum quickly puts the kibosh on that.

"It's Monday and you have to go to school. Trust me, Daisy, it's better just to get on with things."

I'm running late, and as I rush towards my locker, I notice a guy is standing by it. I'm irritated. I want to grab my books and go, and he's in my way. When he turns around, I see that it's Jimmy. He's cut off all his hair.

He looks older and tougher with short hair. He's dressed in a dress shirt instead of a T-shirt, but he has retained his black jeans. I stop in front of him and raise my hand to his head, then I remember I don't know if I'm on hair-touching terms with him and let it fall back. The theme from *Jeopardy!* rings through the halls, the last-minute warning to get to class. Jimmy grabs my hand and pulls me down the hall and out the front doors of the school. We run, although no one is going to chase after us, and stop when we're safely round the corner. He holds me for a long time, and we don't say anything.

Jimmy takes me to the diner. It is not the kind of place high-school kids hang out. I order coffee and Jimmy has a $2.99 breakfast. The waitress calls him honey.

He tells me he's dropping out of school, and then he breaks up with me.

twenty-six

Fall passes slowly, slowly, slowly. I miss Jimmy. I drag myself to school. My mourning clothes are an oversized black hooded sweatshirt, unbrushed hair and extra eye makeup. The first weekends are really hard. For one thing, Mum has become much more vigilant about how and when I'm coming home since I no longer have a "man" to protect me. I resent this sudden interest in parenting. Every weekend she expects me to come with her and look at houses. I trudge behind her, black clad, sullen faced; a caricature of the difficult teenage daughter.

I miss the sex. I wake up frustrated, clutching my polyester teddy bear and feeling like no one will ever want to touch me again.

I never see Jimmy. He never calls. Steve tells me that Jimmy's quit the restaurant and is working for his dad doing construction. I have a hard time imagining him getting up and making it to the site with a metal lunchbox and a hard hat, but this is apparently the case. He no longer goes to the arcade, and although I look, I never see him at the mall or on the bus.

Jude and Cathy have started honing in on me as a potential suicide or Christian. I enter the cafeteria, and they wave me over. They invite me to preposterous events, the United Church youth group's performance of *Godspell* and a fake accident put on by MADD. I hide in the library with Wanda. I wallow in Daphne du Maurier. Wanda finds a copy of *Lady Chatterley's Lover* and reads anything vaguely titillating out loud, making me blush and the librarian cough to remind us she can hear us.

The school is doing the musical *Annie* this year, and I can't face it. The music department is running it, not Gerry and Kleinberg. Damon is doing AV and Jude volunteers as wardrobe mistress. I can't take the singing and the general optimism of Miss Parker, the head of music. I am not hanging around the stage, so I don't get to witness love blossoming between Jana and Damon. Jana is playing Miss Hannigan and has reinstated her commitment to the theatre. Cora forewarns me, so when I arrive at the Joneses' for Christmas cookie decorating and find Damon with his arm around Jana on the Jones family couch, I'm not blindsided.

"Daisy, how are you?" Jana asks me. She is full of concern.

I am clutching presents for Millie and Sinead and a box of homemade fudge that Mum and I made in a rare moment of mutual domesticity. Festive feeling has been flowing through me, but the sight of Damon and Jana ends this brief euphoria abruptly.

"Oh my god, Daisy, you should come carolling with us!" Jana pronounces.

"Carolling?" I am still unwinding my scarf as she pounces.

"A bunch of us are going tonight. Miss Parker is coming,

and we're going to hit a bunch of the teachers' houses. Then, after, a bunch of us are headed over to Roseanne's. You'll know everyone—it should be really fun!"

"That sounds great. You should go, Daisy," Mrs. Jones chimes in, and I hear the concerned encouragement in her voice.

Cora watches me and Damon and Jana with a small smirk on her face, but does not comment.

I try to say no. But Jana will not take no for an answer. I can't maneuver out of this. The three of us leave the house. Two blocks from the Joneses', I pull out a cigarette and light up.

"Are you still smoking?" Jana asks disapprovingly.

"Yeah," I say.

"It's terrible for your voice," Jana—not so long ago a chain-smoker herself—declares. I notice Damon declines the proffered packet as well.

When we meet the other kids outside the school, they all turn out to be dutiful do-gooders. I don't want to be the kind of teenager who participates in school events on the holidays. Miss Parker hands out lyric sheets and points out that, although we are on vacation, we are still representing the school and must behave accordingly. There must be no smoking (she looks pointedly at me as she says this) and no swearing, and we must sing the proper lyrics to all the songs. She's talking to us like we're a bunch of five year olds. We traipse from house to house. Miss Parker has not warned the other teachers that we're coming. Some are full of bonhomie and get their kids to look at us in their pajamas and hand out candy canes. Others look ambushed. At one teacher's house, I am sure I see the curtain twitch, and although the lights are on, no one comes to the door. I stand at the back and mouth the words to "Hark! The Herald Angels Sing." Miss Parker gets Jana to sing a solo of "O Come, O Come, Emmanuel." Jana has obviously been practicing. I shuffle along with the group—with them but apart. I have no one to whisper little barbed asides to and no one's hand to hold and give little squeezes.

I claim a headache and refuse to go to Roseanne's. Jana insists that she and Damon walk me home. It's not far, but it is painfully awkward, and I can't help but think of the last time Damon walked me home at night. This time I'm the third wheel.

"Merry Christmas!" Jana calls to me, as she and Damon depart. "We should do something soon."

"Yeah, sounds great," I say, without much enthusiasm.

I retreat into the shelter of my house and watch Jana and Damon walk away hand in hand.

When she arrives for the holiday, Elizabeth seems more normal. She's been working at a ski resort out west. Her hair is brushed and clean, and she's wearing sporty clothes. She speaks with a strange BC inflection, and is alarmingly optimistic for a Radcliffe female. She refers to "the slopes" and goes out most nights with "friends" from high school that Mum and I have no recollection of her being friends with. I hardly see her, and when we are alone, there is still this strange disconnect. I feel too shy to tell her any of the things I've been saving up to say to her.

Elizabeth takes charge Christmas Day. She insists we play Monopoly in the afternoon and makes sure there is a hubbub of conversation going on, which drowns out the silence of

Donald and Grahame and Jimmy's absence. All this cheerful-ness is exhausting.

After the Christmas break, I become Jana's project. Cora thinks it's hilarious. Jana finds me sitting alone. She sits beside me and interrupts the book I'm reading. Jana comes looking for me in the library. The only thing that keeps her at bay is Wanda. She has a look she gives Jana, the same look she previously used on Jimmy.

"You just need to tell her to fuck off," Wanda says when she sees Jana peering in through the library door.

"She means well."

"Does she? You know what they say about keeping your enemies closer. I think she wants to keep an eye on you."

Jana invites me to go see movies with her and Damon. I decline. She invites me to her house. She stops her car beside me and offers me drives home. She is full of advice. I remind her of her younger self—she means last year. Lost and lashing out—she means smoking. A part of me likes the attention Jana gives me; it reminds me of Elizabeth, or Cora when she had less baby and more time, but with Jana there's always a weird edge.

"Damon told me all about what happened with your parents."

"Oh."

"His mom is so sweet having you over to babysit."

Nothing like learning you're a charity case.

"I know you feel sad, but you don't know what it's like to be clinical. My therapist says I need to be more open." Jana digs in her purse and just happens to flash her antidepressants at me as she looks for a tissue. "This is why I'm telling you I used to be jealous of how close you were with Damon, but now

I understand you're more like a sister or maybe a cousin to him. Carm is such a great lady. I'm sure she will make an awesome mother-in-law."

The winter is a brutal one. Snow mounds in the yard, and ice paintings cover all the windows. Mum and I rush quickly home after work and school. We walk around the house padded in slippers and sweaters. We are gentle with each other, offering cups of tea and sitting in silence on Saturday nights watching *Masterpiece Theatre*. We get used to being alone together and remember the pleasure of small comforts—tea, toast, and lying warm in bed listening to the cold wind howl. When the weather starts to get warmer, it is like we are emerging from hibernation, both of us sleepily coming out of our shared den.

A soft April breeze is blowing my curtains in and out. Mum bawls at me to answer the phone. I can't figure out who is calling me on a Sunday morning.

"Daisy, where are you?" It's Cora.

"I'm here."

"You know what I mean. Are you still moping over Jimmy Hill, or are you mad at me?"

"Yes and no."

"Jana and Damon can babysit. Dad got my car working. Let's go for a drive."

Cora's car pulls up, the muffler making almost as much noise as the stereo. Mum looks askance when I head for the front door. "Her dad says it's fine," I shrug. We drive listening to the stereo and not talking. Cora takes a new pack of cigarettes from the glove compartment and hands me one. We drive north. It's surprising how quickly we get out of the suburbs and into open country, with cows in fields and strange modern farmhouses. Mostly it's hydro wires and sky.

Cora pulls into a gas station. I offer her money for gas, but she waves it away. I lean against the car watching the early cottage-goers heading home. Some of them are taking disgruntled kids to the questionable-looking gas station restroom. Cora hands me a Coke and a Slim Jim. I have never had a Slim Jim before, and when I curl my lip she says, "You'll like it." And she's right, there is great pleasure in chewing down on the salty fatty meat.

We drive for two and a half hours. Eventually, we turn off the highway and roar down a dirt road, kicking up dust. We pull up at a makeshift boat launch looking out over a lake at the end of the road, and get out of the car. Like all lakes close to city, this one is dotted with cottages; some are old and ramshackle, others are new with pink brickwork and multi-storied decks. Across the water is a clearing; Cora points to it. "I used to go to camp there."

"Did you like it?"

"I hated going, I never wanted to and loved it by the time I left. I love the lake."

It's quiet: all we can hear is the lake lapping against the shore. I stick my hand in the water; it is the temperature of recently melted ice. The fact that we have made it here of our own volition, or at least Cora's, on a Sunday afternoon seems miraculous.

"So, why haven't you been over?" Cora asks me.

"I've been busy."

"Bullshit. Damon says you never go out and that you disappear at school."

"I feel stupid around Jana. She makes me feel like a kid with terminal cancer. She told me your mom was only nice to me because she felt bad for me when my parents split up. And it makes sense, why did she need me to babysit when Damon was around?"

"Fuck Jana, she is so full of shit. Mom doesn't trust Damon with anything. Jana's just jealous because we all like you more than her."

Cora bends down and starts untying her shoelaces.

"What are you doing?"

"Living."

Cora takes her clothes off, fast and with determination. She pulls off her pants and underwear in one determined tug and steps out of them. She turns to me. "Come on, hurry up."

I take off my boots and then kick off my socks. Cora pulls her sweater and T-shirt off, then takes off her bra. I can see her back, the shape of her like a cello, curved and round. I hesitate, then quickly get out of my own clothes.

Cora is standing in the water hopping from foot to foot, saying, "Cold, cold, cold."

My need to be covered up and hide my nakedness overwhelms me, and I run in fast, splashing past Cora, and plunging my body in as soon as the water is up to my thighs. The air gets sucked from my lungs. I take a stroke and another, my arms stiff, my skin hurting. I turn back and look at Cora with her arms crossed across her breasts, still only ankle deep, hopping from foot to foot.

"It's as warm as a bath," I say through chattering teeth.

I can hear the sound of a car approaching and Cora must hear it too, because she looks back towards the road, then she hurtles in and is beside me spluttering unintelligibly with a look of horror on her face. "So cold," she manages to articulate. The car drives past, and with the dust it kicked up still in the air, we both rush from the freezing water to the shore and clumsily pull our clothes over our bright red skin.

twenty-seven

Mum is not happy this summer. She walks around with a distant look in her eyes and sighs at odd moments. Her doctor has prescribed her pills, and these just seem to have pulled a fish tank over her head; when she looks at me, I think I must be blurry.

"You should go out more, Mum. Let's go see a movie."

"Not tonight."

"Well, I'm heading over to Wanda's. Do you want to go see any houses tomorrow? I can see if Wanda wants to come?"

"I don't think so. You go on."

I don't know what to do. I head out the door.

When I come home, the real-estate section of the newspaper is open on the table, a small black-and-white picture of a house circled. I peer at the tiny image and imagine us living in it. The next day I walk to my summer job, thinking of different streets with streetcar tracks and fresh vegetables and flowers tumbling out of store fronts and filling the sidewalk.

Ice cream makes perfectly normal-looking people behave

like sociopaths. The man before me is smiling, but I can tell a complaint is coming: there are not enough marshmallows in the rocky road so he wants a refund, he's going to accuse me of short-changing him, or insist that he ordered strawberry and now that his kid has eaten half a container of orange sherbet he wants us to fix the order. I dip my metal scoop in milky water.

"Is this really maple walnut? It doesn't taste right to me," he says.

An older couple comes up and wants to try a few flavours. I give them a taste of tiger tail and then chocolate ripple on plastic pink spoons. I offer them a taste of white chocolate raspberry, and Victor, the owner, comes and stands close beside me.

"Not so many tastes. This is not a charity. And go easy on the napkins too. One. Per. Cone."

I'm closing with Ingrid, who never talks to me unless to say "Do this" or "You're doing that wrong," and Alice, who is sweet but talks endlessly about her cats and doesn't smell quite right. I'm hoping no last-minute customers come after 5:45 p.m. No one ever finishes cleaning by 6:15 p.m., but we don't get paid if it takes us longer than that to mop the floor and cash out.

I wipe out a refrigerated unit that stinks of soured milk. I haven't wanted to eat ice cream since my first week, despite my twenty-five percent discount. The phone rings, and I expect it to be Victor, with instructions to hose down the dumpster or a reminder to count the float twice.

"Daisy! Personal call!" Ingrid yells at me. "Quickly please."

I panic for a moment. Why would Mum call me unless

there's an emergency? It's Wanda from a payphone at Wonderland where she is working this summer. All day she walks around with a flotilla of bobbing balloons trying to sell them to the parents of over-excited children.

"Come out with me. Just for an hour," she says.

"I don't know, Wanda." My feet ache.

"You don't get paid to talk on the phone," Ingrid says to me. Alice looks at me with mournful, sympathetic eyes.

"I'll come. Gotta go."

"Daisy, this floor isn't clean. Get new water and do it again," Ingrid tells me with spite.

I hum to annoy her as I lug the heavy industrial mop bucket to the bathroom. I heave it up and over to tip it down the toilet. Water slops out of the bucket too fast and comes out of the toilet in a wave, soaking my shoes and socks with dirty water. A brown puddle forms on the bathroom floor. "Clean that too!" Ingrid snaps at me.

Alice leaves, patting me on the shoulder. Ingrid has let her go with just enough time that, if she runs, she'll catch her bus. Ingrid waits by the door shaking her keys in impatience as I put the mop away.

Wanda's sitting with Mum, in the living room, with a glass of white wine in her hand. The two of them observe me in a way that indicates I have very recently been the subject of conversation.

"What?" I say.

"This house is great," Wanda says holding up the newspaper.

"It's okay, but did you see the one next to it with the balcony?"

"That house is beautiful, but the location is all wrong."

"Location is everything," Wanda says, and takes a sip of the wine Mum has provided her with.

I fortify myself with a glass of wine in the bathroom as I clean up and change out of my polyester uniform into jeans and a T-shirt.

"Where is this party?" I presume it's in our neighbourhood.

"It's on Oak Street, in the new development."

"Wanda, that's miles."

"We'll take the rec trail."

We walk by houses like ours, houses the same age as our parents, and a Victorian that has somehow escaped demolition or fire.

"That place. Mum should buy something like that place." Wanda and I stop and admire a white painted house with a wraparound porch and a tower running up the side. The paint is peeling, but it remains regal.

As we enter the trail, there is still dusky light. This section cuts between groomed back gardens and industrial yards. The gravel path follows alongside a stream full of reeds, plastic bags, and the occasional shopping cart. Patches of pink foaming stuff float along the surface like toxic bubble bath. A dog walker comes towards us; her dog is small, old, and disinterested in our enthusiastic praise of his cuteness. It's getting darker, and Wanda starts talking about nothing, and I know this is because it's getting creepy in here and we need a distraction. Something makes a noise close to us, a rushing sound like unearthly breathing, and we both stop still. A racoon ambles into the path in front of us. It turns and stares at us with wide yellow eyes, then disappears into the undergrowth.

Both of us start to speed walk. I trip on a root, stumble, and grab Wanda's arm. I look up from steadying myself, and I see an opening ahead of us. We pop out of an arch of trees into the large groomed expanse of park that edges Forest Village, the housing development we're headed to. Out in the open, away from the shadow tricks of the trees, we are braver. Lounging on a picnic table, I hold the flame to the end of Wanda's cigarette and the light from my Bic glows.

"How far is it now?"

"Not that much further." Wanda gestures across to the far side of the park. I see a row of square grey houses. They are all oversize, with tiny strips of dead grass and tall anti-social fences separating them from their identical neighbours.

The night crept down when we weren't looking. Walking down the path through the centre of the park, we hear moths buzz around the fake old-timey lamps that appear at regular intervals along the way. We pass two large baseball fields, a playground, and a parking lot. In the middle of the park, we stop and stand on a little foot bridge, meeting the stream we followed earlier once more.

"So much space," Wanda says, spinning her arms out. This place is empty, except for us. The sky seems huge tonight. There is a bright full moon, and one or two stars starting to appear.

"You can see why people pray to it," I say, throwing my head back to stare.

Wanda lets out a sound, slow at first, then low and loud. She howls at the moon. My voice cracks the first time, but I open my throat wider and let out a matching sound. Our howls vibrate against each other, and in the distance, a dog howls back at us from one of the small fenced yards.

All the streets of the subdivision are named after trees—Tamarack, Elm, Birch, Palm. There are no oaks on Oak Street, only small ornamental shrubs planted in decorative gravel. They look thirsty. Most of the houses have the blue light of the television coming out of their windows. We can tell where the party is at by the bunch of cars lining the curb outside.

"Whose house is it again?"

"Karen's boyfriend, Matthew. I work with Karen. Matthew works in rides. I've only met him a couple of times."

I have my hand clasped around the greasy brass of the door handle, and I'm pulling it shut behind me. I look at Wanda, and I know she feels it too. We don't belong here. Something in the way the lights and the music and the laughter lurch in this house isn't right.

We start by looking in the living room. A bunch of teenage boys are taking hits off a bong. One sits with his eyes closed. *A Clockwork Orange* plays on a large TV screen. The sound is turned up loud, and there is masculine laughter in the room. We back out, not speaking, and look in another room. The kitchen. Two girls are in there. One of them lights a cigarette from the burner heated red on the stove.

They look us over.

"You want something?" one of them says. She's wearing a bomber jacket and Docs. I look at her shoelaces. There's something in her, something hard.

"Karen?" Wanda asks.

"Matthew's girlfriend," the other girls says. She is too skinny, with a band of acne across her cheeks. "I think she's in the garage." She gestures back out into the hall from where we have come.

Laughter comes up from a set of stairs leading to the basement. Hard music comes up from there. Something I don't know. It's jarringly loud and aggressive. My throat hurts in empathy with the guttural words the singer shouts. I can't make out the meaning of the lyrics, only the feeling of them, and it sickens me with the force of its violence.

"Jesus, sorry, Daisy. I'll just find Karen, then we'll go."

We find another door, and it opens into the garage. Light blazes. I blink, adjusting my eyes. The sounds from the other rooms irritatingly clash, neither loud enough to drown out the other and both menacing.

Wanda puts her hand on my shoulder.

There is a man in his late twenties standing against the wall across from us. Shaved head, Docs, a swastika on the arm of his bomber, just like I've seen on the news, but never in real life. He is too old to be at this party. I taste danger. He looks us up and down; it is clear we have interrupted something. Then I see her. Jude is standing with her back to the metal door of the garage. She doesn't see our arrival. Another girl with short, shaved hair is up in her face. "Cadet! You'll do as I say. I think you need to show me more respect. If I say lick my boots, you lick my boots."

"Do it," the man says quietly. "Girls like you like that kind of thing. Don't they, Jude? And Carol tells me she's your superior." He says this in an eerily calm manner, still watching Wanda and me where we stand framed in the entrance from the hallway.

Jude is shaking, her eyes glassy. She might be high or

peaked out with fear. She's only focussed on Carol. Carol is taller than Jude, tall and thick. She puts her hand on top of Jude's head ready to push her down, but first she grins at her audience.

Wanda flies. She leaps and I follow. Wanda grips Carol's shoulder and spins her so she is backed up beside Jude. Wanda drives the palm of her hand into the metal door right next to Carol's head.

The sound of Wanda's hand slamming into aluminum takes several seconds to subside. We are all suspended in the vibrating sound. Then the man laughs, not real laughter, laughter he forces out, a threat.

"Guess you've got two more little girls to teach how to behave tonight, Sergeant."

A smile forms on Carol's lips, even though Wanda still has her pinned to the garage by her shoulder. Carol's pupils are small. She's figuring out what to do next. It takes her a moment, and at once I realize both that she is stupid and that her stupidity makes her even more dangerous.

I'm a few feet away. No one is looking at me.

"Woof. Woof. Woof. Woof woofwoofwoof. Arrrrr ArrrrrrArrrrrrr." I put my head to one side as I bark and howl and roll my eyes around and hunch over. Everyone is staring at me, confused, except for Jude. She wrenches up the garage door and yells, "Run!"

Burning lungs, we keep running until Jude stops, bends down, and clasps her knees. We are in the park. I glance back, sucking in air. No one is following us.

"Don't worry," Jude spits out words between intakes of air. "Carol, is, fucking, slow."

"Fuck, Daisy, what was that?" Wanda says.

"Rabies. I was acting rabid. If wolves are surrounding you, act rabid."

"Jesus."

"Friend of Dad's. Once. Told a story." I take a deep breath. "At a dinner party."

"Thanks," Jude says, first looking at me, then at Wanda. "I didn't think the party was going to be like that. I wouldn't have gone if I'd known Carol was going to be there. She's always been a bully, but I didn't know she was a neo-Nazi."

"It's okay, it's okay." Wanda has her arm around Jude's shoulders. Jude's crying now, letting out the shock and the built-up adrenaline.

We lie on the grass, the three of us with our heads together. A shooting star goes by, and Wanda sticks her hand up and follows its trail.

"Make a wish," I say.

"What did you do all summer?" Jude asks us.

"Nothing," Wanda and I say in unison.

"What about you?" I ask her.

"I learned how to fly," Jude replies.

"As if," says Wanda.

"No really, that's why I'm in Cadets. I'm an Air Cadet. I want to be a pilot. This year I started lessons."

"Holy shit," I say.

"Why didn't you ever tell us?" says Wanda.

"You never asked," says Jude. "And I'm telling you now."

"What's flying like?" I ask her.

"It feels like closing your eyes and falling backwards and knowing you're never going to hit the ground."

twenty-eight

I'm disoriented starting grade twelve. A couple of kids smile at me, but they're all in groups or couples telling loud summer stories or enjoying last-minute kisses before classes start. I walk past Damon and Jana. They're making out across from a group of grade nines, who are trying unsuccessfully to ignore them. My first class of the day is Drama. When I get there, the door is locked. To cover up my embarrassment at being early, I am pretending to be busy looking at my empty day planner when someone taps me on the shoulder. I turn around: it's Jude.

"Hey," she says, and I grin at her.

Gerry comes and opens the door. He's wearing a Hawaiian shirt and greets us with "Aloha, ladies!" The class is split between the musical kids, the play kids, and a handful who take Drama but have thus far avoided the drama of the school play. Damon rushes in at the last minute and plunks himself beside me and Jude. Jana blows him kisses from the door. It's so obvious they are doing it. If it wasn't obvious, I would know anyhow, because Cora came home one day and heard them at it in Damon's bedroom. She said it was a risky thing to do, since someone is almost always home at their house.

Some of the musical kids are singing "Bicycle" by Queen.

"I hate that song," Jude says.

"I know, it's music for people who want to grow up and teach at preschool," I say.

"You guys are such snobs," says Damon. Jude punches him on the arm, and he ducks away in exaggerated fear.

Wanda, Jude, and I spend our lunch hours in the library. Wanda's always studying, determined to get the kind of grades that get scholarships. Our table is pushed up against a large window and is littered with university brochures. Wanda and I sit on the long side of the table facing outside. Jude is at the head of the table, rocking her chair on to its back legs, and reading *Pet Sematary*. I swirl my hands through the glossy publications.

"I don't know why you're so excited. It's just more school," I say to Wanda.

"It's not just more school. I don't want to clean up blood and piss and shit at the hospital like Mom does every day. This is my way out of that."

"I wish I knew what I was going to do with my life." I slump melodramatically on to the table.

"You don't have to know what you're going to do; you just need to do something." Wanda pats my head.

We are distracted by a swoop of birds outside the window. They arrive in a mass and land on the roof. We can hear them, a hundred bird voices exalting their existence chirpily, and pattering on tiny feet above our heads.

"There's so many of them," Wanda says, and we stand up

and try and peer up at them. They take off from the roof again in a swooping formation of organized chaos, their wings making a rushing sound like an outgoing tide.

"A murmuration," says Jude.

"What?" I say. Wanda and I cock our heads at Jude.

"A murmuration of starlings. That is what you guys are looking at."

"A murmuration," says Wanda, with newly glittering eyes.

Jude walks over to the magazine rack and comes back with a science magazine. She flips through to an article entitled "Flight Patterns: Avian Dare Devils" and hands it to Wanda. There's an image of a group of birds, much like the ones we've just seen, stark against a grey sky. Wanda carefully rips out the picture.

She finds out about the place after reading an article in *NOW* magazine. It's far east on Queen. I stare out the streetcar taking in laundromats, seedy strip clubs, and an illogical number of places selling fried chicken. The shop is wedged between an antique store and Lucky 8 Convenience and Psychic Readings. The bottom half of the window displays pictures of tattoos. Skulls with flaming eyes, Playboy rabbits, and four-leaf clovers, but Wanda has the picture in her bag. She wants a cluster of birds to travel across her shoulders.

"I am nineteen. You are eighteen," she says to me, before pushing open the door.

There's a man sitting behind a desk talking on the phone when we come in. He's in his fifties with a pot belly and has a spider web of blurred green ink covering his bent elbow. He waves at us with his free hand and sticks his two free fingers up, then mimes at the phone. I walk down a wall covered in photographs of muscular male arms with portraits of women and various dragons tattooed on them.

"Sorry," he says, hanging up the phone. "Can I help you ladies?"

"I have an appointment with Cherry?" Wanda says, like we're at the dentist or the hairdresser.

Cherry is the kind of beautiful that makes me nervous. Her hair is pulled back in a ponytail, and she is wearing a white undershirt and black jeans. The muscles in her arms move beneath her tattooed skin with every gesture she makes. Her eyes are dark brown and her lashes are thick and black.

She takes us into a back room.

"I have to ask you for ID," she says apologetically, and Wanda produces a license from her purse. It's not fake, it's her cousin's, and I hold my breath waiting to see if it will work.

"Great, Amanda, sorry I had to ask."

Wanda is lying on her front as Cherry leans over her. She has interpreted the picture Wanda gave her. There are twenty-one birds, just black shapes, but with definition at the end of their wings evoking feathers. Each is in a slightly different pose, and they fly from halfway across the right side of Wanda's upper back up to the top of her left shoulder.

"Good," says Cherry. "This looks good. I love it when people want beautiful things."

"Does it hurt?" I ask Wanda. She has her eyes closed. "It doesn't not hurt, but it's not as bad as I thought it might be."

"Yeah, people make it into such a big deal. But it's not

really. You're doing great," Cherry says.

"Those birds are so real looking," I tell Cherry.

"Starlings for darlings." Cherry smiles at me. "What about you? I don't have another appointment booked. You want something done?"

"You could just get a small one. One starling." Wanda is enthusiastic.

"It's a pretty tattoo. You could get one now and if you like it, add to it later," Cherry says. She can see I'm tempted. "Honey, I've regretted many things in my life, but never a tattoo." I eye the flowered garden that sweeps up Cherry's arms.

Wanda talks to distract me, and gets up occasionally to haul up the back of her shirt and admire the new markings on her back in a mirror. Cherry's touch is gentle, and after the initial sharp pain, the area goes numb. It only takes a few minutes. A lone bird on my shoulder, swooping up.

I scoop cones of pumpkin pie and maple walnut for most of Thanksgiving weekend. I fill in on shifts like this once in a while so that Alice or Ingrid can have a day off. Mum is looking at houses with Olivia.

Monday the store is closed. Taking a break from homework, I go for a walk. It's the early evening and I smell turkey roasting, see extra cars parked in driveways and guests arriving clutching pots of rust-coloured mums. Maple leaves have imprinted on the sidewalk, and wood smoke is in the air. It is a perfect Thanksgiving day, and I feel so lonely. I'm being sentimental, remembering Thanksgivings of my youth when Elizabeth and I made placemats by ironing leaves between waxed paper and Dad got the stuffing ready as Mum peeled potatoes. Through my melancholy comes the sound of wheels on pavement. I look up, and Damon is coming dangerously and beautifully down the middle of the smooth street on his skateboard. He makes an elegant U-turn and stops beside me.

"Shouldn't you be eating turkey?" I ask him.

"Nah, we did it yesterday, and now we're all sick of being stuck in the house together." It occurs to me just how small his house is for six people.

"We're skipping Thanksgiving this year. Where's Jana?"

"I don't know," Damon says with don't-ask-questions finality. "Wanna go smoke a joint?"

We walk over to our old schoolyard and smoke, lurking amongst the trees by the fence, and then we sit on the swings, making trails in the sand with our shoes.

Damon pushes me and I swing sideways out of control, laughing. We goof around giggling and half-heartedly shoving each other off course. I write my name in the sand with the toe of my boot.

The weed wears off, and we walk slowly back to our houses. Neither of us wants to go home, but there isn't anything else for us to do.

"You want to come to my place?" Damon asks, but I've already been gone for longer than I should have.

"I saw a house I really liked today," Mum says when I come in the door. "How would you feel about switching schools? I know Wanda won't be there next year. I'm ready for a change. There's nothing keeping us here."

"I'd be okay with moving."

Mum nods. "Do you want scrambled eggs or baked beans?" she says holding the bag of bread in her hand.

I reach up into the cupboard to take out a cup, and the neck of my sweater slips down.

"Daisy." I freeze and squeeze my eyes shut for a moment, before turning to face her.

"You better show me."

I stretch my sweater down exposing the whole tattoo. She doesn't say anything, but when I cover my shoulder back up, she hugs me for a long time.

Christmas break looms ahead once again with Mum and me trapped in the house together, trying to fill the various voids in both of our lives. Elizabeth is vague. She might come, she might not, and then she calls and announces she is coming and she has a surprise for us. I lie awake worrying what this surprise might be.

Mum braves the traffic, and we drive through light snow to the airport to get her. We see her once more through the glass of the security area as she escalates down to baggage collection; she's looking for us, smiles and waves. Mum reaches over and squeezes my shoulder. Elizabeth hugs us when she sees us, and I take her heavy bag. She's dressed in a flowered cotton skirt and a flowing white top. The skirt has bells sewn to the bottom that tinkle like glasses clinking together as she walks. Over this she wears a sensible wool winter coat which makes her seem older and more grounded than usual. We're getting ready to leave the airport when I notice Mum staring at something; I follow Mum's eyes and see the unmistakeable gold band on Elizabeth's finger.

"I eloped." She beams at us.

"Oh, Elizabeth," Mum practically moans. "But why?"

"What do you mean, why? Because we're in love, because we want to be together."

Ian will be arriving to meet us the next day.

Donald is informed of Elizabeth's marital status and says he will book an extra seat for our Boxing Day dinner. The Joneses coo and cluck at Elizabeth's news, and Mrs. Jones says it all sounds so romantic. Cora and Millie ask about the how and where and what was worn. I go to work and scoop gingerbread and candy-cane ice cream and feel cheated out of a bridesmaid dress.

He's old, at least thirty. He has those too-blue Vancouver eyes and a winter suntan from skiing. He owns a coffee shop, which neither Donald nor Mum seems impressed with; they have always viewed entrepreneurship as somehow disagreeable.

I am ready to hate Ian, but I don't. He brings us all presents and lots of coffee. He buys wine and offers to do dishes, and he looks at Elizabeth like he loves her without it being all creepy.

After dinner and presents on Christmas Day, Ian and Mum wash up, and Elizabeth says, "Come on," and I put on the bulky Guatemalan sweater she has given me, and we head out into the crisp, cold air.

"Are you okay?" she asks me.

"I'm okay," I say.

"Good. So what do you think of my husband?" She pronounces the word carefully, still trying it out.

"I like him. He's different from other guys." I'm thinking of our dad and Jimmy.

"Good, he likes you too."

Mum, Elizabeth, and I go visit the house a few days after Christmas. "It's a good time to make an offer; it's been on the market for a while," the real-estate agent tells us. It's small, two bedrooms, and there's a scary dirt-floored basement down a rickety set of stairs. The wooden floors upstairs are honey coloured, and in the front room is an old fireplace with art-deco green tiles and a cast-iron face.

"Does it work?" Elizabeth asks the agent.

A *For Sale* sign sprouts out of the snow on our front lawn. Dad comes over to pick up a few boxes of his stuff. He offers Mum his unsolicited advice.

"It's not a good time to sell in the winter."

"It's not really any of your business anymore, Donald," Mum tells him.

All toothpaste is washed from the sink. We avoid using the living room, and the sofa cushions are constantly plumped. We exit the house at odd times when our real-estate agent alerts of us a showing. On a Tuesday at 7 p.m. we find ourselves driving around, past the high school and then by the town hall.

"I've got an interview lined up for a new job. I wasn't going to say anything, but if it works out I'll have to commute until we can move."

"Where is it?"

"It's at Caufield's Caskets. They make coffins."

"Coffins? Really? Do you want to work there?"

"I'm not sure, but the location is great. It's by that house we looked at, in an old warehouse."

I get home to find her slumped on the couch after the interview. "I screwed it up, Daisy."

"How?"

"She, Mrs. Caufield, asked if I'd felt any hesitation about working in the death industry. I told her I thought it might put more qualified candidates off, and I'd have a better chance at the job."

"What did she say?"

"She laughed."

I answer the phone the next day. "It's Audrey Caufield," I say, handing the phone over to Mum.

"Thank you, yes, I'm very pleased," Mum says into the phone, while doing a silent dance of joy.

In the spring, Damon and Jana star in the school production of *West Side Story*. Wanda and I sit at the back of the audience during the final night. Damon is wearing tight leather pants. As soon as he walks on stage, Wanda grabs my hand and squeezes.

"I don't think he can bend over," she whispers to me.

"He'll never be able to have children after wearing those. They must be cutting off all the circulation," I whisper back. Wanda guffaws. The people beside us—parents, he's in a suit and she's wearing a church-service dress—give us censorious glances. We can't look at each other for the rest of the play for fear of causing another involuntary outburst of noise.

Wanda and I go to the afterparty. We're welcomed into a suburban house smelling of smoke and hot teenagers. I drink beer sitting on the back deck, looking up at the skies trying to see the stars despite the security lights, which come on every time someone moves or opens the screen door. Damon comes out, and Wanda and I groan as we are, once again, temporarily blinded.

"You changed your pants?" Wanda teases him.

"I do not want to talk about my pants. And no, that was not a cucumber."

"A gherkin?" I ask.

"Stop. Or I'm leaving," he says.

Damon lies on the deck between Wanda and me, looking up at the stars, obviously high on his final performance as much as anything else. "I've known you guys forever," he says, and reaches up and grabs both of our hands.

"Easy, tiger," says Wanda and drops his hand. Damon waves his free hand around, gesticulating at the sky we're all looking up at.

"Where do you think we'll all be in ten years?" he asks us.

"New York," says Wanda.

"L.A., I'm going to go to L.A.," says Damon. "What about you, Daisy?"

I think about London or Paris, but they sound too cheesy.

"I don't know," I eventually answer.

"That's your problem, Daisy. It's like you're afraid of wanting things in case you don't get them," Wanda says. "I'm going to get more beer for you, whether you want it or not." She rises, and we are blinded by the light once more.

Damon still holds my hand. "I always thought we'd end up together, but it just never happened," he says to me.

I am acutely aware of how this could go for me with Damon drunk and Jana inside.

"Damon," I say, "you have Jana." I realize as I say this that, although I like Damon, I don't want to be anything other than his friend.

"Oh, Jana." He sings it like "Oh, Donna." "And you have Jimmy."

"Not for a long time," I tell him.

Damon pulls himself up and rests his head on the armrest of my chair. I think something momentous might happen.

"I'm going to puke," he announces matter-of-factly, and walks to the rail of the deck and vomits over it.

That weekend someone makes an offer on the house, and Mum accepts.

twenty-nine

Kleinberg stops me in the hallway, "I hear you're leaving us."

"Yes."

"Well, good luck," he tells me. I sense there's more he wants to say, but a bell rings and I mumble an inadequate, "See ya," before beetling away.

Wanda leaves at lunchtime. "I'm just wasting studying time," she says as she abandons me. It's the end of the day, and I'm clearing out my locker. There's no one left; it's just me and the janitor pushing dust and paper down the hall. Outside, I walk past Jana and Damon standing in the school fountain, making out, as graduates whoop around them. I watch the festivities with jealous interest. At home I sit in the half-packed living room. Three boxes in one corner, with *Donald* written in thick black marker across their tops, wait for Dad to pick them up. I can't imagine not living here anymore, but even more I can't imagine staying.

"I couldn't say no to her," Mum says, as the van backs up in front of the house on moving day. It is a large cube truck.

It is painted black and has a graphic image of a coffin and *Caufield's Caskets* painted in large gothic script on the side. Mum's boss has sent the truck and two of her warehouse workers to help us with the move. The men joke around with Mum and call her Shell.

"Why are they calling you Shell?" I ask her.

"Everyone at work does. I like it. It's less stuffy than Sheila. Less old fashioned."

Our new neighbours gawk as we arrive to unload. Mum and I stand beside the coffin van and wave over to them. Racoons fight in the backyard during the night. Mum and I lie in our separate rooms, listening to sirens and letting the ghosts of our new home get used to us.

They have pet cats in Caufield's offices, to keep down the mice, but also, according to Mum, because Audrey is a softy. I sit waiting for Mum, while rubbing the chin of Eartha Kitty. From inside one of the back rooms where Mum stands, I hear her laughing. She emerges smiling, and as we walk down the street towards the café where she takes me for lunch, she greets people. Over the summer evenings and weekends, she paints the house. Everything is clean and white. Clean-slate white, we joke. The foreman from the woodshop, Bill, comes over. He gives Mum advice on how to refinish our banister, then stays for a beer.

I get to know our new neighbourhood, taking long aimless walks. I go further and further afield, and eventually I discover the sandy shores of the beaches and paddle my feet in the cool polluted water of Lake Ontario.

At the end of the summer, two nights before her parents will drive her to her residence at McMaster, Wanda comes to see our new house for the first time. She admires Mom's paint job and compliments our cute porch and tiny patio. We walk to Broadview Station, then take the streetcar west to the Ex. Wanda's parents took her every year when she was younger, and she tells me about the fun-house mirrors where her dad would pull faces and how her mom would never let her go to see the world's fattest man.

We're both wearing cut-off jeans and our legs stick to the red vinyl seats. Soon the streetcar is full of families with little kids looking excited as mothers put on sunscreen and young fathers heft folded-up push chairs up the streetcar stairs. By the time we get to the gates of the Ex, there's standing room only, and I feel overwhelmed by the people around me. There are so many languages, so many different conversations. Women in saris and punk teenagers with purple hair, and an old, old man with one leg. Everyone is headed to the same place. Wanda can't believe I've never been before.

"It's just what you do at the end of summer. I can't believe your parents never took you."

"Mum says they went when Elizabeth was little, but when I was born it seemed too much bother to cart two kids down."

She also said it was tacky and dirty, and she can't imagine why Wanda and I are going, but I don't tell Wanda that part.

When we get off the streetcar it is like a blast of every-thing—kids crying, people screaming on rides, laughter, yells of anger and excitement. The guys at the games of chance are calling customers in with loud banter, and there is fairground music and the grinding and mechanical screeches of the rides. The air smells of burning grease and meat. It's so crowded at the entrance our naked arms brush against hairy male torsos and bump against the brims of toddler's sunhats.

On the merry-go-round, we find horses that are side by side. Mine is white with a wide-open pink painted mouth, and Wanda's is a black stallion with big white teeth and a gold painted mane running down its head. The music starts, and we start to go round. The wind hits us, and my horse goes up as Wanda goes down. I grin as I look back at Wanda, and she reaches out her hand. I can't quite reach her, but our fingertips touch as my horse goes down and hers goes up.

We walk more slowly as it gets darker, sharing a stick of candy floss. It is so sweet it makes me cough as it melts down my throat. The crowds are gone, but couples walk with hands in the back pockets of each other's jeans. There's a lot of making out going on in the lineups for rides and at the games stalls where posturing men try and throw hoops over sticks or shoot wooden ducks with air guns. The wind picks up. The music plays and all around us the multi-coloured moving lights swirl. We overhear a conversation between two men standing in front of the teacup ride and talking into a radio.

"Looks okay for now, but there's a storm's coming."

"We'll close the rides in ten minutes, that's what they're saying."

"Quick!" Wanda grabs my hand and runs, and before I can think, because if I could think I would have refused, I am being ushered onto the Ferris wheel. They're loading it and there is no lineup. I am being strapped into a rotating cage next to Wanda.

"Oh my god." The ride slowly moves up, so they can load another cage.

"This is great. I'm glad we made it."

"Wanda, I don't know if this is a good idea." I have made the mistake of looking up and seeing how high the wheel will turn.

"It will be great. You just have to relax into it. Relax your stomach, look around. Look at all the lights and the people."

It starts in earnest then. We are not doing the slow inch-by-inch turn anymore. We are spinning and gaining speed, and I feel momentarily terrified.

"Look, look, Daisy!" And Wanda points out that we can see right into the concert grounds and I look.

"And the gates over there, and you can see the lake."

I look around, and I can see the city spreading out further the higher we climb, and by the time the wheel plunges over the other side, I just feel a slight clenching of my gut, but Wanda lets out a "Whoo hoo!"

"Just scream if you have to."

But I don't scream. I laugh and feel the sticky undulating joy of it.

"I feel high," I tell Wanda.

"Well, we are high."

"You know what I mean."

"I know, it's great, isn't it. I love this place."

We stagger from the ride, slowly getting our land legs, and the rain starts gently. It's fat warm drops at first, and we watch as people start rushing for cover. The Ex workers are wearing black plastic garbage bags over their clothes. Not us. We walk through the rain until we hear the first rumble of thunder echo over Lake Ontario, and then we run. The rain comes hard now. There is one crack of sheet lightning while we are still out in the open, and when we hit the streetcar shelter a few seconds later, a crack of fork lightning comes through the sky.

"Close," someone in the shelter says. And everyone nods and gazes out. Most of us are wet with rain dripping down our noses. The rain has washed away the grease of the rides, the film of sugar that coated my hands, and the sweat clinging to my clothes. There are three more close cracks of lightning, and every time all of us in the shelter laugh a little and look around at each other, grateful to be here together rather than out there alone. The street is deserted, all the last-minute people running for shelter have found it. The storm moves off into the distance, and we see flashes of light and hear distant rumbles of thunder as we ride home. When we get to our station, the rain has stopped. Toronto smells clean, like it has had a bath after a week of wearing the same clothing. Walking down the street to the house, we look at men playing cards and smoking in café windows and women up late in laundromats.

"You'll like it here," Wanda says.

"I think I will. It's a lot different."

"There's more life. More distractions from your own head."

"I'm going to miss you."

"Daisy, don't get sappy. I've had enough of that from Mom."

"Okay, but it's true."

I wake up in the night. Wanda is standing at the window in her T-shirt and underwear. One starling is visible on the exposed part of her shoulder. She's backlit by the streetlight, and I am struck again by how beautiful she's become. I want to say something, but my mouth is too tired to form words, and I drift back to sleep.

It's early when she gets up to go. I get up and throw on some clothes, and I walk her to the subway. We are both quiet, and whenever I think of saying goodbye, I feel my eyes get all watery.

There's an alley leading to the station, and we stop before we get to the end of it. This is where I have to let Wanda go on alone. We stand, and I wait for her to hug me. She reaches forward and pulls me to her, her hand cupped around the back of my neck. Our foreheads touch.

"Fuck it," she says.

Then she kisses me on the lips, open mouthed, and I kiss her back. She is soft and sweet-tasting. She lets me go, turns, and walks away. She looks back once, smiles, and then she's gone.

acknowledgments

Thank you to James Langer, Rebecca Rose, Rhonda Molloy, Samantha Fitzpatrick, and everyone at Breakwater Books for the magic they perform turning manuscripts into books.

Thank you to Kate Kennedy, my fabulous editor.

Thank you to the Writers' Alliance of Newfoundland and Labrador, the NLCU, and the Literary Arts Foundation of Newfoundland and Labrador for the NLCU Fresh Fish Award. Winning this award in 2015 gave me the courage to keep writing. Thank you to Brian O'Dea for coming up with the idea for the award in the first place.

Thank you to Alison Dyer for making me feel like I belonged. Thank you to Susan Rendell for editing an earlier version of this book with care, and to Michelle Bush and Dionne Powlenzuk, my first readers.

Thank you to Carmella Gray-Cosgrove and Eva Crocker, two of the smartest and kindest people in the universe, for making me write harder and think wider.

Thank you to Sharon Bala and Lisa Moore, heroes, for being generous with their time and advice. Thank you to Diane Carley, Terry Doyle, and Basma Kavanagh for encouragement, moral support, and friendship.

Thank you to Stephanie Taylor, the best dog-sitter ever, for bringing me up in a house full of books.

Thank you to family and friends, lost and found, for making life interesting.

Most of all, thank you to Colleen for absolutely everything.